Secret Baby For My Ex's SEAL Brother

A Steamy Enemies to Lovers, Billionaire Boss Romance

"Billionaire Silver Foxes' Club" Series

Valencia Rose

Copyright © 2024 by VALENCIA ROSE - All rights reserved.

In no way is it legal to reproduce, duplicate, or transmit any part of this document in either electronic means or in

printed format. Recording of this publication is strictly prohibited and any storage of this document is not allowed

unless with written permission from the publisher.

All rights reserved.

Respective authors own all copyrights not held by the publisher.

Contents

Prologue: Mia	1
1. Mia	9
2. Chris	27
3. Chris	37
4. Mia	54
5. Chris	67
6. Mia	78
7. Chris	85
8. Mia	99
9. Chris	116
10. Mia	125
11. Chris	139
12. Mia	148

13.	Chris	156
14.	Mia	166
15.	Chris	176
16.	Mia	188
17.	Chris	201
18.	Mia	210
19.	Chris	219
20.	Mia	233
21.	Chris	245
22.	Mia	258
23.	Chris	267
24.	Chris	278
25.	Mia	288
26.	Chris	297
27.	Mia	310
28.	Chris	315
29.	Mia	324
30.	Chris	338
31.	Mia	351

32.	Chris	357
33.	Mia	369
34.	Chris	376
35.	Mia	386
36.	Chris	402
37.	Mia	409
38.	Chris	419
39.	Mia	430
40.	Chris	439
41.	Mia	449
42.	Chris	464
43.	Mia	470
44.	Chris	480
45.	Mia	489
46.	Chris	497
47.	Mia	505
48.	Chris	515
49.	Mia	524
50.	Chris	530

51.	Mia	537
52.	Chris	550
53.	Chris	556
Epilogue: Mia		562
Sneak Peek Into "Secret Baby For My Bestie's Ex-SEAL Dad"		570
About the Author		573

Prologue: Mia

You know how they say, "when it rains it pours"?

Well, right now, it feels like a hailstorm, thunderstorm, tornado, and avalanche hit me all at once.

I chewed my lip, trying to find the right words.

"Chris, I've worked hard to get to where I am and—"

"I don't care. I'm not interested in hearing about it."

The domineering energy stifled me.

He stepped forward, towering over me.

His cologne permeated through the air, melting all sense of rationality for a brief second.

Memories of that night, how he held me in a tight, protective embrace, haunted me.

Get it together, Mia!

I slipped back, remembering the situation I was in.

I had to convince him. I rested my hands at my side as I remembered the self-help book on emotional intelligence I read the other day.

"I get it, but I'm the best employee Grant's got."

I spent years of my life balancing college and promotions in the tech world.

I started as a junior programmer but made it here because of hard work, dedication, and my mom's support.

There was no way in hell I was going to give this up because of one mistake. One very dirty mistake I couldn't stop thinking about.

Chris cleared his throat and turned towards the window.

His arm protruded slightly in the casual dress shirt he wore. *For a company billionaire, I thought he'd dress a little nicer.*

But *that* was probably part of the appeal.

He turned back towards me with a scowl.

I looked at the cold, blue eyes that stared back at me, feeling like they saw through every part of me. Almost undressing me.

Like that night.

I pulled myself out of those thoughts. It was an honest mistake. Neither of us was sober.

"I don't know why I'm even entertaining bringing you on."

"Because I told you that I have experience and—"

"You're not capable of handling my assets."

Okay, now he was just making up crap to get me out of this office.

I shook my head and smiled.

"With all due respect, you haven't even *seen* my work yet. I think you know the fact that I made it this far speaks for itself. If you at least give me a chance, I can prove it to you."

Chris grunted and turned away.

"Give me one good reason why I should?"

I bit my tongue as I held back from mentioning that night. *The man didn't even realize he was inside me till I cried out his name.*

I smiled, maintaining composure. "I've worked up the ranks in Arlington, Virginia, for the last ten years. I have the stats to back them up."

I grabbed my phone and opened up the Google sheet depicting our sales. I placed it on the table and stepped back.

"There, proof enough?"

He looked down and scoffed.

"Mere numbers don't mean a damn thing to me, Mia."

"I'm sure I could show you my production quotas for the last five years and my accolades and you would *still* not believe me. But I'm not here to prove anything. I'm here to get results."

That was the truth. This wasn't a side gig for me that I could leave at any time.

This was my life, and I treated this job like my life depended on it.

Chris stayed silent. I leaned forward and smirked.

"Got anything else? Maybe more insistence that I'm not capable?"

He furrowed his brows and sighed.

"No, I just don't think you should be here. This is a strictly professional environment and–"

"Tell me something I don't know, Chris. If anything, *you're* the one making this unprofessional."

"And you're the one walking back into my life."

His words didn't affect me.

I'd dealt with enough rude people in this field that a little bit of aggression from a guy I thought I'd never see again didn't bother me.

"We don't have to like each other, Chris. But just—"

"Get. Out."

"Come on, please be reasonable and—"

"Why should I be reasonable to the woman who broke Casey's heart?"

Seriously? He wanted to bring *that* up right now?'

"That's irrelevant to the situation here and—"

"If you have nothing else to say, then do me a favor and get out of my office. I'll be talking to Grant after this."

No words would sway this man's mind.

Of course, he would be stubborn rather than put that night behind us.

It was a week ago, but it felt like yesterday.

The memories flashed vividly despite the drunk haze.

His hands were on my body as he felt every part of me, not to mention the wanton sounds that escaped me, begging for more.

Ugh! It was so good, but I knew it would *never* happen again.

When Grant approached me with the merger, Chris was the *last* person I thought I'd see.

"Fine, but there's nobody else as capable as I am. So getting rid of me is only going to shoot yourself in the foot."

"I'm sure there's someone else Grant knows."

"No, there's not. Grant chose *me* to be his CTO for a reason. He saw my potential, and how much I contributed to the team. Hopefully, *you* will see it sometime soon."

I didn't need to listen to this crap.

Right now, we'd be in a stalemate if we continued in this direction. I knew when battles weren't worth fighting.

I walked to the door and opened it. I turned around and flashed the fakest grin I could.

"I'm looking forward to working together, Chris. Hopefully, you and I will eventually see eye to eye."

I didn't like him, and he didn't like me. Back when I dated Casey, he always ignored me.

The guy pretended like I was the equivalent of a doormat half the time.

Not to mention, he *barely* acknowledged anything good that happened between Casey and me.

His arrogance, too. The man was so full of himself and didn't care about anyone except Casey.

Even though the night in the club was a drunk-induced night of pure fun, the reality of the situation was simple.

I had recently broken up with Casey.

The last thing I needed to do was fraternize with his super close and overprotective older brother.

I pushed open the door and slipped out of there, refusing to listen to any more of Chris's crap.

But even as I closed the door, my thoughts drifted back to the way he stared.

Those animalistic, feral eyes locked onto me like a predator catching their prey. That primal energy drove me crazy, whether I liked it or not.

I knew better than to get involved, though.

If he wasn't going to work with me, then so be it.

I worked better on my own anyway.

One
Mia

ONE WEEK EARLIER

"Two cosmopolitans. My treat."

"But Nat—"

"I invited you out. You need to let loose. Be immature for once in your life."

I rolled my eyes. *Yeah, immaturity is why I threw away my relationship of two years.*

The bartender slid two drinks next to us. Nataly brought hers up for a toast, and I did the same.

"To a better future!"

"Right. A better future."

It had only been two weeks, but the pain was still there. I needed time.

Nataly didn't realize not everyone gets over breakups by getting drunk.

"Nataly, I don't—"

"Mia, I don't want to hear it. You're going to enjoy tonight and get your mind off things. Plus, there's, like, tons of hot guys for you to get with."

"Sure, but—"

"You broke up with him. Come on, live a little! Problems aren't solved simmering over them!"

I hated that she was right.

The liquid hit my mouth a second later. *Damn, that's good*. I downed the contents and put the glass down. I exhaled and smiled.

Nataly smiled with that same shit-eating grin she always had plastered to her face.

"Want another?"

Dammit, Nat. I knew coming here was a bad idea.

"I shouldn't—"

"Don't worry, Mia," Nataly chirped, winking. "These guys know me. And plus, you need it! Get your mind off your ex, girl."

Before I could protest, another drink sat in front of me. More and more settled, and before I knew it, my vision was a haze.

I slammed my hands on the counter and got up with a smile.

"There we go!" I cried out.

"Finally turned your brain off and forgot?"

I smiled a confident grin.

"You could say that."

Nataly giggled and gestured to the dance floor. "Then let's forget even more."

I didn't need to be told twice.

When I got up, my vision blurred. I shook my head a little, and it cleared up.

"You good Mia?"

"Yeah, I'm fine."

"Alright. Don't need you dying on me now."

"I'm not some stupid freshman anymore, Nat. I'm twenty-eight. I've been around the block before."

"Then prove it!" Nat cried out as she rushed towards the dance floor.

I followed her without a second thought.

Nat's challenging energy helped with the storm of emotions that raced through my head.

My relationship with Casey hung over me like a grim reminder. I wished it worked out, but he never changed.

He ignored every attempt to settle down, whereas I worked and grew as a person.

I climbed the corporate ladder and managed to secure a stable job with a company I liked.

The final straw, however, was when he ran off for a month to be a racecar driver. He *swore* it was just a phase, but I couldn't do it anymore.

At least for now, even though the breakup still sat fresh, I could forget for a while.

We danced together until I heard a low, tenor voice behind me.

"Mind if I cut in?"

I turned and looked at the source of the voice.

Holy shit. He was hot. Tall, dark blonde hair and a muscular frame barely contained in the shirt he wore.

"Sure. She needs it. Gotta forget that pesky ex of hers."

"Wait, Nat—"

Nataly's gone vanished into the throng of people.

I turned back to the tanned hunk, barely visible in the dim lights of the club.

We danced together, hips gyrating and our bodies pressed against each other.

Damn. *He's like crazy hot.*

My hands felt up the defined abs, and I slid my fingers under his shirt.

A feral grunt escaped him.

"Getting ahead of ourselves, are we?"

I pulled back, smiling. I probably look like a freaking idiot right now.

"Maybe. Or maybe I just want to forget."

"As do I. Came out here for the same reason."

Large hands pulled me closer. He trapped me in his embrace.

Our chests touched, and soon, eager lips met.

I moaned, opening my mouth as I felt his tongue dominate me the moment our bodies came together.

Being with this man liberated me. Having casual sex was such a rarity that it became a treat. Something new, not the same tedium that I experienced with Casey.

Sometimes, a change was all a girl needed.

The bass reverberated around us, but right now, I was spirited away into my own little world.

Drunk and desiring this man, I wrapped my arms around his shoulders.

The kisses grew wilder, and I ground my hips against him. He groaned as he reached down to grab a handful of my ass.

"You can't wait either, can you."

"Hell no. Let's get out of here."

The words were raspy, barely audible, but enough to prompt the stranger.

He pulled back and grabbed my hand. He led me through the throng of people to the nearest place we could go.

An unoccupied single-use bathroom.

He opened the door and thrust me inside.

After he locked the door, our lips were on each other again.

Quick hands made work of the lilac dress I wore.

Thank god Nat has a sense of fashion. I trusted her with the attire tonight and didn't regret a damn thing.

The dress sat somewhere in the bathroom. Not like it mattered.

His lips teased my neck with subtle licks and touches. I moaned and clenched against him.

I needed more. His large, inviting hands pulled me in and drove me crazy.

His hands draped downwards to my breasts, teasing them against his fingertips. The touches were slow but exact.

He pinched my nipples in just the right way.

His lips soon replaced his fingers as I felt his tongue flick against the nubs.

He teased me, and I clung to him. The ache burned, but I needed him inside.

While the foreplay was good, my core dripped with an ache for something big to come inside.

And judging from the feeling between my legs, there was a *very* big surprise in those pants.

I could barely keep it together. He's got me on the edge.

He tugged on the nipple a little harder, and I threw my head back.

"You have the most intoxicating moans."

Dammit, why did he sound so familiar? The thought sat there until, once again, he slid his fingers to my aching breasts.

Hungry lips nipped at my neck, sucking on the flesh. I clung to him, barely able to think straight.

I pushed against him, my juices probably smearing his pants.

Not like it mattered. The growls emitted from his lips, animalistic and wanton, shot a fire deep in me.

"Take me right now. Please."

The mystery man slid down to my sopping panties. He teased the outer lip through the outline with delicate touches.

I cried out, spreading my legs as far as I could.

"Stop fucking teasing," I begged.

He growled, and animalistic hands pulled the waistband off. They snapped, breaking apart as he pulled them off.

Damn. There goes those panties.

His fingers teased inside, touching the deepest parts of my inner core. Large and rough, I mewled, unable to fathom anything going on.

Two fingers, followed by three, entered into me.

My body was raw and needy by the time his fingers curled up all the way inside.

He teased my clit with small motions. I clenched my walls against his fingers, crying out broken, barely audible sounds.

The slick touch and sounds of my wet slit made the ache between my legs even more profound.

I could barely wait as baited breaths escaped my lips.

I grabbed his muscular shoulders.

For a second, I admired his build. He was *built,* and his taut muscles felt perfect to hold onto.

But I couldn't wait any longer, and as I felt my orgasm loom over the horizon, I practically begged him to stuff me.

Do it already. Please.

The sound of foil being unwrapped pulled me out of my thoughts.

He spread my legs apart, and for a second, we locked eyes. They were so familiar to Casey's and yet so different.

Holy shit, that's—

I recognized the man instantly. I knew him.

It was Casey's brother, Christian.

Before I could protest, he plunged inside.

All thoughts about how wrong this was silenced by his rod.

He pressed all the way to my core, and my walls clenched, sucking him all the way in.

My hands gripped his shoulders so I could feel every inch of his body.

This was so wrong but felt so right.

I couldn't pull away. Even if I wanted to get the hell off Christian, his member split me open. My body ached.

His large, robust member filled me up completely. It was like he managed to fill me up.

My hands gripped him even tighter as I held him there.

The bass from the club became just a meager thought in the distance. It didn't matter anymore.

What mattered was Christian's body, entwined with me.

I moaned and clawed at his back. *I shouldn't be doing this.*

His thrusts hit deeper than I ever felt before. Not even Casey managed to hit these spots.

I was lost in a trance, mesmerized by the feeling of this man.

He groaned and held me tighter. He didn't see anything wrong with it.

Maybe the guilt of the situation didn't bother him either. At least not enough to stop.

"Shit, Mia, I'm—"

"I am too," I cried out.

It should've been awkward, but it wasn't. Instead, it felt so different and yet so right.

Hot breaths mingled together.

I wrapped my legs even tighter around his waist. He grabbed my hips and continued thrusting inside.

After a second, he reached down and teased my clit.

I looked at him, and when our eyes met, my orgasm hit me.

"Chris—"

My fingernails tightened against his large biceps. As my vision went white, pure bliss seeped through me.

I came down from my high. *What did we do?*

Chris pulled out of me. His wide eyes looked at me, I suppose from hearing his name on my lips.

His jaw dropped, and the realization of who I was had hit him like a ton of bricks.

Shit. This wasn't what I wanted.

"Chris, I'm—"

"Fuck! This should have never happened."

He stepped back and pulled up his pants. I stood there, naked and confused.

"Chris, I don't want this to—"

"It was a mistake. Let's forget this ever happened."

I tried to form the words. It was impossible. *What have I done?*

The door slammed shut a moment later.

I reached for the lock and rested my hands against the sink.

The lingering reminder of him leaking down my thighs made me realize what I'd done. What we'd done.

I just had sex with Christian Hamilton.

My ex, Casey's older brother.

I took a couple of breaths. *Calm down, Mia. You'll never see him again.*

As I collected myself, I threw my dress back on and readjusted my hair.

I needed to forget. There was no way that actually happened.

My stomach churned. I raced to the toilet, this time to throw up the remnants of the last who knows how many drinks.

After I flushed the toilet, I rested my hand on the safety bar.

Breathe Mia. This will never come back to haunt you.

Even as I told myself that, I knew it would be impossible.

A knock at the door pulled me from my thoughts.

After I drank some water from the sink, I meandered to the door.

As I opened it, Nataly's piercing green eyes looked at me, and a catlike grin sat on her face.

"There you are!"

"Hi. Sorry, I'm—"

"Hold on. You look like shit."

Nataly stepped inside and locked the door. I rested against the sink. I clutched my chest as I struggled to catch my breath.

"What happened? I saw that guy you danced with earlier leave and—"

"That was Chris! Casey's brother."

Nataly's jaw dropped.

"Wait, for real? I didn't know."

"Course you didn't," I replied. I reached for a paper towel to wipe the last bits of vomit from my lips. "You never met him."

"Oh. Shit."

"Yeah. This is a problem."

It was so shitty of me to do that. Casey and I only broke up two *weeks* ago. And now, here I am, getting my back blown out by his brother.

This was *not* what I needed.

Nataly rested a ginger hand on my shoulder. She massaged it.

I appreciated her attempt to diffuse this otherwise *mess* of a situation.

"It'll be alright. It was just one night. He wouldn't hold that against you, right?"

I nodded. "I doubt it. Besides, neither of us were of sound mind nor—"

"Exactly! So don't get your panties in a bunch."

"About that."

I gestured to the panties, now ripped in half. Nataly whistled.

"Damn, dude's a freak in bed. Maybe I should get on that."

"Nat, I swear to God—"

"Kidding! It's not like it would matter, though, right? It was just one night, and it won't happen again."

"You're right. It won't."

Although I wish it could because, who am I kidding, the sex was mind-blowing!

"Ok then, let's go back on the dance floor. Shall we? To get your mind off totally fucking your ex's brother and all."

"Do you *have* to remind me?"

"No, but I did."

Goddammit, Nat. Nataly giggled and opened the door.

"Well, now that you're decent, let's get out there. Panties or not."

She was never going to let me live this down, was she?

I followed her back out to the dance floor, and for the rest of the night, we danced with each other. The drunken heat hung over me once again.

Good. We can forget this fuckup.

At least, that's what I hoped.

Two
Chris

A WEEK LATER

"Alright, everything's signed."

I breathed a sigh of relief. *Thank god*.

I looked over at the notary agent, who sealed the signed copy of our merger.

Iris picked up the contents and held them to her chest.

She adjusted her tortoise glasses and nodded quickly. Her caramel-colored hair bounced against her shoulders.

"I'll get this finalized right away."

"Appreciate it, Iris."

Iris slipped out of the room.

As the door closed, Grant Marsden, the man I'd just agreed to a merger that would net billions of profits, smiled.

"I'm really glad we can work together, Christian."

"Hey, the pleasure is all mine."

Grant nodded. "You've come a long way. I remember when William started his business and made his first billion. I'm glad you followed in your father's footsteps."

"Casey and I both did. We promised ourselves."

Even though Casey was a bit of a loose cannon, he did well. We took what our parents provided and made something of it.

"True. How's he doing?"

"Great. Apparently, the guy just won his first Indy 500. I'm trying to get out there at some point to see him."

"Amazing! You've always cared a lot for him, haven't you?"

"Someone had to."

Our parents used to leave us at home a lot, mainly to take care of their multi-billion-dollar business but also to maintain the required social presence that came with it.

So I was the one who made sure that Casey didn't go down the wrong path.

I helped him with high school, watched him go on his first date, and even helped him through his first breakup.

And his most recent breakup, too.

I shook my head as the memories flooded my head. Our bodies thrust into each other. Passion entwined. And then, the reality of who I had fucking hit me the moment she uttered my name.

Mia.

"Something the matter?"

"Oh. Not at all. So with this merger, I'll be in charge of the company's assets." I responded.

"Correct. I trust you with that side of things. The board will still manage the overall profits and financial options. However, this gives you more room to play with."

That was true. With these additional assets, I plan to increase the company's revenue by up to 10%.

Grant was a legend in the tech world however, he was getting up in age.

With this merger, he still had a stake in the company but wouldn't have to directly run things.

"Indeed."

"Yes, and I'm excited to see the future integration between our staff and yours."

"Naturally, it *will* be fine. I'll make sure of that."

"And I'll make sure you do," Grant replied. "Speaking of, you still wanted my Chief Technology Officer to take over that aspect of the company. Correct?"

"Please," I lamented. "That last one performed terribly."

I had recently fired him. I had to constantly watch his work like a hawk.

The man never hit KPIs, and I got so sick of the back and forth. Termination was the only way to go.

"I'm sorry about that. Well, you can count on this one. Trust me, she's worked hard to get to where she is."

"I'll believe it when I see it. Lip service does *nothing* for me."

Grant chuckled. "True. You're just like William. A man who doesn't believe it till he sees it."

"You have to be. Too many liars in this damn place."

"Naturally."

Grant's phone pinged. He glanced down and nodded.

"Speak of the damn devil. She's here now."

"Oh. I didn't know she'd be here so fast."

"I didn't either. Let me get Mia. She's downstairs."

Wait, *Mia*? There's no way it was her. Mia was a common name, right?

My fists clench, and I grit my teeth.

Memories of that night flooded my mind again, as much as I wished to forget them.

Our bodies pressed together, the sweat and sheen decorating them. The thump of the club's bass and the tightness of her pussy.

Dammit! I slammed my fist on the desk.

Grant turned around and cocked his head.

"Something wrong?"

"No. It's nothing," I muttered and looked away. "I just thought for a second I might've known your CTO."

"I doubt it. She worked with our company for a little while. Prior to us, she worked with another tech firm as their programmer. A real smart cookie for her age."

"I see."

"She's young, but I doubt that'll be a problem. Got a good head on her shoulders."

Young *and* named Mia? I sure hope it's a coincidence.

Not to mention, the last thing I needed was to see her. For my own sake and for hers.

My phone buzzed. I looked down and saw Casey's name.

Still down to golf later? I'm back in town and need a break.

Why does this keep happening? Is this some kind of sick joke?

My vision fuzzed for a brief second. I clutched my chest and attempted to breathe. Air barely flowed through my chest.

I took a couple deep breaths in hopes this would go away. Everything stayed frozen in place, refusing to change.

I counted to ten, just like what my therapist taught me. No dice. The vision continued to fuzz.

"Goddammit!"

I reached for my pocket and pulled out a tablet.

Always happens at the worst possible times.

I took the pill dry. I grimaced at the taste. These bastards tasted like shit, even if you took them with water.

My vision cleared just as I heard footsteps at the door.

"You're going to love this guy. He's actually one of the hottest tech entrepreneurs in the field. A real winner in the startup world."

"Great!"

Fuck! It is her. I looked around and tried to calm the racing thoughts. But it was too late.

The door opened, and a familiar head of long, dark brown hair tied up in a ponytail greeted me. Her hazel eyes stared wide and as surprised as my own.

"Chris. This is Mia Thornton. Mia, this is Chris Hamilton."

Mia didn't say a word. I couldn't blame her.

It was like some kind of sick fuck played a joke on us.

"Nice to meet you," Mia said after a few seconds and extended her hand.

I grabbed it and held it for a split second before I let it go.

"Wonderful to meet you." *Yeah, maybe in hell.* I glanced over at Grant, who stood there and looked around. His brown eyes looked between Mia and me.

"You're going to love her, Chris. She's super capable and one of our top tech professionals."

Right. Sure. Mia's fixated gaze sat unwavering.

I nodded and looked at Grant.

"Yes. I'm sure she is. Say, Grant, could you give us a moment to talk?"

"Of course! I'm going to head back to my office. I'll be bringing over the rest of my R&D team in the next couple of days and—"

"That'll be great. I'll contact you when we're ready for that."

Grant's face fell as I spoke those words. *He needed to get out of here before I exploded.*

My hands clenched tighter. Fingernails dug into the palm of my hands as I maintained composure.

The *last* person I needed to see stood right in front of me.

"Alright. I'll talk to you soon, Christian."

He slipped to the door and disappeared in a flash.

Silence settled throughout the room. Mia's eyes looked around.

"Chris, it's uh nice to see you again and—"

"Get out."

She blinked, confused by my words.

"Excuse me?"

"Get out. I cannot work together with you and would prefer if you never stepped foot in my office again."

Three
Chris

The door slammed shut. I sighed as I sat at my desk.

Now what?

A million thoughts sifted through me.

Part of me wanted to just forget about Mia, but that would be impossible.

She *had already* made her presence known.

Regret settled in the pit of my stomach.

If that night I had realized it was Mia sooner, I would've never done that.

Sure, she felt so amazing and tight, but it was wrong.

I couldn't betray Casey like that. Not after how much he meant to me.

A few minutes later, I heard a knock. *Please don't be Mia.*

"Come in."

The door opened, and Grant walked in. He grinned, sliding into the leather seat across from me.

"I saw Mia left."

"Yep. She did."

"So what do you think? Great, huh?"

Yeah, as great as a thorn in my side. I nodded.

"Yeah, she seems alright."

Grant's face fell. "What's the matter?"

"I just wanted to ask if you knew anyone else."

"Why? Is there something wrong with Mia?"

I couldn't explain that here.

I shrugged and looked to my right, towards the bookshelf.

"She's just quite young, don't you think?"

"Young? I mean, sure, but she's more than capable. In fact, she's scored top performance these last few quarters."

Great. Just what I needed to hear.

"I see. But she's still not versed in the way I run the company and—"

"Chris," Grant reasoned. "It will be alright. You know I don't hire just any old person for my teams."

"I know. You've had some award-winning technicians."

"Exactly. And Mia's managed to increase the company's productivity by up to nine percent. Her technological prowess is something you shouldn't discount."

"I'm not, but—"

Grant reached for my shoulder and squeezed it. His eyes narrowed.

Great, I'm about to get a lecture.

"I understand where you're coming from, but please just humor me."

"I make the decisions in this company."

"You do, but discounting her contributions may negatively impact the company," Grant forewarns.

"I decide how the company's going to play out, Grant," I corrected.

I closed my eyes and take a deep breath. "Just find someone else for me. I'm getting rid of her the second I get a chance."

I couldn't be around her. I couldn't make the same mistake twice.

Her sweetness and sinful body were tempting enough.

To feel those legs around me, thrusting me deeper into her... the feeling of being so close to each other would arouse my attention, and I knew that once I got a touch, I wouldn't be able to pull away.

"I'll do my best, Chris. But please think about what I've said."

"Already did. Now please leave."

Grant walked out the door and closed it. *Finally.* At least now I could figure out what the fuck I needed to do next.

My phone buzzed. *What now?* I looked down and saw Casey's name.

Meet at the country club?

Please. The last thing I needed was to meet Casey right now, especially after all that's happened.

I focused on my day, and when four hit, I walked out of there, avoiding Mia as much as I could. Luckily, she got the same sentiment I did.

The less we saw of each other, the better.

I drove my Aston Martin out of my private parking spot and headed over to the Wilson Country Club.

Sure, I could have my driver take me, but I preferred driving myself.

It came with my past as a Navy SEAL. Not being in control terrified me.

At least when I was behind the wheel, I controlled my fate.

Even with two drivers, I only used them when I went to big events.

When I got there, I saw a lime-green Bugatti right next to the entrance.

He was here already. *For once, not late.*

I slid out of the car and locked up before heading inside.

"Great, so it's just us then!"

There was Casey, alright. His platinum blonde hair sat short but shagged right at his ears. His blue eyes, similar to mine, stared with excitement at the country club owner.

Casey looked like my mini-me.

While he wasn't as muscular as me, he had leanness. He always was the smaller of the two of us.

I shuffled inside and approached the country club owner, a man in his fifties with wire-rimmed glasses and a dimpled smile.

"Yes. So far, we have nobody else waiting to use this area and—"

"Christian! There you are."

I couldn't help but smile. Casey brought out a side of me few could.

We shook hands and half-hugged, just like we always did.

Casey pulled away, grinning from ear to ear. His blue eyes widened with enthusiasm.

"I thought you were going to bail."

"Hey, look who's talking. For once, you're the one on time."

"Yeah, well, I'm back in town for a little bit. Thinking about racing next weekend at the track here."

I nodded. "Still haven't given up the sport then."

"You kidding me?" Casey scoffed. "I'm this close to qualifying for the Indy. Hell yeah, I'm going to try again."

I chuckled. Casey's been following this dream for a little while now.

While I didn't understand, I've always respected him.

The manager gestured to the entrance to the eighteen-hole course.

We stepped out, and I sighed with contentment.

"Everything good?" Casey asked.

"Yeah, dude. Just been busy as hell."

"Yeah, we both have. But I'm glad we can make time like this."

"You know I always will," I replied, resting a hand on Casey's shoulder.

We started with the first couple of holes. Casey fell behind from the start.

I laughed as I watched him hit the ball all the way into the sand trap.

"Goddammit."

"You're using too much force," I explained. "Try grabbing the driver near the top rather than the bottom."

I grasped Casey's hand and adjusted it. He rolled his eyes.

"I'm not a little kid anymore, Chris. I'm thirty-fucking-three."

"Yes, but you're still my little brother."

Casey's been like this ever since he turned eighteen. But, with our own parents rarely in the picture, it felt like I had to be the one to look after him.

"I know. And I appreciate it," Casey replied.

He adjusted the driver once more before he swung once again. Sure enough, after I corrected it, it went in the direction it should've gone.

"Shit, you're right."

"Yeah, I am. Always. So, everything going okay?"

Casey walked to where his ball went, about ten yards from the hole. "As good as it can be. Still hurts like hell after what happened with Mia."

I nodded a little bit. I had to hold back from saying anything.

The last thing he needed to hear right now was about us that night.

"I know Casey. You really loved her."

"Yeah, and I wished she'd just goddamn understand! This is a dream, and I love her still."

Just what I needed to hear. "Give yourself some time."

"I know. Thanks for being here for me, though. I can't really confide this to anyone else."

The words dug a knife in my heart. *If Casey found out about this...*

He wouldn't find out. It would be a secret I'd take to the goddamn grave if I had to.

"Anytime," I reasoned. "You're strong, you know that?"

"You think so?" Casey scoffed. "I feel like a fucking pussy."

"Hey, you two were together for years."

"Yeah, and she stopped giving a shit, all cause I wanted to race cars."

"I know Casey. Everything will work out. It always has, even when we were young."

Casey chuckled. "Yeah, true. Besides, the firm's been keeping my ass busy when you know, I'm not out racing cars and climbing and shit. I've got a guy running it, but..."

"Hey, that's a step in the right direction," I reasoned.

Casey's always been the more adventurous and impulsive of the two of us. Probably cause I never got a chance to experience that kind of life.

Having parents who made you but rarely raised you makes you do that.

Sure, we had nannies, but I was there for Casey when Mom and Dad weren't.

Being multi-billion-dollar business owners and socialites was more important to them than raising their boys.

Casey rested on the score marker. "I'm sorry to bring the whole thing down."

"Don't be."

"Anyways, how's my nephew doing?"

"Good. Funny enough, Mom's watching him right now."

That was one of the few things Mom got right. Even though she wasn't there for us, at least she stuck around after all the crap with Alara.

"That's good. Give him a hug and a high-five for me, will ya?"

"You could always come and see him."

"I know, but I'm going back to New York tomorrow."

"Again?" I grunted.

"Hey, I have a new client I'm trying to win. But if I race next weekend, I'll be in town."

"Alright."

I dropped the subject as we played through the holes.

Casey was an adult and, unlike me, didn't have the responsibilities of being a dad. Or the joys that came with it. But it was damn hard when I had an ex-wife trying to drag me down.

Still, a pang of jealousy sat in my heart. *He still had freedom.* As for me, I was trapped.

I never told anyone about it, though.

It was better this way. Suffer alone to ensure the success of others.

At the eighteenth hole, Casey shot first. The ball bounced and then ricocheted off the wall straight into the hole.

"Oh, hell yeah!"

"See? You still got it?"

Casey shrugged. "I don't feel like I do."

"Then what the hell was that?"

"Luck, dude. Like everything else."

I shook my head. "Not everything is luck, bro. Sometimes, you just figure things out."

That's how I got to where I am today.

Sure, my parents had the wealth, but I could've easily pissed it away.

Casey folded his hands across his chest.

"I know. I just, sometimes, wish I was more like you."

"Grass is always greener, bro."

It sure was. Casey still had time.

As for me, I experienced the world and all the hells within.

Dammit, not again.

My head throbbed. My vision became a haze once more. Black spots filled the center of my vision.

I gripped the wall next to me. I took a couple deep breaths as I struggled to catch my breath. My body stayed standing but frozen in place.

When I finally got the strength to do so, I reached for the packet and grabbed a pill. I swallowed it, and Casey groaned.

"Again?"

"Can't help it. Been getting worse."

"You should go see someone."

"I'm fine, Casey," I corrected. "I've been fine for a while."

As fine as I'm willing to let on. I didn't need Casey doting on me like a parent.

"Fine. I just know life hasn't been easy. Speaking of, how's that merger going?"

Great. Now I really didn't want to bring that up. Memories of Mia came back like a rude reminder.

"Good. Grant's given me the rights to his company."

"That's cool. Any big plans."

"Just trying to get more software nailed down. The merger's interesting, and Grant's new employees are certainly characters."

"Glad to see there's some growth. I'm sure the new people under your jurisdiction are some interesting characters."

Yeah. Mia, for one. I would rather die than tell him she's working under me.

"They are. Most are just a couple of tech pros."

"I see. I remember Mia mentioned she might be changing jobs soon. She worked in tech and was quite successful. I'm surprised you two haven't crossed paths."

Oh, trust me! We did cross, alright... in multiple ways!

"Nope," I reasoned. "I guess she just worked in a different sector."

"Right," Casey replied. He looked down, clenching the golf club a bit tighter. "I'm just trying to get over her, man. I loved her."

I nodded. I wished there was something I could do.

The memories sat there, embedded in my head. Bodies touching, and the lingering desire that followed.

"I know, dude. But remember what I said. Take time for yourself."

My watch beeped with a message from Mom.

What time are you going to be home? I'll stay with Jacob till you get here.

Duty called. I sent a message telling her I'd be there in an hour from my Apple watch. I closed the watch and looked up.

"I've got to go."

"Yeah, same. Got an early flight. Let's do this again, though."

"For sure. And maybe I'll bring Jacob to your race."

"Sounds good. I'll keep you in the know," he chuckled.

We parted ways after. As I sat in the car, my thoughts loomed through me.

That went better than I thought.

Still, the temptation to blab and tell him everything threatened to spill. I didn't need that drama, though, at least not from Casey.

I took a deep breath and composed myself. The threat sat there, but I had to ignore it.

Yes, we had sex, but that doesn't mean a damn thing. It was one night, one mistake. We'd never share that again.

Hookups were the only thing I wanted from women. Relationships? *Hell no.*

When it came to Mia, I knew exactly how to handle this.

I'd do everything in my power to prevent our paths from crossing like that ever again, no matter what.

Four
Mia

"Mia! There you are. I thought you forgot about dinner!"

"And miss time with you? Come on, Mom, don't take me for a fool," I replied with a grin.

Mom opened the door, and I followed her inside. Her large green eyes stared at me.

She smiled, even though these last few years were hard on her.

She gained a few pounds. Probably the weight of Dad's death hanging over her.

Her brown hair, the same color as my own, was greyer than brown these days.

She wore a patchwork shirt and Mom jeans. On her feet were Nikes, a few years old and worn.

I entered the living room and looked around.

The same old place, just a little emptier now. Emptier not just cause of me but also because of the memories locked away.

The walls sat devoid of pictures of our family. Those memories sat in private locations for Mom to look at on her own.

I slid into the other chair with a large white plate in front.

Mom spooned the casserole onto my plate. She placed the green beans and the mashed potatoes in the center. I took a bite and savored the taste.

"You've still got it!"

"I always do, hun," Mom reasoned. "I told you that you would never go hungry, even if you worked for hours at the office."

I chewed and swallowed, nodding. Mom always took care of me.

"We're here for each other."

"I know, dear."

We ate in a calm, collected silence.

I spooned a little more potato onto my plate and took a bite.

"So, how are things with the new merger?"

"Good, I suppose. It's just..."

Do I tell mom? She was here for me when I broke up with Casey and encouraged me to follow my heart.

She also consoled me after I ended things with him and the dust settled.

"What is it?"

I chewed on my lips. *I shouldn't bring it up. Mom didn't need to worry.*

She leaned forward and looked at me curiously.

"Mia, what's going on?"

Dammit. No way out of this. I sat, cornered by her words.

"It's just, there's someone that works there now. And I'm not sure if I'm ready to see them."

"Who?"

I hesitated, not sure how I was going to explain this. I didn't want to lie to her.

"Chris."

"Chris?" she asked, looking confused.

Then, a moment later, her face comes to the realization. "Oh, Casey's brother, Chris. Well, I'll be damned. I know he's close to Casey, but I never thought you two would meet up like that."

"Trust me, I didn't want this either," I admitted. "But life has a messed up way of working like that."

Mom looked down and continued eating her food.

I took a few more bites as I tried to quell the racing thoughts.

What now?

"I'm not sure whether to stay or go."

"You know that's going to be a problem if Casey finds out."

"Don't worry, Casey's off being a racecar driver in Europe for all I know. We haven't crossed paths in a while."

"But they're close. He used to mention Chris a lot when he came to dinner."

I nodded. That was a problem. Their closeness could either work out in my favor or not.

"Yeah, but he didn't bring up Casey at all when we talked."

"That doesn't mean he won't in the future, Mia," Mom chided.

"So what? Do I just leave then?"

I couldn't do that. But I worked too hard to get to this point.

"Does Nat know?"

I shook my head. "Didn't have a chance to call her yet."

"I'd suggest talking to her. She means well and usually has a better grasp of these types of situations, better than my old brain."

I chuckled. "Come on, Mom, you're not that old."

"I'm retired. Don't flatter me."

I laughed. Mom always knew when to say the right thing.

"Anyways, yeah. We're working together. He's technically my boss cause Grant wanted to give the company away."

"Now that's going to be a problem, isn't it?"

"I don't know," I admitted. "I'm just not sure how to feel."

It wasn't as easy as just brushing it off. I *wish* it was, but I kind of threw that away the second my lips met Chris's.

Dominating and strong... I melted against them.

"Mia?"

"Oh! Sorry."

Dammit, I did it again.

The sensations of that night haunted me, especially at the most imprinting times.

Mom sighed, shaking her head. "I don't know what's going on, but if you're not careful, inviting Casey back into your life could be a problem."

"I don't think Casey wants to be back. He sure made that clear the second he went off to who knows where."

Risky behaviors were his best friend. He wanted to live that life of immaturity. I gave that up because I knew where I wanted to go.

When he told me he wanted to run off and race, it upset me.

I didn't want to date someone who was at risk of ending up in a body bag because of impulsive activities.

The stress wasn't good for my health.

Not only that, but he also refused to take our relationship seriously.

Sure, I was his girlfriend, but when it came to marriage, kids, and a whole future, he didn't care.

Eventually, I wanted to settle down.

We were two different people with different goals at the end of the day.

That didn't mean it didn't hurt, though.

I regretted the words I uttered to end things. But this was my decision, and I stood by it.

"I don't think anything bad will come of it. I just need time to heal."

His hot brother was *not* the way to do that. Mom nodded and smiled.

"I get it, dear. Just be careful. You just got this promotion."

"I know. You've been cheering for me ever since."

"And I always will," Mom replied. She smiled, and all of the worries disappeared.

Mom was my best friend. Sure, I had Nat, but it was different with mom. Mom always had that sweetness to hear that I couldn't ignore.

She was there for me throughout all my major milestones.

She kept me on the right path. And, when things got hard, she always brought me reassurance.

I looked up and noticed the space behind her.

"Where's that picture?"

"Oh, that one. I placed it in the bedroom."

That was a code word for the grieving pile. I reached out and touched Mom's arm.

"Mom, I know it's been eight years, but please don't put it away because you're worried about me."

"That's not it at all. I just wanted to put some happier memories up."

I nodded. I reached down and grabbed my fork, holding it.

"I'm proud of you, by the way." Mom said, smiling.

"Why?"

"Look at how much you've eaten."

I looked down and realized over half the plate sat cleared. I smiled.

"I'm doing better about that, Mom."

"I know, I just worry. I want to make sure you get good meals, and don't let those feelings overtake you."

I nodded. I wasn't a kid anymore, but the memories of back then and my desire not to eat haunted me.

"You know I've gotten help for that. But thanks for watching out for me, Mom."

"Of course. You know that I always will."

We continued with dinner, dropping awkward conversations about not just Dad but also Chris.

Mom meant well, but I didn't want Chris to be a big deal. He was just Casey's brother and probably hated me as much as I disliked him.

Which was a lot. He wasn't even that nice.

He treated me like a burden. We never liked each other anyway.

After we finished dinner, Mom cleared the table. I sat back and smiled contentedly.

"You always kick ass with your cooking."

"Hey, I'll try Mia. You give me a reason to cook."

"I always will," I reassured her. "But I do need to head out soon. I've got work in the morning."

And *another* lovely day with Christian.

Then again, he probably doesn't want anything to do with me either. So it will be all good.

"You could just stay here for the night."

"Yeah, but I don't want to put you out."

The unused rooms here became storage space both for Dad's memories and other little knickknacks. Mom didn't have the room she used to here.

If I stayed, I'd be on the couch for the night.

Not what I'm feeling tonight.

"I know. I just like having you around Mia," Mom admitted. "It's nice we get to share moments like this."

"I do, too. And I promise that I'll come over again. I'm sure this job won't be *that* taxing."

It'll probably just be what I did for Grant but like with a new *asshole* calling the shots. A pain in the ass when it came to conversations, but otherwise not awful.

Mom nodded. "Alright, dear. I'll walk you to the door then."

I grabbed my purse and followed Mom to the entryway. We stopped there and embraced.

"I love you, Mia."

"I love you too, mom. And I promise I'll be over for dinner again soon."

I pulled back, seeing the happy smile that crossed her face.

"That's what I want to hear. We can make it a weekly thing."

"That'd be great. And I'll tell you about any new information," I replied.

"Good. And Mia? Please just be careful. I know you're focused on your career, but please don't do anything you'll regret."

"I won't, mom," I reassured her. "I know what I want. And that is to solidify this position, get those benefits, and just keep getting more experienced to build my own company."

"That's my girl!"

Mom's enthusiasm always helped so much. Even when it felt like I was all alone, I always had her.

After we said our goodbyes, I walked back out to my car, a Nissan Altima.

I settled into the seat, thinking about what she said. She acted the way she did to protect me.

Mom was there through the good and the bad, through all of the crying sessions and the happy moments.

Right now, I have to focus on my career and my future. While one contained Chris, that didn't mean both had to.

Chris was just the guy I was going to work for. Someone to keep at a distance and only talk to when needed.

I could keep our relationship professional.

I had goals in mind, and he was going to be the stepping stone to get it done.

Five
Chris

"Why didn't you tell me this sooner?"

I clutched the phone tighter in my hand. Mom coughed on the other end.

"I'm sorry, Chris, but I'm sick."

Just what I needed. I slammed my hand down on the desk.

"And you didn't tell me till the last minute?"

"I wasn't sure if it'd get better. But the fever is bad. I'm not sure if–"

"Okay, mom. Let me think about what I can do on such a short notice."

It pissed me the hell off that she couldn't even give me *any* sort of heads-up.

I looked at the clock. The event started at seven on the dot, which was only five hours from now.

Taking Jacob was *not* an option. The less he was involved with my work, the better.

Normally, I'd cancel and tell the others to suck it up and contact me later.

My son meant so much more than a couple of upset people who could, frankly, get the fuck over it.

But this event was huge.

In fact, my not showing up could sour relations with Grant that I've been trying for so long to foster.

"It's only for three hours. I need you to—"

"I would love to, but I don't want to get Jacob sick, dear."

"You don't understand! This event is huge for our company."

Grant invited me to speak at a benefit for the company.

He planned to talk about recent sales and garner support from investors.

However, since this was a joint venture now, he wanted me there to speak, at least for a little while.

I *can't* miss this one.

"I do understand, but it's bronchitis, and it won't go away by tonight."

"Can't you just do what you did last time when you were sick? Let him be in his room and just stay there if he needs help with something?"

"Last time, it was a simple cold, but now, there's that chance he's going to catch bronchitis, which, by the way, you might contract then too. And the last thing I want is for both of you to get sick."

"You don't need to look out for me, Mom," I corrected.

"Yes, I do! I'm your mother I always will look out for you."

I rolled my eyes. *Now,* she's trying to play mother and doting on Jacob. Probably trying to make up for how much she messed up with raising us.

"So you're just going to cancel?"

"I'm not trying to be a pain, Chris! I just can't. Isn't Casey in town? He stopped by briefly the other week."

"No," I muttered. "Casey is now in New York, doing who knows what."

Probably more bullshit to figure out where he wants to be in life. *I swear, that guy....*

"Anyways, that doesn't fix the problem we have here, Mom. I need a babysitter for Jacob, and I counted on you."

Mom coughed, sounding as if she had hacked up a lung on the other end.

I cringed hearing it. *I don't want Jacob exposed to that, but...*

"I get it, hun, but I can't come over with this. It's contagious. I can barely see your father. Why not ask Aunt Margret?"

"She's old and can barely watch the news."

"What about Lisa? She's back from college. Worth a shot."

I pursed my lips. Lisa was my cousin and she *was* reliable.

Unlike the rest of the family, who spent their days chasing the bag, she focused on school and her tea business.

She was one of the few people in our family I didn't mind Jacob being around.

"I'll see if she can. I just wish you didn't cancel on me at the last minute, Mom."

"I know, and I wouldn't have. But trust me, this is for the sake of both of you."

I didn't see how Mom bailing at the last minute benefited me but, on the other hand, I knew she was right in her worry that she could get Jacob and me sick.

"Fine. Just get better soon. Let me call Lisa now and, I guess, find another solution."

"You might want to start considering properly trained babysitters offered by these trusted companies for when incidents like this happen, hun, and—"

"And trust a stranger around Jacob? *Hell no*. I'd rather just call the event off than let just anyone around him."

Mom sighed. "Alright. I'll see if anyone else is available."

She hung up the phone. I sat back and shook my head.

I wouldn't cancel. To cancel would spell the potential failure of this merger.

I needed to plant the seed and get these new investors on my side.

However, all that was about to be thrown away because of mom's last-minute cancelation.

I dialed Lisa, and two seconds later, I heard her voice.

"Chris! How are things?"

"As peachy as they can be. Say, are you free tonight?"

"No. I'm actually with some friends. We're seeing a play in New York. Why?"

"I can pay for your time, Lisa."

The sound of screaming on the other end echoed through the receiver.

Of course, she was with friends. The signs told all as I realized that there was no way in hell she would attempt to make it work.

"Oh, I wish I could, but we're in the heart of the city already."

"Yeah, I kind of picked it up. It's fine. I'll just try to figure it out myself."

I hung up before listening to her response. *Now what?*

There was Alara, my ex-wife and Jacob's mother, but she was the *last* person I wanted to ask.

The witch was probably traveling the world and off doing who knows what.

She claimed she changed, but after demanding Jacob back, her true colors showed.

When I refused, she didn't even bother to call me back.

Good riddance. She was out of the question.

Footsteps approached. I closed my eyes in an attempt to reel it in.

I didn't want people to see any sort of vulnerability.

A knock at the door… I walked over and opened it, seeing the *last* person I wanted to see standing there.

"What do you need, Mia?"

I thought we agreed to stay away.

She didn't need to talk to me, and I didn't need to talk to her. She could go cry to Grant for all I cared.

"I'm sorry for bothering you, but—"

"You're already bothering. Just spit it out."

"Right. Well, I wanted to give you these. That's all. They're the current production stats."

She placed the papers in between my hands.

I snatched them from her and looked down at them.

Up so far. Not bad.

While I hated, well... disliked, Mia and wished she would just quit, Grant was right.

The woman got the job done from the looks of it.

"Got it."

"I'll let you go now. I hope you have a good day."

I furrowed my brows. *Yeah, well, with this newfound stress, I don't think a good day's any close.*

I grasped the doorknob and held it tighter. Mia turned and walked away.

Wait a second. She could help.

I needed this, and she was the only option I've got left at this moment.

Mia met Jacob before.

Back when she was still dating Casey, she had accompanied him a few times when he came to visit Jacob and me.

There were also a couple of times when Casey had offered to take Jacob to Gulf Branch Nature Center & Park, but I remember Mia tagged along once when they went to a pumpkin patch.

I remembered she was good with him and Jacob liked her.

Maybe this could work.

"Wait, Mia."

She stopped dead in her tracks. She turned her head slightly.

"I'll get those stats to you by the end of the day and—"

"That's not what I'm asking you. Come back here."

"But—"

"Are you going to fight me on *everything*?"

My voice lowered, and I saw the hesitation there.

A mixture of doubt and fear sat on her face. *Good*. She deserves to fear me.

Mia turned and walked back over.

Our eyes met, and her hazel orbs sat large and curious.

"Is something the matter? I thought I explained it and—"

"You did. But there is something I need you to do for me."

I gestured inside and nudged her in.

She stepped in, eyes staring wide at me, and I closed the door. I locked it before she could protest.

"Sit."

Mia followed instructions to a T.

She sat there and looked around.

Large, curious eyes looked around the space, avoiding me as I sat across from her.

"I'm sorry, Chris. I don't know what I did and—"

"You didn't do anything wrong. There is something, however, I need you to do."

She shuffled a little bit and crossed her legs. Little bits of thigh stuck out from her pencil skirt.

For a second, the raw desire to grab them and spread her apart threatened my thoughts.

Get yourself together man! I cleared my throat to silence those thoughts.

"I need you to watch my son tonight. I have no other options."

Six
Mia

Was Chris freaking for *real*?

He wanted me to babysit his son. I mean, sure, Jacob was a good kid, but...

"I can't do that, Chris."

"And why not?"

"I'm your employee, for one. And two, you hate my guts. Just stating the obvious."

Chris's face showed no signs of emotions. *As stoic as ever*.

That was one thing I remembered from meeting Chris and spending time with Jacob.

The man barely said anything.

Jacob was a good kid, though. Casey liked the little guy despite not wanting kids himself.

We stepped in and took him to the pumpkin patch a few times.

Chris wanted to go, but he had some kind of excuse. Probably work or other stuff.

"I know. I wouldn't be asking you if my hands weren't tied."

"I can tell."

"This isn't a choice, Mia. This is a need."

"And I need you to understand that I don't want to."

"Why not? I'll pay you for your time."

I stood up and rested my hands on the desk.

"Money doesn't matter. I'm just setting my boundaries with you. And this will break them."

After my conversation with Mom, I vowed to keep all communications with Chris as superficial as possible.

If I could go an entire day without saying more than five words to him, that was a win in my book.

Chris sighed and rubbed his temples.

"I get it. I don't like you either."

"Well, you make that *very* clear, Chris."

"I wouldn't be asking, though, if you weren't my last resort."

"Doesn't Jacob have a mom?"

Chris shook his head. "Not one that I acknowledge to be a fitting parent for him. You, or anyone for that matter, would be more capable than she ever was."

"I don't know if that's a compliment or not."

Our eyes met. The fire that sat there differed from other encounters. There was a hint of something more.

Desperation.

"Mia, I wouldn't be asking if I hadn't tried everyone else. Family can't, and right now, you're the best alternative."

"Aren't there babysitters? I mean, that's what my Mom did whenever she needed to leave me to attend a—"

"I'm *not* leaving my son with someone I barely know."

"So you'll leave him with your brother's ex, then?"

Chris glared, and I smiled.

"I'm just saying, I thought there was an implicit agreement not to speak to one another. And right now, this is breaking all of that."

"I know. But if you do this for me now, I'll never ask you for anything again that isn't work-related. And we can continue like this. I don't want anything more than a babysitter to take care of my son right now."

I paused. *He did seem desperate.* While I'd rather not, he did convince me that he's out of options.

"Alright. Just for tonight, right?"

"Three hours. All I need."

"Damn, you're really left high and dry then?"

His gaze lowered. "I *had* someone lined up, but they bailed; well... had to bail, at the last minute."

They probably got tired of his demanding ass.

"Okay. I'll do it. Just for the night, then."

"Thank you, Mia. This really helps."

"I know. Jacob's a good kid. He educated us on pumpkins when we went to the patch."

That's the most I've ever learned from a child when out doing some family thing.

Chris chuckled and nodded.

"Yes, well, he'll probably just stay in his room."

"Ahh, so we'll both avoid each other. I can work with that."

I always liked kids who would do that.

I used to babysit back in high school before Dad's diagnosis.

Most of the kids interacted with me, but there were a few who avoided me and stayed in their rooms.

The easiest money to make, but it also made me question whether or not I was even needed.

"Thank you. Just meet me at three p.m., and we'll drive over there."

"Not together, I hope."

"God no," he mutters. "You can clock out an hour early. I'll show you inside, make sure Jacob's okay with it, and then head out."

"Sounds good."

Get in, get out. With minimal conversation. Sounds perfect to me.

I walked out of the office after we were done. I didn't want to overstay my welcome.

Plus, I could tell this was not what Chris wanted, either.

I was indeed the *last* option he had. Thank goodness.

I shouldn't have even been doing this. But those piercing blue eyes, fraught with desperation, ignited something in me.

I couldn't leave him hanging.

Plus, if he did this for the company, I would get extra perks too.

It would also mean I could stay out of the picture. I didn't need to attend stupid events.

It was a win-win for both of us. While not ideal, I just had to accept it.

From what I gathered, this also worked in Chris's favor too. The less we saw of each other, the better.

And I was anyways doing it to help his son. Not him.

Seven
Chris

Is she trying to make me late?

I swear, it feels like she's late on purpose at this point.

I tap my foot, looking down at my watch.

I have to be at the convention center in ninety minutes. If I'm late, it's going to be a problem for *everyone*.

I'm this close to just canceling and telling Jacob to get some nice clothes on and come with me. Maybe there's a kid's room I can put him in and–

A pearl-white Altima pulls up next to me. Mia stumbles out.

"Sorry, traffic was terrible."

"I see. Almost thought you, too, bailed."

Mia shook her head and smiled.

"I told you I'd be there, Chris. I don't go back on my word."

Yeah, which is what made even interacting with her hard.

That and the reminders of my actions from that night.

I ignored Mia's words, heading inside. After I unlocked the door, I gestured to her.

"Okay, well, I'm not interested in chit-chat right now. Come in, and let's get this over with."

Mia followed, not saying a word. She stepped inside and looked around.

"Same as before. You don't change the décor a lot, do you?"

"Don't need to. Jacob!"

Small, pattering footsteps echoed above. Jacob leaned against the banister and looked down.

"Dad? What's going on?"

"Come here. I need to talk to you."

A moment later, Jacob stopped in front of us. He adjusted his glasses and looked curious.

"Dad, what's Mia doing here?"

"So you remember Mia? Casey's girlfriend?"

"Yes, she took me to the pumpkin patch! Why's she here?"

Because I have no one else. I shook my head.

"She's here to babysit you tonight."

"Not grandma?" Jacob asked, obviously disappointed.

"Grandma's sick, and nobody else was available. I know this isn't ideal, Jacob, but please be good for her."

Jacob looked past me over to Mia. She waved and smiled.

"Been a while, hasn't it?"

"I guess so. Dad, do I have to listen to her? You told me I was becoming a big boy! I can stay in my room on my own."

I shook my head. Jacob had to be crazy to think I'd allow that.

"You're too young. I told you this; maybe in a few years, I'll let you stay at home."

"But grandma said she was going to watch the new invention I made!"

Mia's eyes lit up for a second as she smiled.

"You have a new invention?"

Jacob stood there and folded his arms across his chest.

"I do, but it's not like you would care. Casey never cared."

"I'm not Casey. And I'm very interested. I didn't know you made inventions."

"He's actually interested in making stuff on his online game," I explained.

"Oh, so like me then! I'd love to hear about it."

Jacob shrugged. "It's nothing. I just made this cool new character. I was going to show Dad, but he's got work..."

I looked over at Mia. Her eyes lit up with interest.

Maybe this could work.

"I would love to hear about it. Sounds like you're really creative."

"Wait, you really do?"

"Yep! I used to play games too. Been a while, but I know my way around character design," Mia replied with a wink.

I looked back over at Jacob and smiled.

"Anyways, you're willing to listen to Mia, at least for a few hours?"

"Yeah, Dad. I know you're busy. I guess I can talk to Mia."

"Yeah, and you told me you were going to carve that pumpkin a while back too."

"The pumpkin patch one? Oh yeah! I took some pictures with my tablet! Let me get it."

"I'm sure she'd love to see them."

I turned around and grabbed the door handle. I looked at Mia one last time.

"Make sure he doesn't forget to eat dinner."

"I will make sure he remembers everything."

"Thanks."

I stepped out the door and closed it. A mixture of both relief and worry washed over me.

I knew Jacob would be okay. But it was Mia's actions that had my attention.

I saw the excitement clearly in her eyes. She didn't mind Jacob, much to my relief.

Good. At least I don't have to worry about her screwing things up or Jacob getting in trouble.

I drove and sped through traffic as much as I could.

As I pulled up to the first spot I could find, I checked the time.

I'm five minutes late.

I swear, Mia tested me and had me on edge from the moment I left.

I adjusted my suit and walked inside.

Grant turned as soon as he saw me. A relieved smile sat across his face.

"Chris! There you are."

"Sorry. I had some personal issues to attend to."

"That's fine. Everything's good now, right?"

"Perfectly fine."

I didn't like Mia, but I trusted her to at least make sure Jacob was okay.

She was capable of that and took responsibility for him before.

Grant led me inside and immediately thrust me into conversations.

Different investors spoke to us.

I talked about my company and what the future merger meant for everyone.

They listened, happy to hear that I wasn't going to screw over Grant's company.

It probably helped that I knew what the hell I was doing, too.

The three hours passed with no issues. I checked my phone. No messages from Mia.

At least she was capable of taking care of Jacob.

The event ended, and Grant waved. I approached him and nodded.

"Good crowd tonight."

"Yes. Thank you so much for giving your speech."

"Hey, I told you. You can rely on me."

"I know. And I hope everything's fine at home."

"It should be. But I'm going to head home in just a few minutes to make sure of that."

"That's alright. I'll take it from here."

We bade farewell, and I headed to the car.

Grant mentioned that we already had three new prospects, all of whom were interested in what I planned to bring to the company. Good. I made an effort, and the rewards sat clear as day.

I drove back to the mansion.

The long driveway shined brightly as the wrought-iron gate opened. As I pulled up, I looked at the row of cars to my right.

Everything was in order. Then again, I did have a state-of-the-art security system in place.

If the wrong person even *touched* my precious cars, I'd have my private security team on their ass.

I looked up and saw the helipad. My helicopter sat there. I liked to take it for long-distance events, but conventions in town were best driven.

I walked up the huge walkway towards the front entrance. I pressed my thumb to the lock and the doors clicked open.

The lights were on in the living room, but the room upstairs was dark. Guess Jacob went to bed.

I pulled my Bentley next to Mia's Altima and headed to the iron-clad door.

"I'm back."

Silence.

I stepped inside and looked around the large foyer. No response from Mia.

What the hell is she doing?

I raced over to the living room, relieved to finally see her there.

She sat there with a book in hand.

Her legs curled next to her body, and those dangerously enticing thighs poked out from the bottom of her skirt. I stared for a moment longer than I should have.

"Oh. Hi, there."

Mia closed the book and readjusted herself.

The little bit of thigh disappeared. I cleared my throat and nodded.

"Sorry. Had a few more things to take care of at the event. Where's Jacob?"

"He went to bed. He talked my ear off for the last two hours about this character he designed on his tablet. And showed me his pumpkin carving pictures."

"Ahh, I see. Did he say much about the pumpkin patch?"

Mia shook her head.

"Not much. But, he does have an interest in computers."

"Really now?"

"Yeah, he kept messing with his tablet, trying to take a picture. I showed him the best way, and also how to share it with you. He sent the photo a while back, but I guess you didn't notice."

Oh. Well, I was at an event.

Jacob's tablet could send pictures. They were often silly pictures. Or blurry ones.

While I hated getting Jacob involved with technology, the teachers pushed it all the time.

I folded my arms across my chest and smirked.

"So you're teaching my own kid how to use computers then. Getting him started on that path early."

"Is it wrong?" she asked with a smile on her face.

"No. You're just not his parent, so I don't know why you care."

"Hey, he's a good kid. He has a passion. I, for one, encourage that in kids. I'm sure you understand where I'm coming from."

Unfortunately, I do. I sat down on the couch next to her and looked upstairs.

"So, he's out then."

"Yeah. He is. And I should get going, too."

She got up and headed towards the door.

Lingering thoughts drifted, ones I know I shouldn't have, *for her to ... stay.*

It was wrong on so many levels to think this way.

I refused to have a repeat of that night. And I wasn't going to. But I just didn't want to end everything on this note either.

"Mia, wait."

She stopped and turned around.

A half-smile crossed her lips. Her mouth looked so plump and inviting I wanted to taste her again.

I knew it was wrong, but the pull was damn strong.

"What's the matter?"

Fuck, what now? I looked away and rested my hand on my thighs.

"Stay. I need to talk to you."

Okay, that wasn't wrong. Mia stayed in place and looked towards the door.

"I shouldn't—"

"It'll be for just a few minutes. Sit."

Without another word, she sat back down on the couch.

Desire overwhelmed my thoughts as I looked at her beauty.

The conflict of interest rose through me, creating a storm of emotions.

She looked at me. Her body tensed as she spoke.

"So what do you need?"

"I just wanted to talk. That's all."

This was wrong. Talking led to so much more. And yet, as much as I wanted to ignore her, I couldn't.

VALENCIA ROSE

I wanted her here whether she liked it or not.

Eight
Mia

Chris's eyes locked on mine with an unwavering gaze. I looked around. What is this? *Could I leave?*

That would make things *so* much easier.

The logical part of me wanted to get out and never talk about this again.

Chris didn't like me, and I only cared about him because of the job situation. And that was all there was.

At least, that was what I tried convincing myself of. Even just helping outside of the office felt wrong *or should have* felt wrong.

My core tingled. Desire held me in place.

I had to admit it to myself... I wanted Chris ever since that night, and whatever it was that he did to me that made me feel sooo...well, satisfied, I should say, even though I knew it was so wrong.

"What did you want to talk about, Chris?"

He didn't say a word and refused to look my way.

"I just wanted to say I really appreciate you helping me out tonight."

"Sure. I mean, I didn't have much else going on."

That was true. Nat had her own stuff going on. Some crap involving a guy at her workplace she was messing around with.

Mom had therapy this evening with her group. They met at a later time, and usually, she didn't get out till nearly eleven. They were her friends, and the camaraderie helped her after dad's death.

My other friends weren't that close to me. From what I gathered, most of them were off doing their own thing.

So, I was off the hook. Chris's darkened expression loomed over me.

"Really, though. It's rare to get help from anyone around here but mom."

"Oh yeah, she's really nice."

"Yes, and *usually* she babysits Jacob. But she's sick."

"I see," I replied, looking around.

The tension stifled the conversation. There was a lot to ask and a lot that I wanted answers to.

"What happened to his mom? I remember there was some drama involving her and—"

"That's none of your business."

"But—"

"It's *nothing,* Mia. There are questions you're better left not asking."

I sighed. *There he goes again.* Keeping me out of the loop and at a distance.

"Why do you do this?" I continued, "You know, act this way. You keep pushing me away, but it's clear you don't want to."

"It's better this way, Mia. I don't want to repeat the same mistakes again and—"

"Like how you ravaged me that night?"

Chris's darkened expression haunted me.

"That was a mistake. I never intend to repeat that again."

"I know. It's conflicting, but—"

The sex was damn unworldly. That night sat, solidified in my psyche whether I liked it or not.

A hunger to experience that again loomed over me. Despite the risk, I couldn't push the feelings away.

And, from the overwhelming stare Chris leveled towards me, I am pretty sure he felt the same way.

"I don't want to cross that boundary again, Mia. I just don't and—"

"What are you scared of?"

"A lot of things. You and Casey *just* broke up."

"That was over a month ago."

"Yes and had sex with you two weeks after the breakup. That was a huge mistake."

"Sure, it may be, but what if *you* wanted it? What if you desired it just as much as I do?"

He looked down and clenched his hands against his thighs.

"I don't want that Mia. I don't want to repeat that same mistake."

"Do you really? Or are you just duping yourself because you refuse to tell the truth?"

His hand reached for my chin and practically yanked me to face him.

I gasped in both surprise and mild pain. *Those hands are strong.*

"You don't know how much your presence has been fucking with me, Mia. I wish I could just forget you! I hate you and—"

"Oh, trust me. I hate this, too. You're mean, cold, and full of yourself."

He gripped a bit tighter. I winced slightly.

"For a reason. I've been through a lot. You don't know the half of it."

"Yeah, you were in the service. I'm just trying to clear the air, and—"

"That's my problem. I *don't* like the way you make me feel. I've kept my distance and been good. Now, you've waltzed back into my life and—"

"I'm not the one who made the first move, you know."

The darkened expression became almost stifling.

His aggression was both incredibly sexy but also terrifying.

He relaxed his hand. I half expected him to pull back and tell me to leave.

"You test my every fiber of patience, Mia."

"You'll get used to it."

His cold, unapproachable behavior drove me crazy. Half the time, it was like talking to a goddamn brick wall.

Chris leaned in, and I braced for his words. To tell me to get the hell out of his face and to never speak to him again.

Instead, his lips pressed to mine.

I wanted to pull away, but they were so strong and dominant.

The alpha energy pulled me in, whether I liked it or not.

He stepped back and grabbed my hair to pull my face up.

"I hate you. This doesn't change that."

"Don't worry, I hate you too."

His lips pressed to mine once again as he drowned every urge to pull away.

He pressed me into the couch, and I gasped.

His tongue thrust into my mouth, and I opened up willingly. Just like the first time. Animalistic pleasure overwhelmed me.

I wanted to forget, to just not think and feel this man against me.

He trapped me in his embrace.

Chris's body overpowered me, and I shivered with delight.

I didn't want to escape.

Clothes disappeared like magic as his hands caressed every part of my body.

I cried out as his fingers teased the tip of my nipples.

I shouldn't want this, but his touch sent shivers down my spine.

"Your breasts are as sensitive as ever."

"Oh, you remembered."

He growled, sucking on the bud fervently.

I clenched, gasping for more.

As he pulled back, a smirk formed on his face. "Not like I'd forget that."

His fingers were like magic.

I leaned into the touch. My panties wettened the moment his larger fingers tugged on my nipples. They skated around the edge of my areola, and I gasped.

The ache grew stronger, and as he continued, the lingering desire for him came back once more.

As he teased me, he leaned forward, until I felt his breath against my earlobe.

"Do you know how much you drive me crazy?" he hissed in my ear as he pinched my nipples.

"Every time you're around, I'm reminded of that goddamn night. And I hate it."

I hated it, too. Despite trying to pull away, he sucked me into the throes of pleasure.

Chris's large, masculine hands turned back and pinched my nipples hard.

He rubbed his palms against the already sensitive buds. I panted and gasped as the wanton need for him grew stronger.

His hands moved away from my breasts and slid downwards to my hips.

I clenched my legs tight, but then he pushed them open.

"No. I know you want this."

I manned in response to that commandeering voice. Chris controlled every situation, and every touch delivered to me.

Skilled hands teased between my legs.

I clenched my thighs, but that didn't stop the finger that drove me to the brink of pleasure.

I bit my lip, trying to stay in the moment.

A million thoughts threatened to pull me out of this. I pushed them away and focused only on this moment.

He pressed the fingers to the tip of my core, and I thrashed about. They were so big, almost like he stuffed me with his own member once more.

A series of moans escaped my lips as I grew lost in the pleasure.

He grunted. Those fingers plunged even further in. At least three sat between my legs. He thrusted them in and out wildly, almost with a fast, violent pleasure, and all I could do was cry out.

I ached for him, and I needed this like I needed air.

"You want this, don't you? Your body says so."

His fingers continued, slamming all the way inside. They moved perfectly against my folds and then as deep as they could inside me.

His lips captured my nipple, and I spread my legs further, lost in the pleasure.

I couldn't even form words anymore, just moans of delight and the ache for more.

Just as I was about to reach my peak, he stopped and pulled them out.

Our eyes met, and I saw the storm of lust and need in his own eyes.

Part of me was disappointed I couldn't finish. His fingers felt so good. But then, a moment later, the thought disappeared.

Chris pulled back and reached for his wallet to pull out a condom.

"But—"

"Don't worry, I won't hurt you, Mia. I just... I don't think I can control this anymore. I can stop if you really want me to..."

The words, strong but with a hint of care, showed me the real him.

"I-I do want it."

He grunted in my ear and nipped at my neck.

"Good. I do too."

His words pulled me in. He sucked me in. I couldn't control it either.

I didn't want to leave until I experienced him again.

He pushed inside, uniting our bodies. Short, rhyme thrusts made me scream inaudibly.

I wrapped my arms around his shoulders and dug my fingers in.

"That's right. Just like last time. I shouldn't do this, Mia, but I can't—"

He thrusted in deeper, and all rational thoughts disappeared.

My whole body sat at the mercy of the man's feral pleasure.

I cried out little sounds, only heard by him.

His hands rested against my hips, and guided himself all the way in.

Every touch felt like it unlocked something more, something deeper inside of me.

And I adored the little touches of his fingers against my nipples with the slightest of motions.

The sounds of our pleasure, combined with my moans and gasps, were the only sounds emitted from us.

Jacob was asleep in the other wing of the house. He wouldn't be able to hear us.

Not only that, but he also slept with a white noise machine on, so I wasn't worried.

Right now, I mentally thanked whatever deity sat above for that one.

Chris held my hips tighter, and then, after a few more thrusts, he hiked my legs over his shoulders.

I lay there, spread and lost, completely overwhelmed by his pleasure.

After a few more thrusts, he held me tighter. A low, guttural sound escaped his lips.

"Close."

It was barely audible. I felt the same way. The volcano of pleasure built up and threatened to explode.

He pressed his member deep into my core, thick and throbbing.

Whites filled my vision as I inaudibly screamed, holding him like a vice grip as my orgasm overwhelmed me.

He groaned, and a moment later, his own release mingled with mine.

We stayed connected. Neither of us wanted to move, to acknowledge what would happen next.

Eventually, Chris pulled away. He walked off to the bathroom to dispose of the condom.

As he left, I sat there. *What do I do now?* I had sex with Chris. *Again.*

I should've left when I had the chance.

This was so wrong. Now, I had to own up to *two* different instances.

And this time, I couldn't just chalk it up to a drunk gal looking for a rebound.

I reached for my panties and bra. At least this time, he didn't rip them. If he did, I wouldn't have complained, though.

Chris returned with boxers, hugging his hips. Damn. He put that big boy away. It was probably for both our benefits though.

My fingers rubbed together as I tried to fathom what to say.

We shouldn't have done that again. This time, we were both totally sober, and we didn't stop.

I reached for my skirt and placed it back on. Chris grabbed his pants to do the same.

"Chris, I'm—"

"Don't worry about it, Mia."

I sat there with my skirt half-on.

"What do you mean?"

He looked over. The lust that filled his eyes disappeared. Instead, that dark, serious expression appeared once again.

"Don't think anything of it."

How was I supposed to do that? He *made* a move on me. He said he hated me so much but then acted like this.

"But Chris, I'm—'

"Don't. You should leave and don't *ever* bring this back up again."

Okay, what the hell? I struggled to find the right words but nothing came to mind. There was no way to win this back-and-forth battle.

"Fine. I'll see you in the office on Monday, *Mr. Hamilton*."

I reached for my shirt and pushed it down quickly.

Without looking back, I grabbed my purse. I put my shoes on and headed out the door.

Chris didn't follow, nor did he bother to say goodbye.

A mix of emotions sat with me as I closed the door.

I fucked up. I had sex with him again, even after I told myself I wouldn't.

All I wanted was to have a normal ass business relationship with Chris.

And now, I felt like I ruined it.

I got in the car and drove off.

With every attempt to forget about what happened, it loomed over me even more. Every regret heightened with each passing second.

My phone lit up when I got to my apartment. A message from Chris.

Thank you so much for watching Jacob. And let's forget everything that happened after I got home.

Gladly.

Nine
Chris

"Here are the prototypes for the new software. Let me know what you think."

I glanced up at Mia. She handed me a file folder filled with different images for software.

Just the person I wanted to see.

I snatched the contents from her hands and left them on the desk.

"Thanks."

"You're welcome. If you could let me know your thoughts and—"

"I'll email you. I'm quite busy and don't have much time to discuss these small matters. I'll get to it when I can. Now you could leave."

Mia nodded as she played with the long braid on her shoulder.

"Sounds good."

"Good. I'll let you know if I need *anything* else."

"Got it."

Mia raced out the door and closed it.

I took a deep breath as I struggled to keep it together.

That damned woman.

I knew I should've let her leave when she had a chance. Instead, I screwed up again.

Mia was like a siren, pulling me in. I closed off those feelings ages ago, but she managed to slither in.

What the hell is wrong with me?

I asked myself this time and time again, but there was no clear answer.

I shouldn't have made those moves that night. Now, here we are.

Much to my relief, Mia took the hint. It meant nothing, and I planned to keep it that way.

Still, her body drove me mad. She sucked me in, whether I liked it or not.

What I wouldn't give to hear those moans again.

A throb between my legs pulls me out of my thoughts. *Goddammit.*

I looked down at the prototypes, which aided in calming my raging hard-on. They looked good.

Mia was capable as hell, and she delivered good work.

A winner in the bedroom *and* in the office. She would be the death of me.

I signed it off and sent over an email. As I did so, my phone buzzed.

Oh great. *Her.*

A woman I hated more than I hated Mia. If that was even possible.

I clicked the ignore button the moment I saw it. But a second later, the phone buzzed again.

Alara.

With a sigh, I opened my phone and held it to my ear.

"Didn't I tell you not to call me ever again?"

I hear a crowd in the background. Guess she's still out traveling the world, and sleeping with every man that she could get ahold of.

"Chris, please just listen to me and—"

"I told you we'll settle this in court."

"Please, just listen to me. I've changed. I really want to be a better parent to Jacob."

Yeah, she wants to be a better parent in hopes of having my son in her life. Fat fucking chance.

"Stop calling me. We're letting the court decide. Only have your lawyer contact me. Lose my number."

I hung up the phone. Anger rushed through me.

I took a couple deep breaths, but the anxiety overwhelmed me.

Why couldn't she understand? She messed up. I never wanted her in Jacob's life.

She's been trying for years to prove she's changed, but I have yet to see any damning evidence.

All I see is a woman who's obsessed with partying and acting like a child rather than one ready to be a mother to a child.

Great. Now I've got this bullshit to deal with. I dialed my lawyer, George Sandler.

"Chris. Everything okay?"

"No. Alara called again."

George sighed in frustration. "Seriously? She didn't learn the last time?"

"An immature woman who preferred partying to being a parent won't. Is there any possible movement on these proceedings?"

"Well, we're meeting with the judge at the end of next month. But the case is heavily ruled in your favor. You'll be fine. She has *nothing*."

That's what I want to hear.

"Good. And I take it you'll make sure if she comes forward with any arguments, that they're squashed."

"Like a bug."

"Glad to hear. Thanks."

I hung up the phone. My hands shook. At least there was some progress on this.

Now, I just have to focus on avoiding Mia and continuing with the ongoing growth of the software team.

I dismissed those thoughts and looked at the budget.

But Alara's message encroached in my mind. *Why? I don't care anymore!*

All that mattered was to protect Jacob. The thoughts overwhelmed me.

I slammed my hand on the table and stood up. My other hand grasped the side as my vision blurred.

Not again.

I stood there, frozen in place and unable to move.

My heart pounded as if it might burst through my chest. My breathing quickened, almost labored, as I waited for it to go away.

Time passed like hours. Every moment felt like minutes, and I struggled to come back to reality.

I fumbled with the drawer with my hazy vision.

Inside sat the pills, which helped with the symptoms. Drugs for when the attacks got really bad. I pulled out a pill and shoved it in my mouth.

They helped when the attacks became too much to bear.

I swallowed and waited. *Any minute now.*

They got really bad under stress. Drove me fucking crazy.

And no matter how many PTSD counselling sessions I attended at different VA hospitals in Arlington, they never seemed to go away.

A couple minutes later, my vision cleared, and I sighed with relief.

I survived another one.

They used to only happen when I got reminded of those nights as a Navy SEAL.

The bombs, screams, and ships that capsized all around me flooded my vision.

I remembered one attack which caused our ship to sink. I was the only one to survive.

All around me, my comrades died, and I was unable to save them.

That dream haunted me almost every night. It happened occasionally in moments of stress.

My brain just shuts down, and the memories flashed in my head like a movie.

I shook my head and focused on the other tasks at hand.

The aching reminder continued throbbing through my head. Eventually, it dissipated.

There we go.

At the end of the day, I closed up the office. I walked out and looked around.

No sign of Mia. Thank goodness.

My hand wrapped around the capsule.

Taking these wasn't the right solution.

I promised my doctor I wouldn't rely on them so much. But, with each passing moment, it felt as if stress might overtake every part of me.

While I hated to rely on them, they were a necessary evil.

Just like Mia.

Ten
Mia

Ugh, not again.

I glanced at the email, well lack thereof, in my inbox.

Chris was supposed to give me an update on the software.

And, of course, he didn't.

My phone buzzed with a text from marketing asking if the software prototype was ready yet.

We planned on releasing new antivirus software that also provided advanced-level security features.

The plan was to start to sell them at the end of the month. But we still had to wait for Chris's approval.

With a sigh, I marched out of my office and then up to Chris's office.

I knocked and waited for his response.

"Mr. Hamilton?"

Nothing for a minute. As I was about to give up, the door opened.

"What is *it*, Mia?"

As charming as ever. I flashed a smile and folded my arms across my chest.

"I wanted to follow up with you on those prototypes. I sent them to you and—"

"And I *told* you that I'd have an answer for you at my leisure."

Here we go again. Even just *trying* to be civil led to these kinds of discussions.

My hands clenched, but I maintained composure like I always did.

"I get it, but I need a response. The marketing team has—"

"The team will get a response when *I* have it. If you come up here to rush me again, we're going to have a problem."

A blind threat. But I knew when to pick and choose my battles. Arguing with Chris wouldn't get me anywhere.

"Alright. I'll let them know. Please give me an answer at your leisure."

"I will do my best. If there's nothing else, please leave."

Before I could respond, he closed the door.

I stood there, feeling a mixture of emotions.

He doubled down on being a prick ever since we had sex that night.

He really wanted to make sure I knew where I stood. Still, I couldn't complain.

At least I still had a job here.

I turned and went back to my office.

I guess I'll work on other projects until Chris gives me that feedback, whenever that might be.

I took a few of the pieces that our security team developed and tested the code.

Halfway through the day, my phone rang.

Please, don't let it be Chris. I was on a roll and didn't need him to yuck my yum.

Nataly's name flashed across the screen.

Thank goodness. Someone who didn't have it out for me.

I pressed the green button and attempted to contain my excitement.

"Hey, girl. How are things?"

"Good! I wanted to talk to you. Just checking in. How are things working out now that you're a girl with a whole ass merger and team under your belt and a fancy corporate job?"

"You flatter me, Nat."

"I'm not! You've just got your shit together. And then look at me, a barista who can barely keep a guy's attention."

A pang of jealousy seeped through me. At least if I had Nataly's problems I wouldn't have to deal with my ex's brother being my boss.

Or maybe I might have to, and it would be just as crappy as it is now.

"I mean, it could be better. You will *not* believe who's my boss now."

"Hopefully, Tom Cruise."

I laughed. I mean, Tom Cruise *might* be easier to deal with than Chris Hamilton.

Sure, he's egotistical, but at least I wouldn't be shut out as much and treated like a piece of dirt.

"No. Chris... as in Casey's older brother!"

Silence filled the other line, followed by laughter.

"Come on, Mia, jokes aren't cool."

"I'm serious! He's my boss because apparently Grant and he agreed to this merger."

"Oh. Shit. So, like, are things okay?"

That wasn't an easy question to answer. I mean, in terms of my professional career, they were.

"I don't know."

"Sounds about right. Shit, that's so awkward."

"You're telling me," I muttered. "I don't know what to do. I told Mom, but...."

I left out the part where we had sex.

Nataly spoke to someone and held the phone over the speaker. A second later, her voice appeared as loud as before.

"Okay. Well, that's something. I mean, it's not like you'd take Casey back, right?"

"Oh, no. Casey moved on, and I did the same."

Breaking up with him was the hardest thing I'd done, but it was for the best.

It gave me a chance to figure out exactly what I wanted.

Plus, being with him made me feel like I was a babysitter at times.

But now, a string of emotions washed through me, including hesitation on what to do next.

"I just don't know what to do. Chris hates me, but…"

"I don't think you should tempt fate too much there, Mia."

"I know, but still."

There was that lingering desire for Chris. I knew it was taboo, but he was so hot he drove me crazy.

Maybe I was just a fool who craved the feelings he gave me.

Or maybe Chris was a man who put me under his spell.

"I'm not going to tell you how to do or not do your job, Mia. But please just keep your distance. He's hot, but you're playing with fire."

"I'm already burned."

"Still. Be smart. Anyway, we'll go out again. This time to a club where hopefully no other weirdos and old acquaintances show up."

"I can only hope."

We hung up, and I sat back.

Going out would be good. Maybe I'll find a guy that'll help me forget about Chris.

Or maybe it'll solidify this storm of emotions inside me as some sort of messed-up desire from my brain.

Either way, I needed a break.

I continued throughout my day thankfully, without any more awkward encounters from Chris.

I drove over to Mom's place.

When I pulled up, the lingering scent of pork chops wafted through the air.

Mom's cooking always helped my aching mind.

I stepped inside, and Mom turned around. She grinned and set the bread next to the pork chops, green beans, and mashed potatoes.

"I could've gotten the door."

"And stop you from working your magic in here?"

Mom rested her hands on her hips. "How are you? Dinner's ready."

I faked a smile, even though I knew Mom would see right through it.

"As good as I can be."

"Well, good. I hope you came hungry. Get to the table."

I sat at our normal spot, and Mom spooned out for me.

I looked at the plate, filled with pork chops, green beans, and mashed potatoes. A side of chicken also decorated the plate.

"Wow, you make it hard to figure out where to begin."

Mom rested her head on her hand and shrugged.

"Wherever is fine. I just want to make sure you get plenty to eat."

"I think we managed that one," I managed to spit out.

I licked my lips and dug into the first bit of food I could find.

We ate in pleasant silence, and after Mom finished, she rested her fork on the plate.

"So, how's the merger treating you."

"Oh, it's been one heck of an experience. Lots of new responsibilities."

"Good. And how's Chris? Everything okay with him?"

I couldn't tell Mom the truth to that question. She would throw a fit and have a million questions.

"Not really. He barely says a word to me."

"That sounds about right," Mom admitted and looked down. "He always did have that aloof vibe to him."

"I had forgotten you had met him once. At some family function Casey's parents had."

"Yeah, and I could tell he was a man of few words, Mia. Not really the friendliest guy."

"You're telling me."

Mom grabbed the plates and put them in the sink. I walked over and grabbed a sponge.

"I'll help."

"Mia, I cooked food and—"

"And I *told* you plenty of times, Mom, that I would help if you did. I want to clean up. You're always making delicious food for me, so at least let me repay the favor."

Mom nodded as she realized my intentions. "Alright, dear."

I washed the dishes as she bagged up the food.

These dinners were an excuse for Mom to make food for the week.

It was part of why I always made an effort to show up. If I didn't, it worried me.

After Dad died, both Mom and I struggled to eat.

For years, I battled with anorexia, and Mom fell into depression, binging and purging.

These days, she managed to keep food down and put the weight on. But there was always that lingering worry that she might fall into that spiral again.

I never wanted to see that happen.

I placed the final dish in the dishwasher and Mom started it.

"Here, check out this puzzle I've been doing."

I followed Mom to the living room, where a large table and puzzle sat.

Half the pieces were put together, while the other half sat in the box. A couple sat strewn around, connected together.

"Oh, nice! It looks super cute."

"Thanks. I planned to put it in that area you mentioned was empty the other week."

I nodded. Dad died thirteen years ago, but it still hung over her.

Sometimes, it felt like he died yesterday with the way Mom acted.

They loved each other. Losing him to prostate cancer broke her heart.

She got therapy for suicidal thoughts, but it still affected how she acted at times.

"How are you holding up?" I asked.

"I'm managing. But what about you? I'm glad you're eating."

I nodded and looked down. "I am. I'm just worried about you."

"Don't be. I'll be alright. But I want to make sure you're okay. Working for Chris seems stressful."

That was one way to put it. I bit my tongue just so I wouldn't worry Mom.

"I'll be alright. Promise. I'm just trying to figure things out. There's been so many changes, and after breaking up with Casey, I feel better but also confused."

That is true. We loved each other, but I craved a stable future. Casey, however, wanted to experience life. I loved him, but we weren't meant for each other.

"I know. But I just want to make sure that working for Chris doesn't open that door."

"It never will. Trust me."

Mom and I talked for a bit longer before I left. Her words hung over me.

Working for Chris may open the door for many things. But it would *never* open up a relationship. He had his own mess, and I had mine.

Plus, he was a divorced man with a kid. I didn't need that baggage.

For now, at least, I had my own life to figure out.

Chris couldn't stand me, or at least that's the way he acted anyway.

Getting together, falling in love, all that stuff was impossible.

And I planned to keep it that way.

Eleven
Chris

"Dad, look!"

I watched as Jacob pressed a few buttons. A picture of a dog sat across the screen that he colored in his online coloring book.

"Good job! You figured it out."

It impressed me to see this.

Jacob was always a gifted kid, even if he was too young for complex computer processes.

I enabled it, and his fascination with computers rivaled only his fascination with video games and going outside.

"Thanks, Dad. I also tried to send it to you, but…"

He pushed it over to me. I studied it and noticed that he forgot to put my name in the address line.

"Ahh. It's because you forgot to say who the picture would go to. Here, let me show you."

I adjusted the address and showed Jacob. I pressed send, and the message went to my phone.

His eyes widened like saucers.

"It worked!"

"Remember, Dad knows how to fix these things," I reassured him.

"I know. I just don't want to ask you. You're always busy."

My face fell at those words. I mean, sure, I was. But I always made time for Jacob, even if my world was crumbling.

He meant everything to me, and I took care of him as much as I could.

"I always leave time for you, Jacob."

"I know, but still. Grandma always says this stuff is boring. She tries to listen, but..."

"Try teaching grandma," I reasoned. "She may want to listen, especially since it means a lot to you."

"Maybe."

Jacob pulled the flash drive out and played with it in his hands.

"By the way. Do you know when Mia will come back?"

Never.

Her watching Jacob was just a one-time thing and nothing more.

I couldn't break his heart, though.

He had told me the next day that he enjoyed his time with her. Jacob had even asked if I could hire Mia to be his babysitter.

And I had told him no. I'd rather not open the door to those feelings.

I kept Mia at a distance for a reason.

Hurting Casey by letting her get close would be terrible. Casey wasn't just my brother; he was probably my best friend.

Casey still looked up to me as a protector, even though we weren't kids anymore.

The doorbell rang. I got up and walked over.

Mom stood in the doorway with her Dolce and Gabbana sunglasses and purse.

"Sorry, I'm late. Your father wanted to go check out some Tom Fords beforehand. He's got a business meeting next week."

"That's fine. We were just working on some computer stuff."

"Oh, that's fun. Well, I guess Jacob will teach me more about it."

I can hear the excitement *dripping* from Mom's words. I sighed and folded my arms across my chest.

"Mom, please. Just let him have this."

"I know. I will."

Mom walked inside. Jacob looked up and smiled.

"Hi, grandma."

"Hi there, Jacob."

Grandma and Jacob both sat down.

Jacob told her all about the computer he worked on. Grandma half-paid attention like she always did.

At least she listened these days. Back then, whenever I had projects, she told me she was too busy to listen.

The nannies would be my confidants, but even then, they barely gave a damn.

When Casey started developing an interest in tech, I refused to repeat the same mistakes.

He managed to follow through with his dreams of building cybersecurity databases.

In a way, we both managed to do what he wanted, but I made sure not to repeat the same mistakes I did with myself by providing Casey with all of the support he needed.

"So you're going out, right?"

"Yes, I explained. "Casey's back in town, and we planned to go out for drinks together."

"Why doesn't he just come here?"

That was a problem. Mom and Casey were at odds a bit.

Part of it stemmed from Mom's disdain for Casey's immaturity and impulsivity.

The other part was Casey's natural inclination to not want anyone around but me.

A real piece of work he was.

"He'll be back later. We just wanted to meet up and talk brother-to-brother."

"Okay. Well, if you need anything, let me know. We'll be here."

"Thanks, Mom. Appreciate it."

Mom, despite her lack of presence when we were kids, tried her best. She might've messed up back then, but she tried making up for lost time now.

That was ultimately what mattered.

I walked out and slipped into my Maserati.

I opened the GPS and put the directions in for Club Fenton, a place Casey recommended to me.

As I pressed the button, my head pounded.

Seriously? Why now?

I rubbed my temples in an attempt to make the headache go away.

It didn't work but instead grew stronger, almost overwhelming. I gripped the steering wheel and took long, deep breaths.

It didn't work. The ringing grew louder and stronger.

Reminders of that night flashed through my head.

The shrill of the bombs as they plunked the water. Some of them hit the ship, while others fell into the cold depths.

The sound of explosions and the uncertainty on whether or not the deaths were from allied, or enemy ships.

The screams of my comrades as they drowned all around me. The sirens emitted from our ally ships.

I clenched the wheel and held it as tightly as I could. These attacks always happened at the worst possible time.

My heart thudded, and I clutched my chest. I took a couple deep breaths, but I hyperventilated.

I grabbed the tablets from my pocket and popped one out. As I took it, the shrill noise dissipated from my eardrums.

Eventually, my vision cleared, and my heart slowed.

I took a couple of deep breaths. Eventually, reality settled back in.

Alright. Take two.

I turned the car on and set the gear in reverse. I backed out and headed to the entrance of my estate.

Just as I put my left-turn signal on, the screen changed.

Incoming Call: Mia.

What is it now? I kept my distance for a reason. I rested my finger against the green button before I pressed it.

Heavy breathing echoed through the car. Panicked sounds filled the speakers.

"Mia? What now? What's going on?"

"Chris! I need your help. I don't know who else to call and—"

"Calm down. Just explain."

Mia sniffled and, a second later, spoke.

"My car is on fire!"

Twelve
Mia

A FEW HOURS EARLIER...

"Okay, Nat, I'll be there in twenty. See ya."

I hung up the phone and adjusted my brown hair. It sat high in a tied-back bun, accentuating my hazel eyes.

I grabbed my lipstick and covered my lips with the mauve hue.

There we go.

I sat back and gave myself one final once-over. It wasn't Nat's handiwork, but it had to do.

I reached for my keys in the front basket and shoved them in my purse.

At least tonight, I can focus on having a good time and maybe meet someone to help get my mind off Chris.

Yeah, easier said than done, but a girl can dream, right?

I trudged out the door and to my Altima. After unlocking and throwing my clutch purse in the seat, I placed my phone in the holder next to the middle console.

I plugged the directions in for this club, a place called Bright Lights.

Nataly *insisted* she had never seen Chris there, or any other acquaintance for that matter. I'll take her word for it.

I pulled out of my parking spot and headed onto the main highway.

Traffic was bad, so the GPS told me to go down a couple of other roads.

Great. I hated back roads. It had already gotten quite dark, so visibility was limited. My phone service was spotty too.

There, some real crazies took the back roads in this area.

I gripped the steering wheel with two hands as I merged off the exit.

Alright. Just got to take this road for four miles and—

A car zipped right by me, cutting me off as I started down the road. *Lovely*. I was already a sitting target for weird people around here.

I took a couple calming breaths as I turned right and drove down the zigzag road.

Where the hell was this club? Most of them were nestled deep in the heart of the city.

I wanted to go out and forget, not go out there and have a grand total of five people to talk to.

I turned right and coasted down the street. Flashing lights appeared behind me, blocking my vision.

"Hey buddy, you don't have to turn those brights that high and—"

The brights suddenly disappeared, and they flashed in front.

Before I managed to get out of the way, the car stopped in front of me.

Crap. There was no way around this. I braced for impact.

The car hit. The airbag deployed. I struggled to get out. Something was on my hand.

"Dammit, I'm—"

The sound of movement pulled me out of my thoughts.

He drove off.

I tried to move, but that wasn't happening. My foot was stuck.

This was bad. I reached for my phone and barely managed to grab it.

A cracked screen. It still worked, though.

I opened it up and dialed 911. They told me they'd be there as soon as they can. Since it was the back roads, they might be a bit.

Figures.

I scrolled down and attempted to find someone else who could help me get out of here.

My friends... Ok, Nat is out in the club. And Toby and Brendon, two of my other friends... I remember them saying they were going out of town this weekend on a fishing trip or something.

I scrolled down. I had to call Mom or—Chris.

Well, I didn't want to worry Mom before I knew anything conclusive about the situation myself.

I hovered over Chris's name. He was the last person I wanted to call. I pressed the button and heard the dial tone.

Please pick up. He was my final hope, and if he didn't, I would—

"Mia, what now? What's going on?"

The annoyance sat palpable on his lips. Tears fell as I struggled to keep it together.

"Mia? What now? What's going on?"

"Chris! I need your help. I don't know who else to call and—"

"Calm down. Just explain."

I looked forward and saw the flames.

The embers started off small. I noticed them as soon as I got hit. But now they grew and threatened to reach the engine.

I took a few deep breaths and composed myself. *I had to get out of here.* I tried the door, but it got jammed on impact.

"My car is on fire!"

"Hold on, Mia," Chris said. "I'm coming. Where are you."

"I'll send my location. And I'll t-try to get out."

"Don't move too much. I'll be there."

I found my location and texted it. The fumes grew and penetrated my nostrils.

All I smelled was gasoline and the encroaching flames.

I tried to move, but it was impossible. Something trapped my foot, and every time I tried to maneuver, all I felt was pain.

Shit, it might be broken. If it is, then…

I pushed those thoughts away. Nothing was broken.

I looked around in hopes that someone would help me.

No other cars passed on by. Despite the roads being backed up to hell and back, nobody else came.

I struggled to see if there was any way to readjust my body so I could get out of the car.

No dice. Everything was trapped, and by this point, numbness settled against my feet.

My strength had already left my body. All I smelled at that point was the pungent smoke.

I can't die here.

Time ticked. I didn't know how long it's been.

The smoke grew more pungent as the fumes reached the engine.

When that ignited, the car would explode, and I'd die here.

Panic settled in.

I tried to force the door. But the door wouldn't budge.

Breathing grew harder as the smoke grew in size.

Carbon dioxide… If I inhaled enough of that, I *would* die.

I closed my eyes. I didn't want to go. There was no sign of anyone, though.

Would Chris save me? Would he get here in time?

I shook my head. *No, don't think like that. Someone will come.*

Someone will come, I thought as my eyes grew heavy and all my worries faded away.

Thirteen
Chris

"Where is she?"

I scoped around. This *was* the location she sent.

All I saw were winding roads, and guard rails that hadn't been maintained in god knows how long.

That was the one thing that sucked about this part of town. Most of it was barely kept.

If someone did get stuck out here, or in trouble, it would be a miracle to save them.

Still, I refused to give up.

I pressed on the accelerator and drove down, taking the turns a little riskier than I cared to.

It didn't matter right now. I had to save Mia.

Plumes of smoke rose in the distance. *There it is.*

I slammed on the gas pedal and took the last curve quickly, nearly drifting against the side.

Casey was the risky driver. I never did this crap. But, when it came to lives, I refused to let people die.

I saw too many in my service as a SEAL. My entire company died in a flash. The memories threatened to encroach, but I pushed them away.

Not now.

I saw Mia's car. I pulled up, and the smoke grew bigger. It became almost stifling.

I smelled the burning scent even as I parked behind her car, a safe distance away.

In case it exploded on me.

I didn't think. I never thought of the consequences when it came to saving lives.

I rushed to the car and pulled on the door.

It didn't budge. Figures. I reached for a part of the guard rail and created a pulley to open the door. It flung open, and Mia's body fell out.

I grabbed her and cradled her in my arms. I pushed her hands under my armpits and cradled her head and neck against my arms.

I pulled her out gently, but her foot got stuck.

Great.

The airbag caught her foot. I grabbed the same piece of guardrail I had before and pushed it against the bag. It deflated.

"Come on, get out," I muttered to myself.

Where the hell were the first responders?

In situations like this, they should've been on the scene even before me.

It was a goddamned miracle the car hadn't exploded by now.

Then again, I did do about 100 all the way to the hairpin curve.

After a little bit of wiggling, I extricated her foot.

I dragged her towards my car and kept her head and torso aligned as we moved.

Basic training. Always make sure you prevent all spinal injuries.

The flames grew, and the pressure of the fuel tank hissed.

Dammit, I had to move faster.

I pulled and pulled. The hiss grew.

The pressure from the fuel tank grew too. While there was a chance that the fuel might not explode, you never knew.

I had no intention of finding out.

Slowly, I pulled the body further away. I leaned down and pressed my ear to her chest.

She was breathing, albeit shallow.

I glanced around. *Why weren't they here yet?*

Thank goodness I knew CPR. Again one of our first basic training.

I checked for seizure-like symptoms. Her fists stayed neutral, and her arms were half-bent. No sign of that, but her breathing was shallow.

"Come on, Mia. Pull through," I said.

Her breathing further shallowed. *Fuck.* There was a chance if I didn't do something now that—

I shook my head. She was alive. I would not let her die.

Sirens echoed in the distance. The embers from the car traveled further, and a moment later, the flames grew double in size.

Close. *If I had been even a moment late...*

The ambulance and firetruck approached. Men got out, each of them fighting the giant blaze without a second thought.

I stayed there, ensuring that Mia didn't have a seizure or stopped breathing.

A paramedic approached. He looked at me and then at her.

"Is she okay?"

"She's breathing. Heartbeat is stable but faint."

"Got it. We've got it from here."

"Where are you taking her?"

The paramedic loaded Mia onto the gurney.

"St. Matthew's. The closest hospital to here. Are you family or her husband?"

I shook my head immediately. We did *not* have that kind of relationship.

"I'm her boss. She didn't have anyone else to call."

"I see. She'll be there in due time."

I trusted them with her. I knew she'd be okay, but my anxiety was still too high.

I knew my battles. They wouldn't let her die.

"I'm going to follow her to the hospital."

"That's fine. You're welcome to."

They got in the ambulance and drove off.

I stood there and looked at her car.

The firefighters hosed down the car with water. Smoke obscured the skies in a pitch-black hue.

Who the hell did this? It couldn't have just been some drunk crazy doing a hit-and-run, or could it?

I'll figure that out later.

Right now, all that mattered was her. I got back in my car and drove over to St. Matthews.

When I got inside, I discovered Mia had been admitted to the ICU.

The smoke inhalation choked her, and she struggled to breathe.

My hands gripped my thighs. I took a couple deep breaths as another panic attack threatened to come again.

No. I had to be strong for her.

My phone buzzed, and I looked down. Crap. It was Casey.

Hey bro, is everything okay? I'm here, but I don't see you.

I need to tell him.

I grabbed my phone and headed to the smoking area.

I hated the smell, but this was the closest place to where Mia was.

I called Casey, and two rings later, he spoke.

"Hey, bro! Everything okay? I've got drinks already."

"Hey Case. I'm sorry, but I won't be able to make it tonight."

"Oh. Is something wrong?"

Crap, how do I explain this? I took a deep breath as I tried to find the correct words.

"I'm sorry, I had something come up. I had to stay with Jacob."

I hated to lie to Casey. He meant the world to me. But if I brought up Mia, that was going to spell trouble with a capital T.

"Oh damn! I'm sorry. Well, if you want, I can come over and—"

"It's fine, Case. Don't worry, he'll be alright."

"Okay. Just let me know if things get fixed, alright? If you need anything, let me know."

As much as I regretted lying to him, I knew talking about Mia would bring up more questions than what it would be worth.

"Alright. I will bro. Thanks for understanding."

I hung up. A wave of regret settled over me.

Still, I couldn't leave Mia alone. I had to make sure she was stable, at least.

I couldn't live with myself if I let her go.

I went back inside and paced around the room.

About a half-hour later, the head doctor exited the ER.

His tired brown eyes looked around the room before he settled on me.

He raised a wrinkled finger, and I approached.

"You must be the one who found her, right?"

"Yes. Christian Hamilton."

He extended his hand.

"Dr. Marcus Grimes. I'm the head emergency doctor here. You're here for Mia, right?'

"Yeah. I'm just an associate. Had to make sure she was okay."

It stung saying that. He nodded as if he understood my plight.

"I get it. Well, she's recovering right now. I know you're not family, but…"

"That's fine. She'll be okay, right?"

"She will be. Luckily, there were no broken bones. You knew how to safely get her out of the car, didn't you?"

"Yes. I was a Navy SEAL for years."

"Well, you responded just like a first responder. She'll make it. Just give her time."

I followed him to room 304, where Mia slept. I took a chair from the corner and settled it next to the bed.

As Mia slept soundly, I thought about what to say.

I saved her because I had to. I always protected people, especially if they meant something to me.

But the longer I spent around Mia, the greater the temptation grew.

A part of me wondered if it was the mere desire to protect everyone around me or something deeper.

That was a question I wasn't sure if I was ready to answer yet.

Fourteen
Mia

Light poured into my eyes.

I opened them slowly. *Ouch!* My body felt as if I had been run over by a truck.

Then again, from what I remembered, that might've been the case.

My vision slowly came together. All I saw was white.

And a familiar head of blonde hair.

Wait, Christian?

There's no way he was here. I remembered calling him, but...

"You're awake."

I turned my head slightly. Chrisitan raised his hand, and I nodded.

"Yeah. Where am…I?"

"The hospital. They got you just in time."

I nodded.

"So I survived then? This isn't the afterlife."

"I mean, unless I died too, no." He tried to lighten the mood.

Chris being the only one I saw in the room brought up so many questions I wanted to ask.

Did the paramedics make it in time, or was he the one that saved me? How do I even thank him if he did?

I slowly rose upwards. Nothing was in a cast, but my chest felt heavy. I looked over at him and flushed.

"What happened to me, by the way? Like did I pass out or…"

"Smoke inhalation," he explained clinically. "The doctor says that you were close to having carbon dioxide poisoning. But I got you away from the scene in time."

"You saved me?"

He chuckled and brushed his hand against mine.

"Did you *forget* I was a Navy SEAL for years, Mia? It's my job to save those in trouble."

Oh. Right.

A pang of disappointment emanated within me. Ok, he said that it was because of that, but still.

"Yeah, you used to be a SEAL, but—"

"I took an oath when I joined, Mia. To save lives wherever I could. I followed that oath even after I completed service and still follow it to this day."

"I see. Thank you."

"But I was also worried. You said there was nobody else, right?"

I nodded.

"My friends were out of town. Nat was off at a club. She would've probably gotten there hours after the fact. And Mom wouldn't have been able to help me. She's not that strong, and I didn't want to worry her."

And then I cautiously continued, "I mean if this was a few months ago, I would've called Casey, but honestly,

I doubt he'd make it in time. He'd probably have gotten the message after the fact."

He nodded.

"I know what you mean."

"I appreciate it, Chris. Really. I could've died..." I cringed thinking about it.

He pulled his hand back and stood up to stretch.

"Well, you're safe now. I'm glad to see it."

"I am, too. I just wonder who hit me."

"That's a question you're better off asking later. *After* you've recovered."

He was right. I touched my chest and noticed a couple of bandages there.

I smiled. "My hero, I guess."

"Yeah, I am a hero," he bragged.

I rolled my eyes. Okay, maybe I'll give him this one. He did *earn* the badge.

I turned a little bit and grinned.

"Again, thank you so much."

"Hey, no problem."

Our hands touched. He held it tightly, and when we locked eyes, the lingering urge to ask him what this meant sifted through me.

I wanted to stay away, for both our sakes. Professionalism would just make this so much easier.

Under his words, even if they were meant solely for protection, I sensed something more.

"There is something more, isn't there?"

He scoffed and turned away.

"No, there is not."

"Chris, I'm—"

"Mia, for your own sake, don't take this the wrong way. I just wanted to make sure you were okay."

I looked down to hide my disappointment. We weren't dating, but I sensed an element of care that differed from his normal actions.

"Okay. I'll drop it."

He leaned in, and our lips sat inches from each other. I smelled the faint hint of cinnamon and expensive cologne.

A pleasant scent, one that I couldn't deny I enjoyed.

"I am glad you're okay, Mia."

He nearly pressed his lips to mine. I sat there, unsure of whether I wanted to close the gap or not.

I mean I wanted to. The desire from each of those nights hung over me.

Plus, it was clear he did like me in some regard. Even if he didn't want to pursue this.

Still, it created tension, which I wasn't sure if I liked.

He pulled back before we could deepen it any more.

"I'll be back as soon as I can."

"Don't be a stranger."

"I cannot guarantee that," he teased.

He walked out the door before I could say much else.

I clutched the sheets as I thought about what happened.

Chris was such an enigma. One minute, he was over here saving me, with clearly deeper intentions. The next, he blew me off.

Still, without him, I didn't know where I'd be.

"Mia?"

I looked towards the door. Mom raced in with tears in her eyes.

"Oh, my baby girl! You're okay!"

Mom enveloped me in a tight hug. I hugged her back just as tightly.

"Hey, mom, I'm okay."

She pulled back and wiped away the tears.

"I was so worried. When the doctor called me to say you were here and unconscious, I drove over immediately."

"I know, mom. I'm sorry to worry you."

Mom looked around the hospital room curiously.

"I heard that someone saved you. Was it Toby? He's always cared for you and Nat—"

"Actually, it was Chris."

Mom stopped and stood there wide-eyed and surprised.

"Oh."

"Yeah. He helped. I called him as a last resort."

"That's good to hear," Mom replied as she smiled. "He's a good guy."

"Yeah, he is," I admitted.

Which made our relationship so much more complicated.

I appreciated all that Chris did for me. But, to cross that boundary, especially after all that happened, just felt so damn wrong.

"Is he still here? It'd be nice to see and thank him."

That's right. Mom did meet him one time at some family gathering that Casey's parents invited us to.

It was awkward. Mom came from a more middle-class family.

The wealth overwhelmed her, and while Casey and Chris's Mom was sweet, there was a clear discrepancy between both parties.

"He just left. He didn't stay too long."

"I see. Well, I'll have to thank him later for saving your life."

"I'm sure he'll appreciate that."

Mom smiled. Her eyes sat tired. She was so worried about me.

I didn't blame her. I thought I was a goner.

Mom and I spent the rest of the day in the hospital.

Once the doctor okayed me to leave, I left with her.

The doctor mentioned if there were problems with my breathing, to come back. Yeah, like that would happen.

This hospital was over an hour from my place. I didn't have a car either.

Mom drove me back to my apartment. When we got there, she turned to me and rested a tender hand on my shoulder.

"Stay with me for a bit."

"But mom, I—"

"I have a car, Mia. I'll make room at the house."

I shook my head. "It's fine, don't worry about it and—"

"No! I'm not going to lose anyone else."

Her voice rose, and her eyes filled with tears.

There was no use fighting her.

"Alright, mom. I'll stay."

Mom hugged me tightly. I hugged her back to reassure her.

My thoughts swarmed with different thoughts.

Would Chris tell Casey about me?

I doubted it, but still.

That was a question for another day. For now, I had to focus on recovering and getting back into the swing of things.

Fifteen
Chris

"You made it! No driver?"

I stepped out of my Bugatti and locked it.

"You know I prefer driving, Casey."

"But then you've got to sober your butt up before you go home! Where's the fun in that?"

I sighed, closing the door of the car, and followed Casey into the restaurant.

He slid into one of the barstools, and I took one next to him.

"Plus, I am supposed to head back to the office soon."

"True. Duty calls, I guess."

I chuckled. "You're right. It never stops."

The bartender got our orders. As he turned back, Casey leaned over a little.

"Hey, so what happened the other day? You *never* miss out on meeting up."

The bartender brought me my port just as he asked. Thank god. I still didn't know what to tell him.

He was right. Casey and I always made an effort to hang out. Even when I had busy-as-hell days, I always made sure to let him know.

We'd sometimes move the times, but we always managed to figure out how to hang out.

This was a rarity.

"Oh, yeah, something came up."

"I see. I didn't want to pry, but I was worried."

"It's all good, Casey. I get it. It was just a personal emergency."

"Personal? Was it about Jacob?"

I shook my head. "No, something else. Work-related."

"Ahh, I see," Casey replied.

He grabbed his beer and took a long swig before he sat it down.

His expression changed. Sadness sat on his face.

"I'm sorry, Chris. It was just off of you to do that."

I couldn't fault Casey for feeling this way.

We were bros, and I always made sure to be there for him.

He had even less support from our parents and also relied on babysitters like I did. I had to provide reassurance every now and then.

"I know. I promise it won't happen again."

"It's just…"

Casey chews on his lip.

I rested my hand on his shoulder as he ruminated on what to say.

"What's up? You never get like this, bro."

"I know, it's just…it's about Mia."

Great. Just the name I needed to hear. After I saved her life, I kept my distance.

I didn't want to open the door to something I wasn't ready for.

"What about her?"

"It's just, I'm trying to get over her, man. It's been over a month now, but I still think about her every day."

"I get it. You loved her."

As I uttered those words, a pang hit my chest. Casey *did* love her. Which was what made everything all the worse.

"I did. Honestly, I know she broke up with me back then because of my immaturity, but I wanted to change."

"How so?"

"I don't know! I'm still trying to figure it out. Having all this freedom's messed with my damn brain. I don't have the direction you do! You've got all your shit figured out."

"Hell no. I don't."

"Well, more than me!"

"Because I had to grow up, Casey," I replied as I patted his shoulder. "I had to be the older brother. And I always will be."

Casey looked down at the beer, now only a couple dregs.

"Yeah, I just sometimes wished I had the confidence that you do. Sure, I act like I'm not hurt, but her ending things still tore me up."

His wound was still fresh. Even the mess with Alara and her cheating on me still bothered me from time to time, and that happened years ago.

So I could understand Casey.

"I get it. Life hasn't been easy for me either."

"I know Chris. But I'm jealous. I really am."

"You've got *nothing* to be jealous about."

I was a Dad trying to make the world as best as I could make it for my son. All while dealing with an ex-wife who occasionally thrusts her way into my life.

Easy? Nah, but I made it work.

"I am trying to see other girls. So far, it's been…interesting."

"Like flings?"

"Yeah, but none of them really bring that spark to me the way Mia did. But she already made it crystal clear to me that she didn't want to try again."

"I'd say just take some time for yourself and figure out what *you* want."

"Maybe. I don't have the answers to that yet."

"Well, there you go. That's where you have to begin. Holding onto the past isn't going to ever make things easier."

Casey sighed. "You're right, dude. And I hate it."

"Remember the goals we went over a while back. Work on those, and I'm sure the right gal will come to you."

"Yeah, I'll do my best."

Casey turned to me and smiled. It was that genuine grin he only gave to me these days.

"I love you man. You've been there since everything. You always know exactly what to say. And you seeing me whenever I'm in town does help with these feelings that seem almost overwhelming at times."

"I'm glad to help."

It bothered me to say that. Was I helping? In a way, I felt like I betrayed Casey with every word.

It wasn't a one-time thing either. I did it multiple times.

How much longer can I keep up these lies?

Casey ordered another beer. I did the same.

As the bartender walked to refill our drinks, he smiled.

"I'm glad we can talk like this. Is everything good with your company? I know there was that emergency, but otherwise..."

"Yeah, we're good."

I refused to tell him anything about Mia. He didn't need to know.

Casey frowned. "You sure? I want to make sure you're okay, too."

"I'm fine, dude. I promise."

"Alright. Fine. I won't bother then. I just want this to be a two-way street. You help me, I help you."

My hand tightened against the counter.

Yeah, it stopped being like that the second Mia and my lips met.

I closed my eyes as I tried to figure out what to say.

"I'm good. Trust me, Casey. I've just got my own lot to deal with, with Alara and all."

"Oh God, is she still doing that shit? She needs to move the hell on."

"Hey, I'm not opening the door to any of that. She's the one who needs help."

I steered the conversation towards that. It helped with the lie.

Still, it was so wrong of me to do this. I *never* lied to Casey before. That was something I always kept true to.

But the more I helped Mia, the harder it was to know what I wanted.

I did help her and I chalked it up to the SEAL training, which was true.

And I'd do it again, too. But there was something greater growing deep within my heart.

I had to push that away before I did something I knew would turn my world upside down.

Casey's phone beeped, and he looked down.

"Oh damn!"

"What's up?"

"I have a race tomorrow evening out in Toledo."

"Ohio?"

"Hey, Toledo has a *killer* racing scene. Hopefully, my new rig can stand up to the competition."

I chuckled. "I'm sure it will. I've got to get back to work, too."

And get something in my stomach. The bar was nice, but the food options were limited.

Mostly just finger foods and fried crap. I maintained a strict diet of balanced foods.

I needed something to sustain me, because I had meetings upon meetings to go to this afternoon.

Something I was *not* looking forward to.

We paid for our drinks, and as Casey exited the door, he turned.

"Again, dude, don't fight the good fight alone."

"I won't."

I told myself this, but I never could let people in. When it came to life, being alone would just make the pain easier.

Especially when it involved long-term pain that was hard to ignore.

"Alright. I'll text you when I'm back in the area. Next time, let's go to the racetrack here! You can check out my sweet driving."

"I'd love that bro. I'll text ya tomorrow to follow up."

"Sounds good!"

After one last friendly hug, Casey headed out of the bar.

I used the restroom, and then headed to the exit.

I still had about forty-five minutes.

I took extended lunches once a week because I needed them.

Occasionally, they were spent meeting with other businessmen.

Collaborations were best served over food.

Tay's Café was right next door. They had foods that fit my diet and also tasted great.

I headed out of the bar and to the café.

I looked in the parking lot as I left. Casey had already headed out.

As I approached the café, something bothered me. I couldn't explain it, but hesitation coursed through me.

I shook it off a moment later. *It must be my imagination.*

I opened the door and heard a familiar voice to my right as I stepped into the small café.

"Oh yeah! I'm actually working on a software project similar to that. Dad would be super proud if he was here with us."

Wait a second, that's—

In the corner of the café sat Mia and a woman who looked similar to her but about thirty years older. Her age-old face smiled at Mia's words and pantomimes.

It was her mom. I had seen her once before, in some family gathering, when Mia was still dating Casey.

Mia looked to her right, eyes wide with surprise, as both of us realized the situation.

Sixteen
Mia

Chris?

I looked back at Mom and forced a smile.

She did not need to know Chris was here.

For one, besides a few gatherings during my relationship with Casey, Mom and Chris barely spoke to each other.

Plus, the awkwardness of the gathering his parents had invited us to still hang over the air.

Not to mention, Mom knew Casey and I's history.

"Wait a second, that's—"

"Hi, Chris," I managed to spit out.

He waved a little bit. Mom's jaw dropped, and she leaned over.

"That's Casey's brother, right? I remembered him from the party."

I nodded. *This is not what we need.* Chris and I *both* agreed to stay away from each other.

This would only make things *more* awkward.

"Chris! Over here," Mom exclaimed, gesturing towards our table.

No, mom, don't!

Chris stopped dead in his tracks. He turned a little bit, half-smiling. He walked over and stood near the table.

"Yes?"

"Oh, my Mom was just—"

"You're the one that saved Mia, right? She mentioned you when I went to visit her in the hospital."

Christian didn't say anything. He glared at me. Crap, he was pissed.

"Mom asked who found me. I mentioned you were a last resort and—"

Mom stood up. "Thank you for saving her. I appreciate it."

Mom enveloped Chris in a tight hug.

I sat there and looked around for any attempt to dispel the awkward atmosphere.

"It's nothing," Chris muttered.

His displeasured face communicated the same thing mine did.

Mom smiled and then turned to me. *Please just thank him and let him go on his way.*

The *last* thing I needed was for her to make this any more awkward than it already was.

Mom sat down but closely observed Chris.

"You know, he really does look like Casey. Just older."

"Yeah, he does."

Oh my god, please let the ground open and swallow me up.

Chris coughed and turned.

"I should probably get lunch and head back and—"

"Really, though. Casey's a sweet guy, but I never really got to know you."

He pursed his lips.

"I'm usually focused on other ventures and don't have time for small talk. You probably met me while I was focused on business."

"Oh, I see. That's nice. You're definitely different from Casey. More reserved."

Yeah, and an arrogant jerk who calls himself off.

"I don't want to burden others with small talk, especially if it's *unnecessary*."

Mom looked down and took a bite of her salad.

"Mom, we should probably let him go."

"You're right, dear. He's certainly interesting."

"Thank you, Miss. Tipton. And I'd love to talk more, but I have a *business* to attend to. Something I'm sure Mia is all too keen on also going back to."

I smiled. I really wasn't.

I had a couple of projects to tackle, but this conversation was already getting awkward.

Please, just drop all this and go away.

"Alright, well, I don't want to eat up too much of your time. I just wanted to thank you for saving my daughter's life. Maybe we'll meet again."

"Perhaps. I hope you have a good day, Ms. Tipton."

With the same brusque tone he just used, he walked away and sat at another table.

Thank goodness. I didn't want to think about the possibility of Mom inviting Chris to sit at dinner with us in the future.

Mom picked up the rest of her salad.

An awkward silence flowed between us. From time to time, I caught her stealing glances at Chris.

"He's an interesting man. Not the friendliest, but…"

"He's pretty abrasive, Mom," I replied. "You know how he was at that function. A little quiet and distant from everyone."

"True. He's different from Casey, though. I remembered Casey struck conversation with me the second I walked in."

Well, that was how Casey did things. He knew how to talk to impress. His social skills made him the life of the party. And what made me fall in love with him in the first place.

Chris was a contrast. Cold, aloof, and closed off.

"I'm surprised he even acknowledged us," I muttered.

"Why would he ignore us?" she asked. "He saved your life, and you're one of his employees."

I bit my lip from confessing our complicated history.

It was just as awkward for him as it was for me.

Mom sighed and turned to me.

"I am glad to see you, though, Mia. Did the insurance company give you money for a rental?"

I nodded. "Yeah, and insurance covered everything. I should have the payout for a new car sooner than later."

"I'm glad. You know you're always welcome to use my car if you don't want to wait."

I couldn't do that to mom. She had her lady's group and the support group for deceased spouses.

She had her life, and I had mine.

Not just because it was ugly but because it was a gas guzzler.

Even just taking it to the office for a few days prior to getting the rental ate into my budget.

Plus, her car was dicey going long distances. Sometimes it would work. Other times, it'd struggle with acceleration. It was an old model, but Mom refused to let it go.

Probably cause Dad bought it for her before his diagnosis.

"I'm good mom. How is your support group doing?"

A sad smile crossed Mom's face. *She's still hurting, even after so many years.*

"It's okay. I finally came to terms with accepting that he's gone."

I nodded and smiled. "Hey, that's a step in the right direction."

"Yeah. Something I should've done ages ago."

I shook my head. Mom didn't need to beat herself up over moving on.

"Don't be upset. Remember, it took me going to the hospital for treatments to finally get the strength to move on. You two were together for decades."

"Twenty-five years, Mia."

"Exactly. My way of coping wasn't healthy, I know, but I eventually figured out alternatives to move on."

And to fight the anorexia that plagued me throughout most of my teenage and early adulthood years.

I cringed thinking about it. It wasn't like I could just forget about the pain it caused me. For years, I struggled with eating after my dad's death.

It was only when I got down to a dangerous 90 pounds and passed out while walking to my high school graduation that I finally realized I had to do something about it.

I got help. I got treatment.

I wanted Mom to do the same.

"I know. It's just nice to be able to finally say this. You know how long It's been bothering me."

"Yeah, quite a while."

"Yes. I just hope one day I can look at those pictures and hang them back up again."

"You will, Mom," I reassured her.

My watch beeped, which indicated I had fifteen minutes left in my lunch break. I stood up and sighed.

"Anyways, I better go. I'll come over for dinner this Friday."

I went back to my apartment shortly after the accident. I didn't want to burden Mom too much.

She didn't take it well at first but understood after I explained.

"Great. And maybe we can try out this new spa kit that Delores gave me."

I grinned. "I'd love that."

I paid for Mom's food, and we embraced. As Mom pulled away, she smiled.

"Remember, you're stronger than you think. And don't let whatever Chris does get to you."

"I won't mom. Promise."

I headed back to work. When I got there, Chris wasn't back yet.

Good. We didn't have to talk about how awkward lunch was.

I made my way back to the office, where I had my first meeting of the afternoon.

It was with the software team, and they showed me some of the products.

I gave them the okay, and they'd send them to Chris. Hopefully, we'll get an answer soon.

I worked through the day, thoughts of Chris still eating away at me.

Why can't he just go away? Why does he have to invade my every thought?

It pissed me off, especially since we both mutually agreed not to engage.

Five came sooner than expected. As I sent out the last email, I sat back and sighed.

Another day was completed.

I moved my mouse over to the power button, ready to shut it down. As I clicked on it, an email appeared.

WE HAVE A PROBLEM. URGENT.

What the hell? I paused, unsure of what to do.

I mean, I was *technically* off the clock. Everyone else was gone.

But the overachiever me couldn't just leave things incomplete.

I opened the email, and as I stared at the contents, I grimaced.

Great.

It seemed that the QA team tried to run some code, but they messed up on some lines.

The products had to be ready for presentation tomorrow.

Chris planned to show them to Alan Hernandez, one of the main product distributors.

Shit.

There was *no* way I could leave this alone.

I sighed and opened the line of code.

Well, guess duty calls again.

The code was a complete mess. I didn't think I'd seen a technician fuck up that bad.

My fingers typed, fixing lines upon lines.

There was still so much to do.

The door clicked open, and I whipped my head around. *Who was still here?*

Piercing blue eyes greeted me as I sat frozen in place.

Christian?

He approached, arms folded across his chest.

VALENCIA ROSE

"Miss Tipton, where is the code I asked for? I expected it an hour ago."

Seventeen
Chris

Mia gestured to the computer.

"It's here. The QA team royally screwed up."

I leaned in and looked. I scoffed and stepped back.

"These people were supposed to be in your charge."

"Yeah, well, I didn't expect them to mess up this badly. I'm trying to fix this, so you have something tomorrow."

I nodded and looked at the contents.

"Well, thanks."

"I'm not doing this for you, Chris. I'm doing this for the company. This merger's hard on both of us, and I'm just trying to do my best here."

"I know. You're one of the *few* people I can count on here."

"I'm glad. Anyways, I don't want to keep you too late. I'll have it in your hands by morning and—"

"Actually, there was something I wanted to ask you about."

Mia paused. Her eyes met mine.

"I thought you and I both agreed not to discuss personal matters during business hours?"

We did. But after what happened at lunch the other day, her mother's words hung over me.

She thanked me for saving Mia. So Mia had told *her* about me.

A conflict of emotions settled through me.

"What's the matter?" Mia asked again.

"Your mother. Why does she know I saved you?"

"Because I told her. Is there a problem?"

"Yes. I didn't want you to."

"Too late for that. I couldn't just lie and say it was a random guy."

"You damn well could have. Now she knows."

She stepped out of the chair and walked towards me. Our bodies were close, and she smiled.

"Why is it a problem?"

"Because I wanted to move on! I never wanted to get involved like this."

Her Mom knowing spelled trouble. She might ask about me even more.

While she knew me vaguely because of Casey, I still never wanted to breach the boundary.

"I know. But it doesn't mean anything. Unless *you* want it to mean something."

I hesitated. I looked around, trying to figure out what to do.

"I don't want it to. I made a mistake twice. I'm trying hard not to do it again."

"So then, why did you have to bring it up? We could've just dropped it, you know? I personally had planned to do so until you barged in here and mentioned it."

I gritted my teeth. "Your mom's going to ask about me again. That's going to open the door to problems and—"

"What problems? She doesn't even know about what happened between us. We can just go back to the way things have been, where you ignore me and don't say a damn word. So what'll it be?"

I pursed my lips as I attempted to figure out how to approach this. I wanted to forget all of this.

"That night never happened, Mia. I'm just trying to forget! Don't bring me up to your Mom again!"

I stormed out of the office. I couldn't take this anymore.

The regret pooled, and Casey's words hung over me.

He still wasn't over Mia.

I was such a piece of trash for making a move. For *still* holding onto these feelings.

What am I supposed to do? The storm of emotions overwhelmed me as I reached the elevator.

I pressed the button.

Suddenly, my vision blurred, and I wasn't able to make out even the lights.

Ringing echoed through my ears. My heart raced, and I clutched my chest. My breaths grew shallow.

Goddammit.

I reached for the wall as I choked out small, baited breaths. *Another attack at the worst possible time.*

I took a few more breaths as I tried to calm down.

Stress triggered these attacks sometimes. I always tried to avoid it, but it was impossible.

I gasped for air, frozen in place. My heart raced so fast that I thought I was having a heart attack.

Not now!

A hand rested on my shoulder and gently squeezed it.

The hand moved to the middle of my back and rubbed against there.

Another hand joined and pulled me into a tight embrace.

What the—Mia?

My heart slowed down. Air came back in gulps. My vision cleared as I looked up.

Her hazel eyes stared at me as a gentle smile fell on her face.

"It's okay. What's going on?"

Her hands were soft, and they held me tightly.

I wanted to push her away, to forget all this ever happened.

Her hands squeezed me tightly and provided reassurance.

"Chris, talk to me! Are you okay? Do you need anything?"

But they stayed there and helped with the lingering feelings.

Reality settled back in. I looked up and saw Mia smiling at me.

"Are you back?"

I stepped back and nodded.

"Yeah, I'm fine. Don't worry about me."

The elevator dinged. I headed inside when I felt a hand touch my shoulder.

"Was that a panic attack just now?"

"Yeah, but don't worry yourself about it."

"I just want to make sure you're okay."

I turned around and looked her in the eyes. All she had to do was leave me the hell alone.

Now we were here, and a storm of conflicting emotions raced through me. *Again.* I didn't want her involved in my life.

She was Casey's ex. It was too much baggage to keep around.

I had to be strong for him and for Jacob. But she just weaseled her way back into my life, like some kind of messed up reminder.

"Why do you care?"

"Oh gee, maybe because you practically had a heart attack right in front of me. Oh, and don't worry. This doesn't have to change anything."

I looked up. Her sweet, caring hazel eyes stayed laser-focused on me.

I took a deep breath as I maintained my composure.

"They happen sometimes. I don't like to have them in front of others. I make sure they never happen in front of my son."

"There's nothing to be ashamed of Chris. I know you've been through a lot and—"

"Yeah, and that's why I'm leaving. Have a good night."

Damn. The elevator had left already. I pressed the button again and a moment later, the doors opened.

I walked into the elevator. One of my feet stepped inside. The other stayed outside.

Why? Why couldn't I leave?

It was like a pull from the universe, magnetizing and keeping me there.

I turned around, and the fight in my heart continued.

I wanted to leave, and yet there was no chance I could.

Even though my head told me otherwise, I knew I had to tell her. If only to get the burden off my chest.

So I did.

Eighteen
Mia

Christian stepped out of the elevator. It closed.

He didn't say a word. Instead, he brushed past me and headed into my office.

That was his implicit way of telling me to follow.

It conflicted me to see him like this.

I wanted to know the truth, to find out what I could do to help him. But I also knew that if I asked, it could cause a whole ocean of trouble.

Was I ready for what Chris went through?

I stepped into the office. He sat in my chair, head in his hands.

I grabbed one of the other chairs in my office and sat a comfortable distance next to him.

"How are you doing?"

"Fine, I guess."

I reached for the jug of water and a water cup I kept in my office.

I always made sure to hydrate. It helped me stay focused, and with last-minute projects out the butt, it was the perfect way to wake up.

I poured a glass of water and handed it to him.

"Sorry if it's a little lukewarm. I planned on dumping it after I finished the project."

He took a couple of trepid sips and nodded.

"Thanks."

I reached out. He grabbed my hand but didn't say anything.

"I'm alright. It's just…that's the first time I didn't need to use the pills."

"Pills?"

He reached for a container in his pocket.

"Anti-anxiety pills prescribed for panic disorders. Including my panic attacks."

"So you take these?" I asked.

"I've relied on these for so long that I didn't know if I could ever come down without them."

"I'm glad you didn't have to rely on them this time."

He shrugged. "Yeah, but still. I never wanted to show that side to you. It's just complicated, to say the least."

I nodded. "I see."

It had been quite a journey for Chris. I remember Casey had mentioned once that Chris had some mental health issues and went to therapy. I didn't expect this though.

"I'm sorry for having one in front of you. I always have them in private places. If they happen in front of Jacob, I retreat to the office. He knows when to leave me alone. If they happen in front of my mom, I just go to another room. At the office, I just stay in my place or head to the bathroom."

I know for some people, having these is shameful. Chris, being as prideful as he is, probably sees them as a sign of weakness. I hated that.

"You don't have to be ashamed for having them Chris. I know how hard it can be to fight your battles."

"And what would you know about that?"

I bit my lip. It pissed me off that he thought I didn't get it.

"Oh, maybe the fact that I literally lost my Dad thirteen years ago and then battled with anorexia for three years?"

He looked up. *Shit, maybe I shouldn't have trauma dumped.*

"I'm sorry," I added quickly.

"No, It's fine. Casey never mentioned that."

"Yeah, well, I tried not to bring it up too much. He knew about Dad but not the fallout."

I touched my ribcage. The aftereffects still lingered.

I ate these days, but it was still in smaller portions. Whenever I felt my ribcage, it bothered me.

The reminders of back then haunted me. They reminded me of the battle I went through.

"Anyways, I know what it's like to fight a battle you can't tell anyone. I only got help after I passed out during graduation, and they had to call the paramedics for me."

"Wow."

"Yeah."

We sat in silence. Christian's face softened ever-so-slightly.

"The only person who knows about these panic attacks is Casey. And my ex-wife, but she's not in the picture right now."

I nodded. The realization of the intimacy of this moment made things awkward.

Where do we go from here? Do I want to forget, to pretend like nothing ever happened?

"If you want, we can just not talk about this and—"

"No, I can't do that. You were the first to calm me down without the aid of medicine. Even Casey couldn't do that."

I nodded. "Yeah, Casey tries to understand mental health, but he sometimes has trouble."

"That's the problem with him. He says I'm supposed to get over it. He doesn't understand it's not possible for me to just say a magic word and wish these away. If I could, I would."

"Don't push yourself, Chris. Really. But I'm glad that you're doing better."

"Thank you, Mia."

We didn't say a word. A thought lingered, bothering me for a moment. It tempted me to ask. And I did.

"Why do you have these attacks? What prompts them?"

"I can't explain it yet, but I've been through a lot in the military. I just never bothered to tell anyone."

"Understandably."

"I'm not ready to tell you. But I do appreciate you listening. It means a lot."

His jaw relaxed slightly. A movement that almost looked like a smile crossed his face.

"I'm glad to help. I know I shouldn't, but you helped me. I should at least try to return the favor."

"I appreciate it."

Desire flooded through me. I knew I shouldn't listen to it, but it ate at me like a nagging wound.

Chris sighed and stood up.

"I don't know how to feel about you, Mia. Part of me wants to just never say a damn thing to you ever again. But then I can't bring myself to. I feel like I'm the bad guy every time I feel this way."

"I get it. I feel that way too."

He reached out and touched my face. Those large, protective hands felt overwhelming against my skin.

I wanted to feel them so badly in other places.

His lips lingered over mine.

"Mia, I should not feel this way about you. I'm such a mess and—"

"Maybe you need to stop thinking with your head for a bit and think with this."

I pointed to his heart. He frowned.

"I know, and thinking with that is what got me in this mess in the first place."

"You can't deny it either, though. The feelings you have for me."

"No, I can't, and it's what makes me want to kiss you right now."

"So do it. Do what you want. We can keep this between us, just like the other times."

Why the hell was I saying this? I shouldn't even be *entertaining* the idea of being with Christian again.

We *promised* to not let this get any further again.

And yet, neither of us pulled away.

We could at any time. I could extricate myself and go back to the coding.

And he could leave and go home to his son.

Instead, we stayed here with our breaths intermingled and lust in between our bodies.

"Mia, you make me feel so many things."

"So figure them out. But until then, do what *you* feel is right. Whatever you choose, I won't judge you."

I expected him to pull away. He didn't want this, right?

Instead, his lips drew closer, closing the gap between us.

I should have pulled away. I was trying to move on.

Plus, the breakup with Casey still hung deeply over my heart.

I didn't, though.

Instead, I wrapped my arms around him and settled against his dominating lips.

All rational thought disappeared as soon as he kissed me.

Or maybe this was the right choice after all.

Nineteen
Chris

Dammit, why do I keep doing this?

This is wrong of me! I told myself it was a mistake and I shouldn't make a move.

But was it really a mistake when I felt this damn good?

Mia kissed me back. And soon, I was lost against her lips. They were plump, and the faint scent of peaches had me hooked from the start.

I pressed her against the open part of her desk and kissed her passionately. I hated to admit it felt so good.

Just like the previous times, I refused to pull away. Not when this felt so good.

My hands brushed against her soft, subtle curves.

She moaned softly, and I pressed my hands forward towards the front of her suit jacket. I undid the buttons and practically tore the bottom ones off.

I had to be careful or I might tear them again just like I did with her panties that night in the club.

I didn't care anymore. My member throbbed as I ached to feel again what I had experienced before.

I'm going to regret this.

I kept telling myself this.

And yet, deep down, I didn't think that was the case here. Maybe this was what I secretly wanted, and Mia knew exactly how to pull those feelings out of me.

I dominated the kiss, and she moaned against me.

I pulled back and kissed down her pale neck. She moaned again, and every sound she made drove me crazy.

She had this way about her that sucked me in.

And while I told myself I shouldn't do this; the reality was right there.

I wanted this, even if it wasn't right.

I kissed her collarbone and sucked on the flesh.

She clenched against me and gave me a complete view of the flesh that throbbed there. I wanted to bite it, to mark it, but stopped myself.

The last time I did that, I remembered seeing the little mark she had the next day at the office. It drove me crazy wanting to do it again. And again.

I couldn't get any work done. I refused to repeat that.

I slipped down, my hands following.

Every touch felt like I was making a mistake. Any minute now, I'd wake up, and the crushing reality would settle in.

And yet, there was a part of me that knew I was in the right place.

Kissing her passionately, indulging in every part of her, and savoring the taste.

Desire overwhelmed every rational thought once again.

That pull to have something more, and to experience every part of Mia that I could.

I pulled the final buttons on the jacket aside and pushed her suit jacket shirt off her body.

Her breasts sat in a nude-colored bra, ready to spill out. I caressed down and teased the flesh as it borderlined her breasts.

"Mia..."

What the hell was I doing? I broke my promise *again*. But maybe that promise wasn't correct after all.

The truth was right here.

Mia did something that nobody else could. Even Alara never managed to talk me down.

I needed this. I didn't care what it took, but I had to savor this moment together with her.

I slipped my fingers into the back of her bra and pulled it off.

Desire crossed my body as she sat there, topless for me.

Her breasts looked perfect. Her thin, lithe body was so perfect, and I wanted to envelop every part of her against me.

Dammit! I couldn't pull away.

My lips dipped down and captured her nipple against my lips. My fingers brushed against the tip of her other nipple.

She moaned and instinctually wrapped her arms around me.

The sweet mewls ignited that fire and turned it into a blazing inferno.

There was no way out. I needed her, and the ache became almost unbearable.

I tugged on the nipple hard, just the way I knew she liked it.

Those delicious sounds that escaped her mouth goaded me for more.

"You like this, don't you? You like it when I just disrobe you right here and take what's mine."

"Yes," she breathed out, the sound barely audible.

Not that I needed any goading. All that I needed was Mia and the things she did to me.

I flicked my tongue against the other nipple, basking in the sounds uttered from those sweet lips. My tongue lapped the bud in circles and savored the sounds that came from her lips. A mixture of pure pleasure and passion combined with a little stifle of regret.

Yes, I need her.

I deepened my touches, pulled a bit harder, and did everything I could to hear those sounds again. Mia's cries were like a litany.

They reminded me of the pleasure I refused to avoid.

My rod ached in my pants and practically ripped through the middle. I had to feel her.

Every part of her sat there, just waiting for me.

I slipped my hands into her stockings and pulled them down. Her shoes came with them.

I pushed her skirt up until I got to see enough of her pussy. She was glistening and looked absolutely perfect.

I spread her legs apart and rested my hand against the outline before I teased her folds.

She whimpered and closed her eyes. Little gasps escaped her even before I put a finger in.

"Chris…"

"Just relax," I assured her and then whispered to her, "I love hearing the sounds that come out of you. They drive me fucking crazy."

That was true. They pulled me in, sucking me into the vortex of a desire I so desperately wished to escape from.

There was no way out. Even if I wanted there to be, I knew the reality of the situation settled there like a grim reminder of what I really desired.

But, of course, that didn't stop me from fighting for what I wanted.

One touch of my lips to her wet core was enough to silence all of those thoughts.

I flicked my tongue against her folds, tasting her sweet nectar. She was so wet for me.

I pushed her legs all the way apart and she reached for my head. Her hands touched my hair and gently tugged at it, begging for more.

"You want this?"

"Yes. It feels so fucking good."

That goaded me and drove all the potential regrets and thoughts away.

I lapped my tongue against her entrance, and with each pressing moment she held me tighter, practically begging me.

She filled my mouth with her sweet cunt, and I couldn't pull away.

I needed more.

I pushed my tongue inside. She clenched up and cried out my name.

All I heard were the mewls of desire. All I felt were her hands as they tightened against my shoulders.

She sent me into a different world, one that I knew was taboo.

And yet, I couldn't leave.

I pushed deeper, tasting everything inside.

She clenched harder against me, and when I found that sensitive spot within, I teased it.

My fingers traced her clit before I rubbed my thumb against the tip.

She cried out and rested her hands against my head.

Fuck. If this was wrong, I never wanted to be right.

I continued to savor her.

I felt her hips grind against my face, her wetness driving me crazy.

I knew I shouldn't like this. I knew that it was a betrayal of trust.

But the only thing I wanted right now was her and her alone.

I continued thrusting deeply inside until I felt the hand clench tighter against my head.

She held me like a vice grip, and soon, I heard the sweet sound of my name.

She threw her head back as pleasure enveloped her.

Goddammit.

I pulled away and locked my lips. I still tasted her there.

I looked at Mia, naked minus her skirt, eyes clouded with lust.

If we did this again, there was no way around this.

I could never go back from this.

Did I want to, though?

The reality of the situation hung over me as I started to fumble for a condom in my wallet.

I pulled my pants down far enough to free my member. As I wrapped myself up, I looked at her.

Spread out and inviting. *Just the way I liked it.*

I pushed myself between her folds and groaned.

Fuck she was tighter than usual. It was like she was waiting to experience me once again.

Once I got all the way in, an inaudible cry escaped her. She smiled a moment later.

I didn't move, surprised by the way she looked.

"Mia, I'm—"

"Please, Chris. Don't stop."

I didn't intend to. We could discuss the ethics of this later and what it meant.

Right now, I needed to experience every part of her and to have that body entwined with mine.

I reached for her hips and held them partially off the desk. I wrapped her thighs over my shoulders.

"You'll love how this feels," I stated with a smile.

Before I could utter anything else, I slammed inside...hard. I moved at a rhythm, and she clung to me.

"Yes, yes!"

"Good. I need this, Mia,"

"I need it too and—"

She thrusted her hips upwards as a high-pitched moan of desire escaped her lips. She squeezed me tightly.

It was like she wanted to milk everything from me. If we continued like this, she might just do that.

I continued, indulging in the moment, and the ache grew.

After a few more thrusts, Mia clutched me tightly. Her hands moved upwards to the collar of my suit.

"Chris, I'm—"

Her orgasm exploded. Her walls squeezed me so tight there was no way I *could* go any longer.

I pulled her against my body, and as my orgasm filled her completely, we stayed like this.

And again, my thoughts came... *It was wrong. I did it again. I made the same mistake again.*

Or did I? I looked into Mia's eyes and saw the same desire that mine had.

I pulled away and buttoned up my pants.

She sat there, biting her lip as she tried to figure out what to say.

"Chris. What does this mean?"

I wished I had the answers to that. I refused to dismiss it like last time.

"I don't know Mia. And I don't know how to stop myself when we're close."

The truth was, I wanted to tell Mia things I never thought would cross my mind. Hidden truths about my past I kept from everyone.

She saw but a part of my secrets. I wanted to let her in, even though I knew there were many things that could go wrong once I did.

"Alright. I guess we'll just leave it at that, then."

"Yes, let's leave it at that."

We got our clothes back on. I looked over at the computer, where a half-finished project sat.

"You should get that done."

"I will. It'll be in your inbox first thing in the morning."

"Thanks, Mia."

"Chris?"

"What?"

"I don't know how to feel either. But I like this, even if it is terrible of me."

I nodded. Casey would kill me if he knew the truth. I didn't know what I'd do if he ever figured it out.

It was better not to tell him.

"I feel the same."

I left the office with a heap of regrets. But, as things started to change, I realized the truth was obvious.

I couldn't get enough of Mia, and from the looks of it, she desired me too.

Twenty
Mia

"By the way, Alan loved the software. Everything worked perfectly."

I stopped dead in my tracks. I nodded but refused to look Christian in the eyes.

"I'm glad they did."

"Yes. You've done well so far, Miss Tipton. I hope I get to see more of this from you."

I nodded.

"I'm sure you will."

I headed back to my office and closed the door.

My heart thumped like it was about to spill from my chest.

The situation *was* complicated, but I've never felt like this before. Even just one compliment made me heady.

Every time I slept with Chris, it felt like all of my rational disappeared, replaced with that innate desire for him.

It bothered me because this felt too soon after Casey.

My phone buzzed, and I looked down. A message from Nataly.

Hey girl! Katie and I are getting drinks tonight. Come out with us!

I needed a break. I told her, of course, I would join them and placed my phone down.

At least then, I could figure out just where I wanted to go and what Chris did or did not mean to me.

At six on the dot, I left the office and drove back to my apartment.

I threw on a simple black dress and combed out my brown hair.

After I placed some sleek, black heels on, I drove over to The Foxy Grove, a bar and eatery that Nataly loved to go to.

Well, more specifically, where she loved to meet guys.

After I drove around for thirty minutes to find parking, I headed inside.

A tanned hand waved as soon as I stepped through the door.

There they are!

Nataly sat in a blush pink dress at the bar, sipping champagne as her green eyes stared directly at me. Her red hair sat in some wild updo, which worked for her.

Katie sat next to her. Her black hair was chopped into a pixie cut. Her pale skin contrasted Nataly's tanned features. Ruby red nail polish decorated her fingernails, which matched her dress of the same color.

"Hey! Sorry for the delay."

"All good. Duty calls, right?"

"Hey, you made it out here. That's what matters," Katie insisted.

She was right. We hadn't had a night like this in a minute due to our conflicting work schedules.

Katie worked night shifts as the senior stock manager at a warehouse associated with Amazon.

Nataly was a fashion blogger, so she worked her own hours unless she had to cover a piece.

I, of course, had the simplest schedule, being a 9-5, but with all of the recent work, I haven't had a moment of peace.

The bartender headed over, and I ordered a glass of champagne. He disappeared after he mentioned he had just the thing.

"Dang girl," Nataly whistled. "He's got it bad for you."

"No, he doesn't. He's just being nice."

"Mia, 'nice' guys don't just get a girl top shelf because she ordered it."

The guy came back out with a bottle of Moet and Chandon. He poured the contents into a glass and held it out.

I sat there and stared blankly at the contents.

"I'm sorry, I can't afford—"

"It's on me. My name's Nick."

He scribbled down his number on a card and handed that, along with the champagne, over to me.

Katie and Nataly both cried out as he went to handle other patrons.

"Damn girl, you just scored a date."

I looked at the card. Nick Wilders. Nice guy, but not really my type.

For one, the guy looked like he was barely old enough to be working here.

Two, after what happened with Chris, I didn't know what I wanted.

I folded the card and shoved it in the bottom of my purse.

"I'm not here for guys, Nat."

"I know, but still! By the way, has anything happened with Chris?"

I bit my lip, unsure of where to begin. Katie's brows furrowed at the name.

"Chris?"

"Yeah, remember Casey's brother."

"No. Way. Mia, you didn't—"

"I did," I admitted. "And I did it again, too. And again."

Nat's eyes widened at my words.

"Wait a second, you slept with him *twice* after?"

"Yeah, but I'm not sure how I should feel."

"Clearly, the sex must've been good."

"Yeah, too bad the guy's unapproachable and closes himself off the second he allows an inkling of emotions in."

That was Chris's problem. Even when I tried to let him in, it was like he pushed me away.

I sighed and looked down.

"I doubt it'll ever turn into anything."

"Hey, you never know."

"Guys like that don't just have sex with someone three times, and it means nothing."

"I think it's just physical. I mean, I liked it too."

Chris knew his way around a woman. He knew how to get my body where he wanted it.

And made me do things I regretted.

"Besides, he's Casey's brother. I know they're close. If word gets out, then…"

"Casey's probably over you by now," Nat muttered. "He's a guy and rich at that. He's probably started talking to another gal already."

"I doubt it."

"You like Chris, though, right?"

Did I?

I mean, we did have sex, but I felt like I barely knew him.

Other than the discussion of his panic attacks the other night, our conversations were brief.

"I don't know."

"I mean, you clearly feel something if you aren't even trying with Nick over there," Katie pointed out.

"Nataly hooks up with guys all the time. It's not like I can't have a little fun."

"Yeah, but what if the fun means something more to you?"

I looked at Katie. I hated that she did this. She always managed to say things that provided food for thought, sometimes better than Nataly ever could.

"I don't have an answer to that. All I know is we've had sex a few times, but everything feels the same. He says it's a mistake and then doesn't want anything to do with me."

"Sounds to me like *someone* is in denial," Katie mused.

"Or maybe both."

Nataly and Katie giggled. I rolled my eyes.

"Anyways, enough about me. How have you guys been?"

"Oh, you know me. Always getting out and meeting new people," Katie replied.

Nick came back out. His eyes stayed glued to me, but I looked at my phone, barely paying attention.

"Can I get you guys anything else?"

"You can get me the same as her," Nataly said.

"Oh, I can't give that to anyone and—"

"Come now, is that a way to talk to a *paying customer*?" Nataly teased.

She slipped a card under the palm of his hand. "Besides, my friend isn't interested in you. She's got her own guy she's hung up on."

"Nat, it's not like that—"

Katie laughed. Nick stood there, red in the face, as he looked away.

"I'm free in thirty minutes."

"Good. I am, too."

He headed to the back, and Nataly grinned.

"See, that wasn't so hard."

"Nat, what the hell are you doing—"

"Getting him to forget about you, Mia. You've got it bad for Chris, and I'm not going to stop it."

I sighed and rubbed my temples.

"It's not like that! I'm just—"

"I think you've got to do a little bit of soul-searching there, Mia. I'm not going to stop you either," Katie insisted.

There was no way of fighting either of them. They built this narrative, so I'd just have to go with it.

Sure enough, in thirty minutes, Nataly conveniently disappeared.

Katie watched her walk off and shook her head.

"That Nataly is always up to something."

"Yeah. Sometimes, she's a blessing and a curse to deal with."

"I know. But hey, figure out your lot. I'm sure that, when the time is right, the answers will be clear."

That sounded like some fortune cookie nonsense. I understood that Katie meant well, but geez.

"Alright. I'll try. I suppose."

Katie's phone vibrated. She looked down and frowned.

"Oh fuck, they want me working a night shift. Some idiot called out last minute."

"Can't you tell them no?"

"And miss out on overtime? Hell nah!"

I nodded. We all had our means of making ends meet.

"I'm glad I got to see you again."

"Hey, you as well, Mia. And don't get too upset about Chris. I'm sure if it's meant to be, the universe will bring you two together again."

Katie left a fifty to cover her drinks. I didn't even get a bill.

I guess Nick covered both mine and Nat's drinks.

I headed home, trying to piece together how I felt. Chris did make me feel things.

Things I knew I shouldn't feel.

Maybe I should take Katie's advice and see where things go.

The worst that could happen is nothing does.

I stumbled inside. My phone buzzed with a message from Chris.

Meet me in my office tomorrow. I need to speak with you.

Twenty-One
Chris

"There you are!"

Mom's voice echoed from beyond the foyer.

I walked inside and saw her in the theater with Jacob. His eyes sat glued to the screen, where the latest episode of Paw Patrol played.

"Hey. I'm home early."

"I'm glad. Jacob was curious if you'd be home earlier tonight. The last few nights have been pretty late."

"For a reason," I muttered.

Well, sort of. One of the nights involved Mia. I didn't dare tell Mom about that.

The other nights involved going over a couple of final quarter stats to make sure everything was aligned. We were in the black so far.

I was glad. Grant entrusted me with this partnership, and it prided me to know I was at least running the show well.

Still, it wasn't right of me to leave Jacob like this.

"I know. Is everything okay?"

I nodded. "Yeah. Just been pretty crazy the last few days."

"I can imagine! Do you know who actually called me the other day? Casey?"

I folded my arms across my chest and cocked my head.

"Really now?"

"Yeah. Apparently, this racecar driving stint is going well! He won in Toledo, and he's going to be competing in Dallas. He *insists* on all of us going, but with your schedule and Jacob...."

I looked at Jacob, who waved and grinned.

"Hi, Dad! I want to finish this episode."

"Go for it. Grandma and I are going to talk outside."

I didn't want to interrupt his show. The kid loved that series, even if I didn't get it myself.

Then again, things were much different for him than they were for me back then.

Back then, I didn't have half the technology that he does now. While I'm not really happy with him using all the technology, I've warmed up to him.

Plus, he listens when I tell him to put it away.

Mom and I moved out of the theater. She left the door open a crack. A smile crossed her face.

"Yeah, he's really bent on having us see him. It could be good for you."

I shrugged. "I'll think about it. Casey and I usually see each other whenever he's in town anyway."

It made things easier between my schedule and Casey's races.

We made time, so I didn't have to travel too far.

Mom reached out and touched my shoulder. A smile ghosted her face.

"Something the matter?"

"No, it's just that you look happier."

"Nothing's changed, mom. I'm just enjoying my job."

"I see. Any new girls on your radar?"

"Mom!"

She laughed and leaned against the doorframe.

"Come on now, Chris. Haven't you thought about maybe settling down in the future?"

I shook my head. "You know the answer to that better than anyone."

"I know, but still. I'm not sure what's going on, but whatever's bringing you this happiness, let it in."

I didn't know what she was getting at. My relationship with Mia *didn't* bring me happiness.

In fact, I wasn't sure what it brought me.

Probably a headache.

"I'm not doing anything differently. Just trying to ensure that this merger continues going as well as it has been."

"I understand. But maybe you should think about a girl at some point."

'Mom, I've told you before, after the mess with Alara, that's off the table."

Mom rolled her eyes. She pestered me about this so much it drove me crazy.

"I know. Worth a shot."

"Yeah, and you should stop trying. I just want to pick up the pieces and fix the damage she created."

"Well maybe you should consider letting someone else help you with picking up the pieces. Just a thought."

Yeah, like that would ever happen.

"If we're done here, I'll be in the office. The chefs should be done with dinner at some point. Tell Jacob I want to eat with him."

Mom's face fell.

I knew her game. She wanted to continue this conversation until she got some kind of agreement from me.

Well, that wasn't happening.

I knew what I wanted in life, and that was to give Jacob the best I could. He was my world, and this company provided him with everything he needed.

I'd be damned if I let anything get in the way.

The chefs prepared dinner. Roasted Peking duck, some steamed veggies, rice on the side, and chicken tenders for Jacob.

He was picky, so I made sure they cooked up some organic tenders from cage-free chickens when possible.

He loved rice, though, so he'd eat that. Veggies? Not so much.

I took a bite of the food. Good as always.

Hiring that professional chef did a number on my diet. Instead of a roulette on whether I'd get a decent meal or not, every night, the chef cooked up amazing food.

It was nice, to say the least.

Jacob and I ate dinner together, not saying much. After he finished, he looked up and smiled.

"Hey, daddy, I have a question."

"What's up?"

"Is Mia going to come back?"

I placed my fork on the table and took a deep breath.

"Mia's busy. She was only babysitting you that one night."

"Aww, okay. She's really nice."

"I'm glad you had a good time," I muttered.

The less I saw of Mia, the better.

I still didn't know how to feel.

Part of me wanted to accept the feelings I had for her. That other part of me knew better.

But they were entangled in the heap of desire she brought me. It was so messed up of me to want this though.

Casey wasn't over her. And she loved him. They broke up on friendly terms.

He still thought he had a chance. If I told him the truth, then…

"Daddy?"

I turned and smiled. "Yes, Jacob."

"If you see her again, tell her that I drew a picture of the dog she liked, and it looked cool."

I chuckled. "I will."

After we had dinner, Jacob and I said goodnight. He went to bed.

Mom left hours ago, saying she wanted to have dinner with Dad.

I retired to my office to look at a couple more emails. A few of them came in during the day before a couple meetings.

I scrolled through them until I got to the last one.

You're invited to a Premier Tech Networking event.

What the hell is this? I clicked on it and read the contents.

Oh. Holy shit, this was Pierre Novak.

He was another guru in the tech world and someone our marketing team wanted to collaborate with for so long.

He was having a tech soiree where some of the hottest masters in the field could converse.

This *could* be a great way to get in better with everyone. I looked at the details.

The event was in two weeks in New York City, at The Carlyle. Its purpose would be to introduce people in the tech sphere to others who have similar interests.

I scrolled down. Pierre mentioned a plus-one.

I mean, I could bring her...

I shook my head. No, that would open the door to *so* many things.

I was trying to keep my distance, and the idea of taking her would completely ruin my intentions.

But, on the other hand, it may be good for me to do. Plus, I could invite her as a colleague.

Yes, that's it.

I typed a message back and told Pierre I'd be going and bringing a plus-one, my Chief Technical Officer in charge of software development.

That is a good enough excuse if I do say so myself.

I tapped my fingers. I bit the bullet.

Now, I need to figure out what to do next.

I grabbed my phone and looked at Mia's name. It'd be so much better if I invited someone else.

Hell, even going with Grant would be better than this.

There'd be no temptation, and we could get the job done.

I didn't want to, though.

I *wanted* to bring Mia.

The temptation she brought me, combined with the excitement of desire, overwhelmed logic.

I opened up the text box and wrote my message.

Meet me in my office tomorrow. I need to speak with you.

The deed is done. Now, I just had to wait.

The next day, I headed to the office. The entire time, I thought about how to approach this.

Do I just ask her to be forthright and see what happens? That seemed almost too upfront, but it might be the best option.

At eight on the dot, Mia's heels clicked in the hallway. She knocked on the door, and I opened it to let her in.

"Thanks."

She stepped inside and took the chair across from me.

I joined her and rested my hands on the desk.

Our eyes met. Her hazel eyes were full of life. They were so beautiful that they had me lost in a trance.

"Mia," I began. "I've been impressed with your work the last couple of weeks."

"Oh. Thank you. I'm shocked I made that much of an impression."

"Indeed you have," I continued. "Which is why I'm offering you this opportunity."

I reached for the keyboard and typed in a couple words. I turned the screen around to the invitation from Pierre.

"No way that's—"

"Yes. Pierre Novac."

"We've been trying to secure him for a while."

"Yes, well, I was given an opportunity. And I would like for you to come with me."

Mia stiffened, her hands gripping the hem of her skirt. My eyes caught a glimpse of her thighs, practically ripping the nylons atop.

"Why? Wouldn't Grant be a better option—"

"He's busy. I asked, and he said due to personal engagements and his desire to retire, he is unable to make it. Normally, I'd never ask you to do this, but…."

She nodded. "I see."

"This doesn't mean anything else, just so you know."

"Oh, trust me, I know this too. I'm just happy to be invited."

"I'm glad you are. So yes, you'll be coming with me then."

"I will go."

I stood up and extended my hand.

"Good job, Mia. You've already made sizable contributions to the team."

She gripped my hand and shook it with hesitation. I wondered if she felt the sparks too.

"Thank you. I'm glad that I have."

"I'll let you get back to work then."

Mia nodded, "Thanks, Chris."

Mia left the office.

My heart lurched, and desire flooded my thoughts.

This was wrong.

I shouldn't have ever offered her this opportunity.

But now I have. While I shouldn't even be thinking of doing something of the sort, I did.

And yet, I didn't regret it.

Twenty-Two
Mia

"Wow, it's...impressive."

I looked at The Carlyle that laid before me. I'd never been here before.

New York City was so overwhelming, and it felt like I was in a whole different world.

But no, this was real.

It reeled me to think about it. Chris coughed, and I looked at him.

"Are you planning to go inside? Or were you going to gawk all evening?"

"Oh, right. Sorry about that. It's just a new experience for me."

"Yes, well, there's plenty more to look at."

He led me inside, and I followed him.

The whole place reeked of wealth.

Gold walls greeted us, along with large murals depicting various scenery.

The marble floors clicked under my heels.

Chris led me towards the elevator.

When he stopped, he turned to me. "We have the suite on the top floor."

"Okay."

He pressed the button, and the doors opened a moment later. It was an elevator with large windows. New York sat in front of us.

As the elevator went upstairs, my eyes took in everything.

It was a whole culture shock from the daily tedium. But it was quite beautiful.

When the elevator dinged, we stepped out to reveal a dimly lit lounge.

Servers walked around with flutes of champagne. People talked, and Chris led me towards some of the people.

We stopped right in front of Pierre Novac. He looked up, eyes wide with surprise.

"Christian?"

"Good to see you, Pierre."

Pierre whispered something to a couple of people and walked over.

"Wonderful to see you! And this is..."

"Mia Tipton. She's my CTO."

"Oh how wonderful to meet you!"

He extended his hand, which showed signs of age and wear. I grabbed it and shook it.

"Nice to meet you. Right this way."

He whisked Chris over to one of the chairs nearby. I followed him and sat down in the chair next to Chris.

"Well, this is quite the surprise. I'm shocked you actually came out of your hovel for a minute there, Chris."

"Well, sometimes you need to live a little, Pierre."

He chuckled, the low sound almost biting in the air around us.

"Indeed."

"I wanted to talk to you about a possible—"

"Collaboration," I interjected.

Chris flashed a look, but I nodded.

Pierre adjusted the wire-rimmed glasses on his face.

"Really now? And you think I'll listen to you because..."

"I'm his CTO. And he trusts me with ensuring the technology provided by Hamilton Corporation is to the highest standards."

Pierre whistled and gestured to me.

"Did you train this lady, Chris? Because damn, I've never had someone who worked under you talk to me with such...confidence."

"Mia is a rarity, after all," Chris replied coolly.

I stiffened upon hearing this. I mean, maybe I was. Chris's eyes stayed fixated on me.

Think carefully, Mia. The wrong thing could cost you.

"So what do you want to do then, Mia? I'm assuming *you* will be taking control of the conversation?" Chris asked.

I nodded and smiled at Pierre.

I moved next to him as Chris stepped back to give us space.

"I would like for you to see the range of our products and discuss a potential collaboration. Here's a file depicting everything and—"

"No thanks. You're new, and if I wanted a rundown of the products, I'd just ask Chris."

Damn. Just as rude as Chris, I see. Chris looked at Pierre with the same glare he gave me.

"And what makes you think *you* know everything? Mia knows all about our products."

Pierre laughed almost sardonically.

"Because I know how you are, Chris. You see everyone as just a statistic."

"Is that a problem?" I asked pointedly.

Pierre looked at me, surprised at my words.

"So you believe everyone's just a means to an end and not a customer to sell to?"

"Not at all. But we do need to look at our relationship as transactional. However, that doesn't mean you *won't* be taken care of."

The din of the other people around barely stifled the tension. Pierre sat there, glaring daggers.

He was definitely not happy.

I knew how these guys worked. Part of it attributed to Chris, but the other part of it came from my experience in this field.

"Interesting. So you believe everything's a business then."

"It is. But, again, that doesn't mean we have to disregard the feelings of others. I have a large, expansive catalog filled with a variety of different products. I'm sure you'll be able to find something you'll enjoy."

I handed him the tablet I front-loaded with our top-selling software products.

Pierre looked it over for about two minutes.

I'm surprised he didn't just throw it back at me.

He placed it on the table and then sighed, folding his hands.

"Well, you certainly make an interesting case, *Mia*."

"And I can make it even more interesting if you're willing to listen."

Pierre's eyes darted between Christian and me.

There was both curiosity and hesitation in pulling the trigger.

"Well, now, you've certainly intrigued me, Mia. Women like you are a rarity in this industry."

I took the compliment and smiled.

"I'm happy to hear that."

"Tell you what," Pierre sighed as he stood up. "I have your email, right? Let's talk turkey on Monday, just the three of us."

He opened his phone and put our meeting on the schedule. After he put it away, he nodded.

"It was nice meeting you, Mia. Chris. You've got one hell of a saleswoman on the team."

"Glad you think so, too."

Pierre walked away, and Christian turned to me. His eyes bore no emotion.

"That was a stupid move, you know."

"It was stupid, but it worked. Maybe you should thank me instead."

"And maybe you should watch your tongue and—"

Chris raised his hand and brushed his body in front of mine. A server gasped, and water spilled all over Chris's lap.

Oh shit.

I looked around for a rag, desperate to clean him up.

There was now the fiery anger simmering on his face.

As if things couldn't get even more awkward.

Christian got up and sighed.

"I'm going to get some fresh air."

"Chris—"

He didn't say another word. He stormed off, and I sat there, trying to figure out what to do next.

Did I make the right decision? I don't even know. But the way Chris looked at me felt different like there was something more there.

My stomach was in knots, but I knew what I had to do.

Find him.

Twenty-Three
Chris

I raced through the throngs of people until I finally found the outside terrace on the top floor.

It was a private location. Nobody was out here yet.

Good. A place where I could catch my breath and get myself together.

The water stuck to me. Flashes of memories from back then hit me hard.

I clutched my chest.

Come on, Chris, get it together! This is the last place you need to have one.

It was no use. My heart raced, and my breathing grew ragged.

I closed my eyes and attempted to count to ten.

It didn't work, but it might offset the effects.

I reached for the pills in my pocket.

Oh fuck. They're not here.

I thought I put them in my suit jacket.

Then, I remembered. A couple of pills spilled out, and I had to refill the prescription.

I sent a maid to get them tonight while they were out doing grocery shopping for the week.

Shit. Just what I needed.

I held the railing as my heart quickened, feeling as if it might just jump out and fall to the ground.

I squinted my eyes and hyperventilated.

Stop worrying. You're fine and—

"It's okay, Chris. Everything will be okay."

My breathing softened as it returned to normal. I opened my eyes and looked to my left.

Mia stood there with her hand on my shoulder.

It was both a welcome sight and one I dreaded. She rubbed my shoulder blade with delicate strokes, and I slowly came back to reality.

"It's a beautiful night outside."

I looked forward. Amongst the buildings and busy city traffic, it was.

My vision slowly cleared, and I turned to face her. "Thanks. I needed that."

"It's fine. I got a napkin. I'm sorry for making you lash out like that."

"All good."

She leaned forward and dabbed my suit jacket. She smelled delightful.

The urge to touch her hair raced through me.

No, don't do it.

The wrangled emotions threatened to explode as I took a couple more breaths in.

When Mia finished, she stepped back. She went to the trashcan nearby and tossed the napkin.

"There we go."

"Thanks. You didn't have to do that."

Mia scoffed. "And let you have a panic attack on your own? Chris, you looked like a mess."

Fuck. I looked around to see if anyone was up there.

"You're fine. Nobody saw."

Oh. That's good, at least.

"I see. Thanks again. You should go back inside. I don't need you for the rest of the night. Enjoy yourself."

Mia shook her head and folded her arms across her chest.

"You can't keep running away from this."

"I'm not. I appreciated what you did and—"

"No, not that," she stated. "I'm talking about the panic attacks."

I tensed slightly. Mia wasn't ready for the story. I shook my head.

"It's best you drop it right now."

"I'm not going to Chris," Mia retorted.

"You've been hiding it from me. You told me I'm the only one who has seen you and takes them seriously. I deserve an explanation."

"You don't deserve anything."

"You and I both know that's a lie."

She was right. Mia's the only one who's managed to talk me down from these attacks.

As much as I wanted to avoid the subject, she deserved an explanation.

Her hand rubbed my shoulder. I wanted to push it away, but I couldn't. It felt too nice.

"Fine, I have to admit you do deserve to know," I began.

"Thank you. Now, take your time. Don't push it."

"I'm not," I grunted. "It's just a little hard for me to admit."

That much was true. The only time I've ever thought about telling someone about my attacks was Alara.

That was, of course, right after I got out of the military. But, after she changed and left me with Jacob, I withheld that information.

"As you know, I went into the Navy and joined the SEALs shortly after high school."

"Oh yeah. You had mentioned that a couple of times when I was with Casey. And I remember whenever Casey needed help with the yacht he had, you would show him how to navigate. He used to tell me you were a whiz at that."

"Yeah, well, I went into the service to find myself. A sort of identity. I thought that the Navy would give me some kind of direction."

"That makes sense."

"Yeah, unlike Casey, who was more spontaneous and jumped from job to job, I wanted to have a stable job. My friends in high school suggested it, and after I talked to a recruiter, I thought it was the right way to go."

She nodded. "I get it."

"Well, I went in, and I experienced hell. I saw people die, even when we were in supposed 'safe' territory. I was a part of the scouting battalion. Our job was to look for places to allow the attackers inside. We also searched for people who were thrown overboard, drowning, or otherwise in trouble."

"That explains why you jumped in to help me."

"Yeah. But, over time, it took a toll on my mind and body. I started to see things. Visions of danger. I rarely got a good night of sleep."

She reached out and touched my shoulder.

I could feel the tension in my body as I relieved my memories.

"The breaking point was when I was part of a secret mission along the Kuwait coastline. It was during Desert Storm, and we were supposed to find a way inland for supplies. But that event ended up changing me."

I pursed my lips as I took a deep breath.

She reached out and rested her palm against the top of my hand.

"If you don't want to talk about it, you don't have to."

"No. I do. You deserve to know. While we were out there, our initial survey team didn't check for mines. Big mistake."

"Like the ones underwater."

"You've got it. Our ship grazed a mine upon entering the inland. What we didn't know was it was an ambush."

She listened to every word. "I'm so sorry."

"I lived by some goddamn miracle, Mia. I shouldn't even be here, telling you this story!" he cried out as he slammed his hand on the railing. "I should be dead with the rest of them."

She shook her head. "There's a reason you're still here today."

"Yeah, I'm a fucking coward. I should've gone down with the ship, but I refused to stay. After we hit the mine, everyone went to the bow to fight. I was building and storing munitions, so I wasn't directly on the front line. But when I heard the bell which signified everyone to battle stations, I knew I had to fight. And yet...."

I looked forward and sighed.

"I didn't."

"What do you mean?"

"I didn't fight back. I knew it was a fool's errand. Instead, I dove into the water and used one of the detectors we still had on the ship to find some mines. Eventually, I swam all the way back to where our ship was. Ten fucking miles, and yet I did it."

"Chris this is awe-inspiring, to say the least. To think you went through so much, all to stay alive... It's crazy. I didn't know that was even possible."

"It shouldn't have been. In fact, I was supposed to die back there. I should've died back there, but I didn't."

"I understand where you're coming from. I mean to go out there and be the only one left seems utterly terrifying."

She continued, "You're strong, Chris."

"Maybe. But nobody else in my battalion made it out. The mine took out half the guys, but the other half was done in by the gunfire from enemies. However, when I got back to the main ship with the news, my team took that information and prepared. They sent squadrons on both land and sea with the significant information I gave them. They were able to take out my squad's killers and enact vengeance on them."

She listened as my head hung low. She reached around my shoulders and hugged me.

"Thank you for telling me this, Chris."

"It's hard, Mia. I haven't ever told anyone what happened."

"Well, you did now. That's a progress, isn't it?"

"I suppose."

She looked up at me and smiled.

"You're not alone, Chris," she said. "You've shown me this unique side of yourself."

"You don't hate it?"

She shook her head. "We all have our battles. Acknowledging them is the beginning."

"The next part is to overcome the past," She added. I nodded.

"Thank you, Mia. It feels…good saying this."

"I'm glad. If you need to get anything else off your chest, feel free."

"Thanks."

She looked up. Our lips were mere inches from each other. Just like that night in the hospital, I wanted to close the gap, but fear settled in.

Did Mia want this, too?

I waited, desperate for the answer. But when Mia's lips met mine, all thoughts disappeared.

What mattered right now was to heal.

Twenty-Four
Chris

As I kissed Mia, it felt like the foundation I built for so long crumbled down.

The walls that I had kept up for so long now shook precariously.

I wrapped my arms around Mia, and I held her close to my body. Our lips refused to leave one another.

I pressed my tongue to her mouth, and she opened up. I kissed her passionately and refused to let her go.

She listened. She *understood*. She didn't toss me to the side like Alara did.

But instead, she stayed there and let me get it off my chest.

I still wasn't ready to pursue anything more.

I didn't know if I'd be ready to. But even letting her in, just a little bit, felt right.

Even if a part of me hated it.

I pulled back and grasped her hand.

"Follow me."

I whisked her away from the terrace and back to the elevator. I pressed the button and waited.

Come on. Faster dammit!

The doors dinged, and I swept her inside. I pressed her to the elevator and devoured her lips.

Her magnetizing pull drove me crazy. It made me want to give up the fight.

I knew I shouldn't, though.

But every second I spent with her drove me closer and closer to the brink.

I pulled away and caught my breath. The elevator dinged, and a small meeting room sat to our left.

"Over here."

She nodded and followed me. The door was unlocked. I quickly pulled her inside and locked the door.

Inside was a leather couch. A projector sat at the end of the table, off and facing a large screen left pulled down. A couple of shelves with books were on the left wall, and a laptop sat near the projector on a small desk.

The room was big, not that I cared.

I pressed her against the arm of the couch, and she lay there.

Her backside stuck straight up in the air. I growled and pushed her dress up. I nibbled on her creamy thigh, which caused her to gasp.

"Chris, you're—"

"I don't have time, Mia. I can't wait anymore."

That was literally the truth. At some point, Pierre or another executive could come and find me.

I was already gone for quite a bit. It was a miracle nobody came to the roof.

Right now, all that mattered was Mia and taking her, showing her the desire that built up in my body and the ache that grew with every passing moment.

I pushed her panties down far enough so I had access to her.

My fingers pressed inside, and she cried out.

"There you go. Good girl," I grunted.

My fingers plunged deeper inside, savoring the wet heat. I needed to replace them with something else.

I could barely take it. The ache between my legs grew stronger.

I pressed my pants against her cheeks and rutted there.

"Chris! Stop teasing."

"Why should I?" I whispered in her ear. "Maybe I like teasing you."

She cried out my name, and I groaned.

Damn, she makes it so hard for me to hold back.

I needed to split her apart, to savor her warm, tight heat.

I undid my pants and zipper and pushed them down far enough to allow my member to spread.

I didn't have time for fancy foreplay.

What I needed, was to be inside her. I needed to hear those sweet little noises just as I hit those spots that made her toes curl.

I grabbed a condom and sheathed myself.

She adjusted her body and stuck her butt straight out.

I playfully slapped it, and she gasped. "Chris, please—"

"You stuck it out. I needed to give it what it deserved," I whispered in her ear.

She adjusted her body and gently pressed herself against the couch.

Seeing her rut against it, like an animal in heat, was enough to make me forget all about the morality of the situation.

What I needed right now was to feel her pussy.

I spread her open and she adjusted herself, trying to drag me to her.

I ran a hand against her frontside and rubbed her clit. She gripped the couch and mewled.

God, what a tease. I had to have her.

I pressed my member inside and slammed in there. Her tight walls sent me into a fury.

Her dress slid all the way up to her waist at this point.

I grasped her hipbones and held them tightly as I thrust in and out. She gasped, and moans of desire escaped her.

Every second she clenched around me felt like an eternity.

A lifetime of pleasure, just between the two of us.

I wanted nothing more than to melt in her embrace forever.

I continued, holding her tighter as I moved even faster. My hips moved wildly, almost violently, against her.

Every slam elicited gasps and cries of pleasure.

"Chris, I'm so close!"

"I am too, Mia. Fuck. I'm so close and—"

I groaned, holding her against me as I exploded inside her.

She closed her eyes and moaned. Her hands clawed the couch as sounds of her orgasm flooded the room.

Perfection.

We stayed like this for what felt like forever. I didn't want to leave.

Eventually, reality settled in. This time, the regret didn't consume me.

I ached for her, and after she talked me down from the last panic attack, I wondered if there was something more here.

It's terrible of me to want this, but the longer I spend around Mia, the more I entertain the thought.

Even if a part of me absolutely hated it.

I adjusted my pants. Mia grabbed her panties and put them on. She re-adjusted her dress so it sat cleanly against her thighs.

Our eyes met. So many emotions overwhelmed me.

"I enjoyed this Chris."

I stiffened. I wasn't ready for an actual relationship.

Sure, Mia was hot as hell and fun to mess around with. But a relationship?

I couldn't do that to Casey and to myself.

"I did too, but I can't keep this up anymore. It's wrong of me."

"So what? You'll just keep pushing me away."

"Maybe. I don't know. I haven't let anyone in like that, not since–"

I stopped myself. Alara wasn't Mia's problem. There were things I'd best keep to myself.

She nodded and smiled.

"I get it. You don't know what you want either. Frankly, I'm still trying to figure it out myself."

I longed for her. Every second I spent with her tempted me to throw it all away.

I knew I couldn't. There was still so much that happened after Alara left.

Mia didn't know the half of it. Not to mention, I felt like a fraud every time I talked to Casey.

"I'm sorry, Mia."

"It's fine and—"

The elevator dinged. I looked at the door. Footsteps approached and knocked.

"Is someone in there?"

I rushed to the door and unlocked it. Pierre and another executive I recognized stood before me.

"Oh, hello there, Pierre."

"Hi. I wasn't sure if this meeting room was occupied. I don't even know *why* this was occupied."

I looked around. I should've taken Mia back to the hotel room. But I wasn't ready.

"There was a business complication, and I wanted a place to talk with Mia about it."

"I see. Well, if you're done in here..."

"We'll be down shortly."

I gestured to Mia, and she walked out.

The lingering guilt sat there, but also something more.

The temptation to do it again, to break down all the walls, and experience more.

Even if it was wrong of me to do this.

Twenty-Five
Mia

"Alright, looks like software sales are up."

I checked all the boxes on my agenda. *Looks good.*

Since that networking event, we have had a ton of sales. Pierre liked what I offered and sent in an order for a hundred new antivirus units for his business.

What I didn't expect was the ripple effects that came with it.

More people ordered, and soon, I was getting a hundred orders a day. I ensured that the fulfillment team took care of it, but it was unprecedented.

I couldn't complain though. It set me up for a nice bonus at the end of the quarter.

Still, while things were good at the office here, I felt conflicted.

The biggest problem was Chris.

We shared a connection that night. And the sex... it was toe-curling. Even just thinking about it made my panties wet.

But there was something more.

Chris told me about his past and showed me vulnerability he never did before.

There was more underneath that. I didn't pry, but I wanted to question it.

I knew it wasn't right of me. He didn't have to tell me anything. But still, there was that temptation that bloomed in my mind.

I mean, surely, after all this, he must have *some* feelings for me.

I was so tired of beating around the bush that it drove me crazy.

What *did* Chris think of me?

I couldn't figure it out.

Sometimes, he'd be a little more open and inviting. Other times, he'd push me away and respond to me with just one word.

A true enigma.

Plus, there was the Casey matter to think about.

It'd been a couple months now, but that didn't help things.

Sometimes, I wondered if I was making a mistake, jumping to Chris just like that.

There was also the matter of their closeness.

A conflict of emotions, if I ever felt one.

I went to my office and sat to check my email.

So far, just a couple of personal messages from some traders we worked with. At the very bottom was an email from Pierre regarding a shipment.

I would like for a possible collaboration between my partner Neil and your company. Please advise Chris and let me know what you think.

That could be advantageous. Neil Gunn was an associate of Pierre's. I'd seen his name a few times on Chris's paperwork, too.

A powerhouse in the cybersecurity field. Having him on our side could prove useful.

But the decision was up to Chris and not me.

I sighed and stood up. As much as I didn't want to talk to Chris, I'd have to.

I walked to the elevator and pressed the button. As the doors opened, a familiar pair of blue eyes met mine.

"Oh, Chris. Just the person I was looking for."

"Mia. What is it?"

"I wanted to discuss a possible partnership with Neil Gunn. Pierre mentioned me and—"

"Let's discuss this in my office."

"Ok."

I stepped into the elevator, and Chris pressed the button. The elevator cascaded, and an awkward silence followed.

Tension rose. Memories of the time we shared just a couple weeks ago flashed through my head.

What is it with elevators?

Chris's lips had pressed to mine as he dominated the kiss in the elevator, and it overloaded my psyche.

Come on, Mia, keep those thoughts away. You're at work and—

The elevator dinged, saving me from further dirty thoughts.

I followed Chris to his office, and he opened the door. When we got in, he settled into his chair.

I opened my phone and showed Chris a copy of the email.

"So this is from Pierre. He wants a possible collaboration."

"That sounds good. Tell him I'd be more than willing to discuss matters with him."

"Okay. I'll let him know."

I looked up and saw the same look on Chris's face that he always had. One that conveyed a desire to say something more.

"Do you need something else?"

"I wanted to ask you something, Mia, but maybe it's…better if I ask outside the office."

"I'm here, though."

"Yes, but it's not related to office matters."

Okay, what the heck does he want? The man's been all over the place with his feelings towards me.

"I'm here right now. I may be gone early tonight."

Chris cleared his throat and nodded.

"I see. Are you free next Saturday?"

"I think I am. Let me check."

I opened my phone and checked my schedule.

Nat and Katie were busy next weekend with family and college events. My other guy friends were off at some reunion they got invited to. They offered to let me tag along, but that wasn't really my scene.

"Okay, I am free. What's up? Do you need me to put more hours in?"

"No, it's not that," Chris mutters, looking away. "There's just something I wanted to ask you."

"Spill it. I'm listening."

Chris hesitated and looked down.

"I shouldn't even be entertaining this thought. He's going to kill me."

Who is he referring to? Casey?

"What do you mean?"

"I was wondering if you wanted to come over for dinner."

I paused. Dinner wasn't just a little thing. People who like each other get invited over for dinner. I hesitated, unsure of how to feel.

"I don't want to intrude."

"You're not. Jacob's with his grandmother for the weekend, and I guess I just wanted some company."

Oh. This was surprising, given how much of an enigma he's been.

I pushed a couple of flyaways behind my ear.

"I mean, sure, if you're fine with it."

That was my big worry. I didn't mind the idea of dinner. It might be good to figure out everything.

But still, it could open the door to other problems.

Chris nodded.

"I thought about it. I want this."

"Okay. Then I'll come over," I replied with a smile.

"Great. Six on the dot. I'll have the food ready by then."

"I'll make sure not to be late," I replied with a wink."

I walked out of the office. My heart practically jumped out of my chest.

He just invited me to dinner! Whether or not this meant something, I didn't have the answers to.

But, if nothing else, it made me happy knowing that there was a chance. It might help with these feelings, too.

Still, I had to keep my distance and make sure I didn't cross any boundaries I wasn't ready to cross just yet.

Emotions settled deep in the pit of my stomach as I finished for the day. Anticipation for what was to come seeped in.

But also a worry that this might lead to something else.

I had feelings for Chris. Maybe it was desire, or maybe it was just the presence and power he had over me.

And I couldn't deny it anymore. He had a pull, one that drove me crazy and one that I couldn't ignore.

Whether or not this would change things was still unbeknownst to me.

Right now, I had to just accept what I was given.

Eventually, I'd have to figure out for myself what I wanted, and these feelings lay within.

Twenty-Six
Chris

"Make sure everything's perfect."

"I'm doing my best, Chris. You know how I do things," Cecilia replied with a friendly smile.

I knew this. Cecilia and the other chefs made masterpieces of courses.

But that didn't settle the aching anxiety that rushed through me.

I checked the clock. She'd be here in fifteen minutes.

The conflicting emotions still simmered in my mind. I thought that maybe seeing Mia tonight might help.

There's no denying it. I felt something for Mia.

The problem, however, was eventually telling Casey. And, of course, if I wanted to pursue things further.

The doorbell rang and pulled me out of my thoughts.

I looked over at Cecilia, who smiled. "It's all ready. I'll go out the back."

"Thanks. And remember, not a word to anyone else."

Cecilia was the chef for my parents as well.

A sweet woman, who had become like a friend to me, but if you didn't tell her to keep her mouth shut, she'd run it.

Luckily, she listened if you said something, though.

I heard the faint sound of the door closing in the distance and then, walked to the door and opened it.

"Good evening."

"Hey. Here I am, six on the dot."

I stepped back and gestured inside. Mia walked in, and my eyes looked at what she wore.

A simple mauve low-cut shirt and tan capri shorts framed her body.

On her feet were a pair of white Adidas sneakers. Her hair, while in an updo, sat elegantly. A couple of strands danced against her shoulders.

She looked radiant. Even though her outfit was simple, she was beautiful.

"I'm glad I didn't need to dress up too much," she said with a teasing smile.

"Yes, well, we're here. I must say you look quite lovely."

"Thanks," she replied as she set her bag on one of the rack hooks.

"This way," I encouraged and gestured down the long hallway. Mia walked down and looked around.

"It somehow feels bigger than it did the last time I was here."

"You'll get used to it."

Or not. I didn't know if I was ready to let her be *that* close to me.

We walked down to where the table was. Mia took a seat across from mine and looked at the food.

"This looks so delicious!"

"Thanks," I replied. "It's a simple dish of breaded chicken with sun-dried tomatoes on a bed of rice. But I made sure the cooks prepared it to the best levels they could."

"Well, it sure looks good," Mia gushed, licking her lips as she took in the sight.

"Have at it," I encouraged.

We ate in silence. Both of us hesitated to speak any further.

For me, it wasn't that I didn't want to talk to Mia. But there were a series of emotions which continued hovering over me. A desire for her, but also the constant feeling of how wrong this was.

"So, how's Jacob doing?" Mia asked.

"He's good," I replied. "Mom took him to some playland event. She wanted me to have a weekend to myself."

"So you're spending it with me then?"

I paused and grabbed my fork.

"Guess so."

"I see. Well, Jacob's a good kid."

"Yeah. He likes you."

Jacob still mentions Mia on occasion.

It surprised Mom when he heard her name because she always associated Mia with Casey. I explained to her that Mia helped babysit the night she was sick.

Mom was happy about it and appreciated her generosity. But I couldn't possibly mention to Mom the whole whirlwind of emotions that had settled in.

"I'm glad," Mia said with a smile. "He always was a good kid. Really curious about the world."

'Yeah. He's been working on these kits for kids to learn basic science concepts. Got him one where he learns how to build a basic robot with these little circuits already pre-made. He gets it but does need some help from myself or mom."

"That's really cool," Mia replied and smiled.

"Yeah. The kid's my world."

I looked down as the heaviness settled over me.

I planned to keep Jacob in my world and keep him away from Alara or anyone who would harm him.

Mia frowned as she looked at me.

"Something the matter?"

"Nothing, it's fine," I muttered.

I didn't want to dampen the mood by mentioning Alara. Not just that, though, I wasn't sure if I was ready to tell Mia about her.

She was painful to remember. But it was also the reason I did everything I did.

I made sure Jacob was safe so he didn't have to deal with her ever again.

"Okay. Well if you want to talk about it, feel free. No pressure though."

"Thanks."

We continued eating in an awkward silence. My eyes stole glances at Mia.

She looked so sweet, and I felt a desire to open up whenever I looked at Mia.

There was that pull there, one that I couldn't shake even if I tried.

It was what made everything so much harder.

We'd been doing this back and forth for what, like, two months now.

At some point, I had to make a decision.

What would be my answer when the time came? I wanted to respect Casey's feelings, but…

The more I spent time around her, the harder it was to follow through with that.

Mia looked up and smiled.

"This is so good."

"Thanks. Compliments to the chef. Not to me."

"Surprised you don't cook."

"I do," I replied. "It's just not as often as I should."

"I see. Maybe someday I'll get to taste your food."

Maybe. But if that happens, I feared the wrath of Casey.

"Maybe so."

We finished dinner and later, after we left the items for Cecilia to put in the dishwasher, I looked at Mia.

She stared out the windows at the little garden outside.

"It's such a charming garden."

"Yeah, the groundskeepers are preparing it for the spring and summer."

"For a good reason. It is so pretty here."

She was right. That was the allure of Virginia. Pretty, but also a mild climate for the most part.

"Yeah. Anyways, there's something I wanted to show you."

"What is it?"

I chuckled. "You'll have to follow me to find out."

Mia flushed slightly and nodded.

"Right. Where do we go?"

"Over here. It's something I haven't shown anyone. Not even Jacob's been up here."

Mia's eyes widened slightly. "Really?"

"Yeah. It's dangerous, but I think you can handle going up there."

"Alright."

I walked up to the second floor. Mia followed, and we headed through the door at the very end of the right hall.

When we got there, I pressed the button, and a series of stairs erupted from the ground.

"Woah."

"Cool, isn't it? I had these stairs installed a few years ago when I put together this room. It's kind of a personal place for me."

Why was I taking Mia up here? Was it because I hoped she would like it?

Was it because I felt comfortable showing her more and more of myself when, in the past, I always closed it off?

My feelings were still conflicted.

I stepped up the stairs, and I heard the faint sound of Mia following me.

When I got to the landing I pressed the second button for the ladder.

As Mia reached the landing, I gestured to the switch.

"Press that, will you?"

"Okay."

She did, and the stairs came up.

"Thanks. I always put them up after reaching the landing. For security reasons."

"Seems a little excessive, though."

"I'm always excessive, Mia."

"Oh, trust me; you don't have to remind me. Excessive and extra, to a fault."

I rolled my eyes. "You read me so well. Let's go up."

I ambled up the ladder and got to the top. I lit one of the small lanterns and placed it on the table.

Mia followed, and when she stood up, her eyes looked up at the world above.

"This is—"

"It's my personal stargazing room. I come out here on a clear night to look at the night sky. It calms me."

I built this after Alara entered my life once more. She stressed me out, and I constantly had panic attacks.

It got so bad that I thought I was having a heart attack. When I talked with my therapist, she recommended a personal space just for me.

Now of course, I opened that space to another person.

"Have a seat."

Mia did so, and I sat next to her on the soft, gossamer cushions. We looked up; the stars twinkled above us. Mia took in the view.

"It's so beautiful."

"It is. I love coming up here. You can see *everything* up here."

I pointed to the big dipper, Capricorn, and even Virgo.

"Wow, you can. And I didn't know you were an astronomist like that."

"I'm not," I assured. "I just like the stars. Something about looking into an infinite abyss that you don't even know the ending to brings relief."

"It makes you wonder about the different possibilities out there."

I nodded. "Yeah. Exactly."

Like the possibility of us being together.

I shook away that thought. We just sat there and kept looking at the stars.

The words lingered on the tip of my tongue. I had to tell her.

I looked over and saw Mia's eyes lost in the skies. I touched her shoulder, and she snapped out of it to look at me.

"Oh! Sorry."

"It's fine. I get lost in the stars too. I just wanted to tell you something that I've wanted to say for a while now. It's not a big deal, but..."

"Go ahead," Mia encouraged.

Her sweetness was like a drug. I took a deep breath as I prepared to bring Mia back into my personal world again.

"I've been having fewer panic attacks, especially after telling you about what happened during my SEAL days."

Twenty-Seven
Mia

I listened to Chris's words, fascinated by them.

I helped him with that.

I never thought that'd be something I'd ever hear from the man.

He was such a contrast to Casey. With Casey, he'd tell me everything and anything.

Chris, however, was more reserved.

But, when Chris said compliments, it was like they mattered so much more. Like they came from the abyss of his heart, only to be heard by me.

"I'm really glad about that."

"Yeah. I still have the Paxil, but I've used it maybe once since I told you a couple weeks ago. I feel calmer."

"That's really good to hear."

"Yeah. It just makes everything all the harder for me."

I blinked and adjusted my body, confused by his words.

"What do you mean?"

He looked down, and his hands balled into fists.

"It's just this whole relationship. I don't know if I'm doing the right thing or not. Every time I'm around you, I feel conflicted."

"Like you want this but are worried about the consequences?" I ask.

Cause that's exactly how I feel. Even just being here with Chris makes me feel conflicted.

It's been almost two months, but the wound still feels fresh, like I've made a huge mistake in the process or just jumped into a rebound relationship; well, that is, if you could call this a relationship.

Chris sighed and nodded.

"Exactly that, Mia. And I hate that I feel this way."

"What can you do about it?"

"I don't know! And it doesn't help either that I don't know if I even want a relationship."

That's where I was at. If we did pursue this, then what?

I could tell Chris had his own reasons for not pursuing this further. Besides Casey, of course.

I reached out and touched his hand.

Asking this might open Pandora's box, but there was still so much I didn't know about Jacob's mom and the details surrounding that.

The little bit of information I *did* know was from Casey. He had mentioned that Chris and his ex-wife got a divorce, and things were very rough for a while.

There was also word of a custody battle.

But I wanted to hear it from him, straight from his mouth.

"What scares you about having a relationship?"

"I just don't do them, Mia. It's better this way. Nobody catches feelings and—"

"Judging from the way you're acting, it's a little too late for that last part."

Chris sat in silence, unsure of how to respond to that.

"It's more than just that though. Mia, I've been through a lot. And well, I'm always worried that I'll meet someone who is the same as Alara."

"So am I like Alara?"

"No, you're not but—"

"Then why do you keep pushing me away!"

It was time to ask whether or not he wanted to have a relationship.

The back and forth was getting on my nerves.

"I'm not sure. I don't know if—"

"Chris, I'm right here with you. If that doesn't mean something, then I don't know what will."

He paused. *There we go*.

I managed to get him to realize just how useless this continuous fighting was.

Chris sighed and looked down.

"Fine, you want to know, right?"

"I do, Chris. Tell me."

He clenched his hands together in fists. The anger bubbled.

I reached out and rested my hand atop his.

"Chris, you've let me in once already. You've told me about your past as a SEAL. Why not do it again?"

He nodded slowly.

"Yeah. You're right. The more I fight, the worse it will be."

He looked up, and I saw in those blue eyes sadness, vulnerability, and anger.

Chris had to do this. He needed to get this off his chest.

To do otherwise would stifle whatever this relationship was for good.

Twenty-Eight
Chris

Mia's sweetness sickened me.

She made me realize just how much of an asshole I was, hiding all of this from her. I took a deep breath and looked up at the sky.

"After I came back from the war, I went into software engineering much like you did. I started working, and with the help of Mom and Dad, I built the company I have today."

"Wow! Explains how you built it so quickly after your time in the service."

"Yes. When it comes to business, I know my shit, Mia. What I don't know is women. Shortly after I got back, I went out and mingled with others. One of the women I mingled with was Alara, Jacob's mom."

I sighed and rubbed my temples.

"I hate myself, looking back at it. In a strange way, she was like Casey."

"You mean she was the life of the party and knew how to say the right thing at the right time?"

"Yep. And she loved to party. The woman would go out almost every night to different parties. Soirees, clubbing, hell, even just hopping from one fancy bar to the next. I used to get us in because of my connections."

Mia nodded. "I get that."

"Those clubs were kind of my home for a bit. Well, we eventually fell in love, got married, and had a kid. However, after Alara had Jacob, everything changed."

I remembered it was almost automatic. The woman I fell in love with became an absolute shell of the person she was before.

"How so?"

I pondered how to put the next part. I didn't want to make her sound terrible, but she did things I didn't approve of.

"Well, she didn't want to be home as much as I wanted to. You know I like being here with Jacob."

Mia smiled. "You're always with him, whenever you can."

"Yes. Because I love him so much. And I want to give him the experience of a parent being around. Something I never had."

I bit my lip as the feelings of betrayal and anger seeped through me.

"Throughout my childhood, my parents were too busy at parties and mingling with others in their field. They didn't bother to raise us. I didn't want Jacob to experience that type of life."

"That makes sense," Mia encouraged. "Kids need their parents. I feel like, without my Mom and Dad being there and supportive, I wouldn't be half as successful as I am today."

"Yeah. I practically raised Casey. He probably told you this, didn't he?"

Mia nodded. "Yeah, it's why he always held you in such high regard."

I imagine. I always looked out for him because I knew the struggles of having nobody.

"I didn't want my own son to share the same fate. I stayed with Jacob, whereas Alara wanted to go out, meet new people, and try new experiences."

Mia sighed and nodded.

"Similar to Casey."

"Yes, but different. She did this because she was business-driven. Casey is well…"

"Still trying to find his path," Mia replied as she looked down.

Dammit, the last thing I needed was her upset.

I reached out and wrapped a hand around her shoulder.

"Casey's a good guy."

"He is, but he never grew up."

"Yes. Alara exhibited similar traits, but she wanted to focus on her business. Mingle with the right person, and travel halfway around the world for a business deal. She didn't care about our family. And one night, I got upset because she kept putting business over her own family. When Jacob turned one, we broke things off. I filed for divorce and I got custody of him."

I sighed. "And things were great until three years later when Alara came back. Jacob was four at the time, and she insisted that she changed."

Mia scoffed and shook her head.

"Well, she thought that after she'd seen the world and tried everything, combing back with the conclusion that all these things were superficial compared to your child's true love would fix the damages. I, however, didn't want this. She had already left me once with Jacob and had refused to be a mom, which hurt me."

I gritted my teeth. I remembered the night she showed up at the door after three fucking years.

Jacob didn't know who the hell she was, and I just told him to go to the other room. Because I just wanted to spare him the bitter truth that that was his mom who had returned after leaving him high and dry for years.

"We talked, but everything seemed so fake."

"Probably because it was."

"Indeed. I told her I couldn't do this anymore and that I wouldn't give her Jacob back. She got upset and eventually took it to court."

Mia's eyes widened slightly.

"What...happened?"

"Nothing. The court sided with me automatically. Since then, Alara's tried to snake back into my life. She still calls me, begging for Jacob back. But I would never agree to that."

Mia nodded.

"I mean after what she did, I don't think she deserves him."

"No, she doesn't. In fact, I want her to leave my son alone. But she's still adamant. Neither of us like each other. That ship sailed forever ago and was over and done with when she said our child was a 'barrier' to her success!"

I slammed my fist into one of the pillows. Remembering how she tossed both Jacob and me to the side angered me.

Mia's hand rubbed my shoulder. I leaned into the touch.

"I'm sorry about that."

"You have nothing to apologize for," she replied sweetly.

"It's just the audacity to think that you still have any claim to your child after you left them bothers me."

"No, it's definitely gross. She left you two behind."

"I picked up the pieces, but…"

There was still that anger I felt. Her betrayal, which still created ripples in my life.

She destroyed all that for selfish reasons.

I sighed and shook my head. "I don't seriously date for this exact reason. I fear getting hurt again."

"That's a valid reason."

"Not only that, when Jacob met her, he didn't want anything to do with her. In fact, he told me that she was a witch."

Mia chuckled. "I mean, maybe he was onto something."

"She did have fire engine red hair with white streaks. In a way, I don't blame the kid."

"It hasn't made it easy for me to trust anyone. During the custody battle, she badmouthed me to high heaven. She went on this whole tirade about how I was a bad father, and if Jacob lived with me, he'd grow up to be a troublemaker. All she cared about was control."

"That's horrible."

"It is. I felt like I was the bad guy when Casey and my Mom told me that I wasn't."

I looked down again. The regret grew into a festered wound.

"I still regret sometimes opening up to the wrong person. Sometimes, I'm not sure if I'm ready to trust again after the hell she put me through. But whenever I'm around you, I feel like I can. The thought worries me, and I'm trying to let it go but..."

Mia's hand reached for mine and gently held it. She stroked my fingers slowly.

Her soft hands relaxed me. It made talking about this even better.

"I'm sorry for changing the mood and—"

"No, don't be Chris. You had to get this off your chest."

I nodded. "I did. And I feel better admitting it."

Whether I was ready for a relationship or not was still up in the air. But to bear this piece of myself to Mia like that felt right.

For me as well, it also indicated something else.

A chance to move on.

Twenty-Nine
Mia

I didn't expect the words Chris uttered to come out of his mouth.

But I was glad to hear them.

The man bottled everything up and fought his battles himself. Sometimes, opening up was good for a person.

It gave them a chance to get that heavy load off their chest and to finally build closure.

I squeezed his hand tighter and smiled.

"You've fought hard. And all by yourself."

"Yeah," Chris admitted. "I don't talk about my feelings. It's just easier to fight my battles alone."

"It's not healthy, though. You have to get it off your chest."

"Yeah, but if the wrong person gets that information, they can use it against you. Alara did. She used my PTSD as a weapon and said that I needed to get over it."

"You can't, though."

"Yeah, well, not everyone's as caring as you, Mia."

I flushed at his words. I tried to be here for him. I knew just how rough the battles could be.

"Well, I'm here now. And I understand why you keep your distance."

"Yeah, because letting those walls come down honestly scares me. I don't want the wrong people to know these things."

"So why me then?"

It was a valid question. If Chris didn't want to open up, how was I different?

Chris looked at me, and he squeezed my hand.

"Honestly, I don't fucking know. You've managed to come back into my life every time I tried to push you away. I've tried to keep my distance, but at this point, it feels like I'm *supposed* to tell you these things."

I smiled and nodded. "I feel the same way."

We looked at each other. Chris reached out and caressed my cheek.

"Mia, I don't know how to feel about you, but I can't let you go. I want to tell you these things because it feels right."

"It does."

He closed the gap, and our lips met in a soft, tender kiss. I moaned softly as I slowly fell under his spell.

I couldn't pull away. Chris just had that effect on me.

He pulled me into his lap, and we made out under the stars.

Our tongues danced, and his hands reached down and felt up my backside.

His large, dominant hands squeezed my cheeks, and I gasped.

He pulled back and smirked.

"I love hearing your little noises."

I smiled at his words. The walls I put up were long gone, replaced with a pull for Chris. A storm of complicated feelings led me back to him.

Chris stood up and took my hand.

"Let's go back downstairs. It's cold."

I nodded as I realized the implications.

"Maybe your bedroom could warm me up," I replied with a teasing smile.

He led me downstairs, and after he put the stairs back up, we walked to the other wing. He opened a lone door that led to a large bedroom.

A black bed sat in the center, with a matching black bed frame and sheets. The bed, amongst the contrast of white, looked elegant.

"This is—"

Before I could say the next word, Chris pushed me into the mattress.

His lips overtook me once again, and I wrapped my arms around his shoulders and clung to him.

Chris's rock-hard shoulders felt so strong and masculine underneath my hands. Our lips intertwined, desperate for each other.

My hands skated down to his pecs and felt them up. They traveled southwards and I caressed the outline of his chiseled abs.

His sexy body drove me crazy, and I drank up every minute I could.

"You're fucking amazing, Mia."

His hands fiddled with my shirt and pulled it, along with my bra, off in one motion.

Eager hands explored my body, and I gasped slightly.

Chris pulled back and pushed a couple strands of hair out of my face.

"I can't get enough of you Mia. You drive me fucking crazy."

My face heated. I knew I shouldn't get attached, but...

Dammit, Chris, why do you do this to me?

I knew deep down that he wanted me, too.

His lips trailed down my body and peppered soft kisses against my neck. I shivered with delight as he kissed me sweetly.

The ache between my legs throbbed and my core heated with anticipation.

I needed him to fill me up and feel his weight on top of me.

Chris's hands maneuvered down my body and laid soft touches against my breasts. His fingers played with my nipples like a harp. Soft, steady, and exact.

I closed my eyes as I felt the tug and the overwhelming pleasure fill my every thought. He twisted and teased the nub and I cried out.

"Beautiful. Just the way I like to hear it."

His fingers pinched my nipples harder. My eyes shot open as the moans continued to escape.

He growled, and I could feel the palm of his hands tracing the outline of my nipple.

My face warmed, and soon, his lips nibbled on my collarbone.

I gasped, and he flicked his fingertips against my nipple. I gasped again as I gripped him tighter.

His hands continued to pinch and tease.

Soon, his lips trailed southwards, capturing the tip of my nipple with a small suck. His tongue flicked over the bud, and it hardened just from his hot breath.

My heart raced, and my core throbbed. I was so wet my thighs quivered with delight.

His lips continued to suckle and tease my nipples, pinching the bud that wasn't between his lips.

I was going insane. The pleasure grew, becoming almost unbearable.

"Chris, please! Fuck me!" I spat out.

He looked back and cupped my chin.

"Really now. I want to hear you beg for it."

The desperation grew stronger.

"Please, Chris. I need you to take me and fill me with your cock—"

His hands reached down for the fly and zipper of my shorts. His hands gripped my thighs and caressed them.

"I could worship these. They're so soft."

I flushed, and the ache grew almost to unbearable levels.

Without a second thought, he pulled my thighs wider and slid the garment off my body.

I shivered as the cold air hit my nakedness.

His hands teased my entrance, and as he moved my legs apart, pushing them above my head, his tongue teased my folds and then inside.

I clenched as the pressure started building up inside me.

I wasn't going to last.

Every moment I spent with Chris, every touch of his hands against my body, sent ripples of pleasure through me.

I had to though.

He pulled my legs so they were over his shoulders and he thrust into me. It split me apart, and choked moans of pleasure filled the room.

"That's right Mia. Let me hear you."

The gentle encouragement goaded me forward.

I clenched around him, and he angled his digits, thrusting them deeper into my core.

His fingers were hard and rough, but they were exactly what I needed.

My walls sucked him up, and I gasped with pleasure. It was like he knew exactly where to touch.

As he caressed the upper walls of my womanhood, I closed my eyes.

Pure, sweet bliss.

He added a third finger and pressed them inside. Meanwhile, his thumb encircled my clit, with small sensual touches.

I clutched the sheets and cried out Chris's name with every passing second.

He smiled and leaned over me.

"You're so sexy when I'm fucking you."

The growl in his words was enough to drive me crazy.

I cried out his name as he plunged them deeper inside and he pushed his thumb hard against my clit, teasing it with forceful strokes.

I couldn't hold back anymore. I knew what I wanted, and it was him.

He kept pressing his fingers and teased my clit with hard, forceful touches.

I tightened my grip against his head, almost ready to explode.

My vision went white as my orgasm penetrated my very core.

Chris's name escaped my lips, along with a whole litany of moans that refused to stop falling.

He finished kissing and touching my slick, and as he pulled back, he looked into my eyes.

"Mia, I'm—"

"Don't worry about it. I'm here," I reassured.

I knew he was going to say that despite all his attempts to pull back, he needed to feel every part of me.

He smiled and nodded.

"You get it."

He spread my legs apart, and then I felt something hard penetrate me.

Oh. He's even bigger than before.

For a moment, I thought about protection.

But then I remembered I always had a morning-after pill in my purse since after Casey, I had stopped taking birth control.

Guess right now was one of those moments where I needed one of those pills.

His member thrust all the way inside with a quick and forceful motion to begin.

Every thrust after was so hard that I shot up as he stuffed me.

His hands teased my clit and pinched it with subtle sounds. I closed my eyes and screamed silently. I could barely take it.

He rubbed the nub with small strokes, but it was nothing compared to the thrusts of his massive member.

All I thought about was him.

I closed my legs around him tighter and he groaned.

"You want more. Right?"

"Yes! Deeper. Fuck me deeper—"

He slammed inside and my head rolled back as a moan of complete bliss escaped my lips.

My vision went white, and I could feel the bubbling orgasm looming.

Breathy moans were the only sounds I could make as our bodies moved rhythmically. I could stay like this forever.

His hands explored me and pinched my nipples.

Choked moans of pleasure, barely processed from my mind, were the only things I could hear.

Soon, the ache grew. Even though I didn't want to cum yet, I knew that every thrust right against my sweet spot inside, drove me closer to the brink.

My fingernails dug into him as I closed my eyes.

He continued with his thrusts, and as they grew stronger, I was getting closer to my peak, but I tried to last a bit longer.

I knew he could fill me even deeper and I needed him to do that.

"Chris stop teasing me, dammit I'm—"

He moved a little bit faster, about halfway inside. I moaned, feeling as if I was going crazy.

A moment later, he slammed all the way in after a bit of teasing. As he angled my hips, I gasped and held onto his shoulders.

"I'm—"

The words failed to fall from my lips. All I felt was pure pleasure.

I held his shoulders until my knuckles went white, as my orgasm filled every crevice of my mind and body.

Chris grabbed my hips and plunged inside again.

He held me tightly, like a vice grip, and as he spilled inside, I moaned against him.

This was perfect.

It was what I needed. We stayed like this, basking in the pleasure of each other.

Eventually, I moved off, using his large, sizable shoulders to balance. While I felt like jelly, my whole body basked in the pleasure.

That might have been some of the best goddamn sex of my life.

Chris didn't say anything. Instead, he laid down in bed next to me. His arms wrapped around me and held me tightly.

A mixture of emotions filled my mind.

And mainly, the usual question I always asked myself; *What did this mean for us?* Would it be...something more?

I didn't want to jinx it or rush things. But I liked where we were right now.

As sleep overtook me, the words fell from my lips.

"I like where we are, Chris."

Thirty
Chris

The explosions reverberated through my ears.

"Hold on! Get your ass over here and—"

The cries followed. A body fell, lifeless, as the rest of the guys.

I trod water. My eyes darted about, desperate to find someone, anyone who could save me.

Who could get me away from this hell forever?

Nothing. There wasn't a soul available.

Everyone left as the fighting continued. The gunshots echoed through my ears.

I have to live.

I told myself this, but all around me was death. The bodies of my comrades surrounded me.

Along the shoreline, I saw the gunfire lighting up the night. Bombs leveled at the ships that were on the edge, barely within the line of fire.

Where do I go? How do I get out of here?

The question haunted me as I started to swim.

I looked up. The north star sat twinkling in the sky. I had to follow it.

That was where we were stationed.

Eventually, I'd find the rest of the crew and give them the information needed.

I dove into the water as the bombs continued to go off all around me.

A hell of mine flanked my right and left. The spikes sat there as a grim reminder that if I went the wrong way, I would be screwed.

I have to live. I have to get out of here and—

The ensuing bomb next to me rang through my ears. I grimaced, trying to get away from this hell.

"Someone! Anyone save me..." I recognized those voices. They were from the second battalion, the one I was supposed to help.

With desperation, I swam over there, ready to help them. As I surfaced, I saw the ship there.

"Oh, thank God you're alive, Captain! We need help and—"

CRASH!

The bomb went off right in front of me. The ship sank, engulfed in oil flames.

Screams filled my ears. Pleas for someone, anyone, to come and save them was all I heard.

"Please, God! I don't want to die here!" The man's voice became nonexistent as death overtook him.

I have to find survivors.

I clung to a part of the ship and pulled myself up on it.

I looked around as smoke plumed and choked my throat.

"Anyone! Please find me and—"

A hand reached for me. It tried to pull me back.

I stepped away and punched the man who tried to grab me.

"Get the hell away from here, you—"

Anger rushed over me, unable to form the final words.

I reached out, and as the enemy, masked and obscured, lay on the ground, I had to get payback for my comrades.

I reached forward and grabbed the son of a bitch's neck.

"You'll pay for this! You will die here for—"

"Chris!"

I opened my eyes. Below me laid Mia, and my hands were around her throat.

Oh my God.

I pulled myself back and shook.

Did I just put my hands around Mia's neck and—

Mia put her hands around my stomach. My breathing hastened as I felt the ache in my chest.

What have I done?

My heart raced faster, and the pain grew overwhelming. I could barely breathe.

I reached for the nightstand, grabbed the bottle of Paxil, and took a pill.

I couldn't come down with Mia's assistance after this one.

My heartbeat still quickened, but Mia's arms never left.

"You didn't hurt me, Chris. It's okay. You had a nightmare."

The words filled my ears, but I didn't listen. I couldn't because the regret of what I felt suddenly hit me like a ton of bricks.

Finally, after what felt like forever, I managed to catch my breath.

The choking plumes, which reminded me of the smoke I inhaled, soon dissipated.

My heart rate finally settled. It was over.

I moved forward, out of Mia's embrace.

I looked back at her as a combination of regret and anger settled in the bowels of my heart.

I could've killed her right then and there.

The nightmares were only bad when I was really stressed.

Usually, I just woke up and took a pill on my own.

But with Mia here, I took it out on her.

I hadn't ever done that.

Even with Alara, I managed to get myself to the bathroom to calm down after an episode.

Mia's hand stroked my shoulder.

"You need to leave."

"Chris—"

"I could have—" I trailed off, not even wanting to say the words out loud.

The realization that I might've actually killed her if she didn't pull me out of this unsettled me. It built guilt, which I couldn't shake.

"You're not the bad guy here, Chris. I know it's stressful, but—"

"I can't do this, Mia. I just can't."

I didn't want to hurt Mia. But not just that, I knew I couldn't handle having her this close.

She was better off with a guy like Casey. Or hell, someone less fucked in the head than I was.

Mia pulled her hand back and reached for the sheet.

"Chris, let's talk about this."

"No, I don't need to tell you anything!"

"How can you say that after last night? You revealed so much and opened up."

My hands clenched as anger seeped over me.

"Yeah, well, maybe I was a fuckup for doing so."

"You weren't a fuckup! I don't want us to end like this and—"

"Well, I do! I can't keep doing this anymore!"

My fingerprints were etched against her neck. Her neck was bright red.

Fuck. I really fucked up this time.

I shook my head.

"There is nothing to talk about Mia. That wasn't okay and—"

"Maybe it wasn't, but that doesn't mean you have to fight these battles alone, you know!"

"And possibly hurt you again? No, Mia. In fact, I don't know if we should even…"

Be together. I had to say this.

Mia didn't deserve a guy like me. She had so much innocence and kindness.

Yes, Casey was immature, but at least he was not dangerous; being with a guy like me, on the other hand, could ruin her.

"I'm here right now. If I didn't care, I would've left."

"Yeah, well, maybe you should."

Mia sighed and covered her body.

"Chris, I knew what I signed up for when you told me about the panic attacks. You're strong but suffering."

"This is my battle to fight! Not yours."

"Then why the hell do you keep doing this back and forth, Chris."

Because, damn, I don't know what I want.

"Because I'm not the man for you. I'm too fucked up for you, and I don't want you to *worry* if I'm going to attack you in my sleep. I think it's better if we just keep our distance for now."

"After we just had sex, and you told me about Alara?"

"Yes," I muttered and looked towards the window. "You don't need a guy like me. I'll be alright. Find yourself a better, less fucked up man."

"But—"

"I get you want to help, but you're not my goddamned therapist, so leave me the hell alone!"

The sheets ruffled behind me. I felt Mia's presence behind me.

Why can't she just leave me alone?

Mia's hands wrapped around me. I pushed them away.

"Stop, Mia."

She stepped back, eyes wide with hurt.

"But Chris, I thought—"

"Just get away! I can't keep doing this."

Mia's hands rest on her hips.

"Why can't you just let me in? You pull me in one moment, tell me these things, and then push me away."

"Because I can't give you these goddamn burdens, Mia!"

I didn't want her to suffer like how I did. She didn't deserve it.

Mia sighed and turned away. Her hazel eyes were filled with tears.

"I hate this. I hate what you do to me."

Trust me, I hated it too.

"Mia, I need some space and—"

"Oh, don't worry, I'll *give* you your space, Christian," she replied through tears. "In fact, I'll just get out of your life."

I stood there as the words cut deep.

No, I didn't want that.

I wanted Mia, but every emotion hung over me and stifled me.

"Mia, please, I just—"

"No, Chris. You keep leading me on. Last night, I thought that I meant something to you. Now I know you're a man who can't choose what to goddamn do with himself, just like your brother. And I'm tired of it."

Hollowness settled in. I regretted the words I uttered.

"I'm sorry, Mia."

"I'm sorry, too. I'll just let you go. I know you're better off without me. I forgive you for what you did but you should seriously take some time and think about what you really want."

Trust me. I planned to.

I had to get Mia out of my head.

"I know."

"Yeah, I plan to as well. Ugh, I should've never pursued any of these feelings. I regret it all!"

Mia grabbed her clothes and hastily put them on. I should have stopped her. I couldn't, though.

Every time I wanted to my body froze in place.

The regret heightened all of my thoughts and showed me how I really felt.

I was a fool.

The sound of the door was the only thing I processed. After a few minutes, I was able to move my body a little bit.

I grabbed my robe and threw it on. As I headed down to the front door, I looked out the window.

Mia's car was gone, and the gates were closed.

Should I have done that? Probably not. But right now, I don't know what to do.

I was better off just focusing on myself and keeping these feelings at bay.

It was for our own good.

Thirty-One
Mia

I hate that things ended up like this, but I guess the truth was there.

I'm not the one for him.

As he admitted himself, he was too fucked up for me. I was sick of the constant runaround.

Maybe now I'll get a moment of God damned peace.

I went back to my apartment and immediately dialed. Two rings later, she spoke.

"Hellooooo, bestie."

"Hi, Nat. I'm sorry for calling this early and—"

"Hey, you're fine, love. I was actually home last night."

It surprised me to hear. Usually, Nat partied all night.

"So what's the matter? You sound stressed."

That's obvious, huh? I took a moment to compose my thoughts.

"It's Chris. He's a prick."

Nataly chuckled, and I rolled my eyes.

"It's not funny Nat."

"I know, hun. I get it, it sucks. But the way you uttered it did make me chuckle."

"Anyways, I'm so sick of the back and forth between him and me. I need a break and—"

"Why don't you come drinking with Katie and me tonight."

"I can't. I'm—"

"Mia, you're not tied to *anyone*. And I know you think I'm leading you down a bad path, encouraging you to get your ass out to the club, but you need it."

"And why do you think that?"

"Because you're chasing after a guy who apparently doesn't give a fuck about you, who keeps leading you on and then pushing you away every second he can. He doesn't know what he wants, and you're better off not worrying about guys like that."

She was right. Chris *was* stressing me out.

Then again, a part of it was my fault.

"I was stupid for thinking there was a chance for something, anything with that guy."

"Hey, don't beat yourself up. You need to forget about his fickle ass and just live a little bit."

"I mean, maybe."

I doubted this would fix anything. Chris was always doing this crap, and it drove me crazy.

"There's a club called Diamonds near the DC border. I heard that it's got some seriously amazing music. The new owners are dope, too."

"Yeah, sounds fun," I muttered.

"Oh my God, Mia, you've *got* to get over this guy. Chris is just going to stress you out even further. Now let's go out tonight. Get your mind off things.'

Yeah, easier said than done.

I mean Chris *didn't* choke me hard enough to leave a mark, and I could cover it up with foundation, but I'd eventually have to confront him on Monday at the office.

"We work together, Nat."

"So what? Just say you're busy and hide in your office. Work with other members of the team. He'll get *over it*. And if he really does care about you, he'll figure his shit out. You don't need the extra anxiety, love."

"Yeah, but still—"

"Mia, you can separate work and your personal life. Besides, maybe a killer hangover is what you need to get your mind off stupid guys."

I laughed. Maybe Nat was right.

"Alright, fine, you win."

"There we go! I'll have the Uber driver pick you up. It's about twenty minutes from your place. And I promise, *not* some isolated ass club where a crazy person will rear-end you.."

"Fair enough. Thanks, hun."

I hung up the phone. Nataly had that natural ability to make me feel just a little better about everything.

Even though my life was a constant shitshow, at least I had her.

And it gave me some time to focus on something else rather than have Chris's bullshit hanging over me.

I swear, it pissed me the hell off. I thought I was strong enough to handle the bastard's burdens, but I guess that was thrown right out the window.

The man was broken, and maybe I'm just not the one to pick up the pieces.

Maybe it was because of Casey and I. But I had moved on.

Now, I didn't know if I should even bother with dating.

My phone beeped. It was Nat.

Yo, so Katie says that Diamonds is kinda lame. She says we're going to Velvet Gold, a club with amazing drinks. She says the owner's some rich guy.

Yay, another rich bastard who only cared about himself.

I rolled my eyes but held back from saying anything.

I told her fine and then put the phone away.

A storm of emotions seeped through me, but there was only one thing I could do.

Just live a little, party my ass off, and get my damn mind off Chris as much as I could.

Thirty-Two
Chris

"Coming."

I walked down the stairs. I half-hoped. Maybe it was Mia.

Then again, if it was her, I doubt I'd open the door.

I didn't want to see her. I regretted hurting her, but still. I needed space to figure out what I wanted.

When I didn't expect it, it was Casey standing right across from me. His blonde hair was cut short, and he wore a baseball cap atop his head.

He wore a simple black wifebeater and jeans.

"Casey. What are you doing here?"

"Oh hey. Sorry for showing up randomly. You didn't answer my texts last night."

Shit! I left my phone in the bedroom when I was with Mia.

"Sorry about that."

"No, it's fine. Just a bit weird for you. You always answer me."

Fuck he was right.

"I had some company over yesterday. Sorry about that."

Casey's eyebrows rose.

"Company?"

"Just a friend."

"I see. Anyone I know?"

Yeah, your ex-girlfriend, whom I was fucking like an insatiable bastard.

"Just a friend. Someone I met while I was at an event."

Casey nodded. "And here I was wondering if you finally managed to find someone special."

I did. And my problem right now was I couldn't betray my brother. It would kill Casey on the inside.

And I wasn't ready for the potential fallout that this would bring.

"Nah, nothing much. You know how I am."

"Yeah, you don't *date*. You're constantly alone."

"For a good reason."

"I know, bro."

"Right now, my focus is on Jacob."

"Oh yeah. Speaking of, where's the little guy?"

"With mom."

Casey's brows furrowed. "Oh."

"I'm sorry. I know that—"

"It's fine, Chris," Casey muttered. "She and I just have our differences. It's good she's here for Jacob, though."

"Yeah, I appreciate everything she does now."

Even if Mom refused to be a part of our lives.

"Anyways, just wanted to see what's up. I know you're busy with work and all."

"Feel free to drop by if you're in the area."

"I will. And I'll make sure to text you. Hopefully, next time you answer."

"I will do my best," I replied with a chuckle.

It was shitty of me to forget, but I was so wrapped up with Mia that I kind of forgot. Now that's out the window.

"Actually, you want to go shooting? We're near the range." He said.

"Sure, I'd be down," I replied.

We got in the car and drove over to the range.

Shooting guns got my mind off things.

Even though I felt guilty for hurting her, it felt like an open wound in my heart after I told her so much about the past.

She didn't know how strongly I felt for her. And how terrible it made me feel. I hated it.

We shot for the next couple of hours and made some small talk.

Casey fired his final rounds and then looked up at me.

"You know, I am trying to meet some new gals. But the whole being on the road thing makes it hard."

"I'm sorry."

"Yeah. I hate to say it, but maybe Mia was right. That I should have figured out my life a while ago."

"There's still time," I said, stilted that he said the 'M' word again.

"Yeah, I know. And being with you always helps."

"I'm always here, bro."

"Yeah. Unlike anyone else."

Casey's phone beeped, and he groaned.

"Ugh, dammit!"

"What's up?"

"I have to go, Chris. I forgot I got invited to this party for racers, and they're blowing up my phone now."

There he goes again.

I understood why Casey's impulsivity bothered Mia. Because sometimes it annoyed the shit out of me.

"Duty calls," I replied as I masked my feeling of disdain.

"I'm so sorry, Chris. But I'll tell you how it goes."

"I'd love to hear it."

Casey left, and as I stood near the edge of the counter at the shooting range, a mixture of anger and annoyance filled me.

Again, I had to get over her.

Could I, though?

I swear, it was like every time I thought I did, she managed to come back into my life. And every time she did, it was impossible to extricate myself from this.

I turned to my left, where the shooting range owner, David, stood.

He raised a tanned hand and nodded. "Something the matter?"

He walked over, and I shrugged.

David was a good friend of mine and the owner of this place.

I came out here a lot, especially when I first got my hunting license.

He took care of me and eventually Casey when he was old enough to get his license.

David was the same as always. Silvery hair that went down to his mid-back, piercing brown eyes, and tanned skin that was well-worn from working on the farm he owned.

"Nah, man. Just need to shoot for a bit longer."

"Ahh, I see," he encouraged.

"I need to fire off a few rounds," I muttered.

He chuckled. "Got it, my friend. Well, stay as long as you need to. I am not going anywhere."

"Appreciate it."

David gave me more rounds, and for another couple of hours, I continued to shoot. It helped with the annoyance, but Mia still lingered in my thoughts.

If I could cut them away and forget them, I would.

After I finished, I headed over to the car. As I settled into the seat, I put my phone in the holder.

It rang, and I half-expected it to be a call from the office or maybe a partner.

Instead, the sender was unknown.

Who the hell is bothering me on a damned Saturday? I swear if this is a scam.

I opened my phone and listened to the voice.

"Hello, is this Chris Hamilton?"

I didn't recognize the voice. I was half-tempted to hang up right then and there.

"Speaking?"

"This is Roy Jones. Child Protective Services."

What? Why the hell was CPS calling me?

"Excuse me?"

"I'm sorry to bother you, sir. How are you doing?"

"Fine until you called," I muttered, annoyed that they had the audacity to not only call me on my day off but also a call from *them,* of all people.

I hadn't heard from them in years. Not since Alara took me to court for Jacob's custody.

And now, these sons of bitches were back.

"We recently got a notice from Alara. She wants to appeal the decision and—"

"Tell her that there will be no further discussion. I have *no* desire to take this matter any further."

The man cleared his throat on the other line.

"I understand your frustration, Christian, but we recently have new evidence."

Are they insane? Did they think that Alara's pleas would be listened to?

I knew Alara. She was desperate to get Jacob back, but I'd stop at *nothing* to make sure that she never saw Jacob again.

"There is no evidence. I'm sure she's come up with new lies again to corrupt my image in the courts. I have been a fine father to Jacob."

"Well, this appeal needs to be investigated in the courts again. My colleague will forward you the paperwork. I just wanted to call and—"

"Well, thanks for that. I will have my lawyers be in touch with you."

I hung up the phone and sat back. Anxiety shot through my body.

Why are they bothering me?

CPS took my side back then, and they'd do it again.

Alara was *desperate* because she threw away a life she could've lived for some cheap thrills and fucks.

My heart raced as the anger shot through me. My throat tightened, and I clenched the wheel.

No good. I can't drive like this.

My vision grew spotty as the worrisome thoughts rose through me.

I reached for the glovebox, where I kept a backup bottle of Paxil. I pulled it out and realized it was new.

Weird. I could've sworn the bottle I had was half-used.

Whatever. I took a pill and gulped. It settled into the pit of my stomach, and the foreboding symptoms of the panic attack subsided.

I sighed, almost relieved that it happened. I swear, I felt as if I was going crazy.

I adjusted the mirrors and started driving home.

Many thoughts sifted through me, and I knew that I had to forget them.

After I got home, I checked on Jacob. He was at an event with my mom and having a great time. Mom said they wouldn't be home till later tomorrow.

Good. He deserved it. He needed to be a kid. Right now, I had to get my head together.

At seven, I got dressed up. I didn't know what would happen tonight, but there was only one thing that I wanted to do.

VALENCIA ROSE

To forget about the problems I had currently, and to get drunk at a club somewhere.

Thirty-Three
Mia

"Oh my gosh, you look *so* hot."

"Thanks," I replied with a smile as I stepped into the Uber.

Okay damn. Nat and Katie really shelled out for little old me.

It was a hummer limo with plenty of space. There was also a minibar.

"How could you guys afford this."

"Oh, my new squeeze gave me some money," Katie replied as she downed a flute of champagne.

"You got *another* sugar daddy?"

"He's not a sugar daddy," she corrected. "He's, like, a total sweetheart."

"Who also just happens to be fifteen years older than you and is a widowed man," Nat chimed in.

"So, a sugar daddy," I muttered.

"Hey, I'm not complaining. If I want something, he gets it for me."

I chuckled. At least Katie had someone. She'd been a mess, dating everything and anything.

Recently, she turned to being a sugar baby. While I didn't condone it, she got paid serious cash, so she got by pretty well.

And being in Arlington she could easily travel to New York or Washington D.C. to meet more men.

The Hummer limo rolled and took us to the club. When we got there, Katie stepped out.

"So, like, my new man's friends with the owners. Apparently, they have us on the list already."

"Alright," I replied.

We went to the door, and sure enough, the bouncer had us. He let us in, and soon, the throbbing sound of techno music filled the room.

Finally, a chance to forget.

We headed towards the bar and the bartender got us all complimentary vodka sodas.

I took a long sip and felt the alcohol seep through my head.

"See, isn't this great?" Katie asked.

"Yeah, it is," I admitted. It sure helped me forget alright.

Not just about Casey, but about his *lovely* brother as well.

We ordered another round. I felt a presence behind me. One that felt overbearing and just plain weird.

I turned and saw a man with jet-black hair and brown eyes wave toward us.

He wore a simple blue shirt with a gold cross against his chest. He wore jeans that hugged his thin, shapely legs.

A total contrast from the gruff, muscular Chris, that's for sure. Still a looker though.

"Hi there?" I finally asked.

"Hey, can I buy you a drink? Damien by the way."

I looked over at Nataly and Katie. They both smiled and encouraged me.

"Sure, I'm down."

He slid in between us. The guy was attractive and ordered us another round and me a cocktail.

The bartender settled them in front of me.

I started with the vodka seltzer, which was bubbly and perfect to sip on.

"So, what's a pretty girl like you doing here?"

I looked around. Nat and Katie were already gone. *Dammit!*

I faked a smile, but inside, my heart raced.

"Oh, just trying to spend a nice evening with my friends, but they probably went to the dance floor. Maybe I should too."

"Well, I wouldn't leave you alone if you came here with me," he said, slightly slurred.

He extended a drunk hand and I hesitantly took it.

"Why don't we go dance and you can tell me all about yourself," he offered.

My heart was still racing.

Why the hell did they leave me alone here with some random guy?

Thoughts swarmed my head.

Sure, he was attractive, but there was something that bothered me about this.

He didn't ignite that spark that Chris did. I mean, I could fuck around, but something about that felt wrong.

Like I shouldn't.

I wasn't even *tied* to Chris. Fucker didn't even know if he wanted to date me or not? Why the hell was I worried about a guy like him.

I shook it off.

"I mean, maybe we could dance a little bit."

"I'd like that."

We headed towards the dance floor.

My heart raced as I looked at Damien. The thump of the base drowned away these thoughts.

We danced together, and for a bit, I felt good.

The nagging feeling of dread disappeared, if only for a bit.

Damien's hands first landed on my waist. A safe space.

But then he leaned in, and I looked at him.

"Uhm, what are you doing?"

"Isn't it obvious? *Dancing*."

His hand landed straight on my ass, and he grabbed it gently. I stiffened up.

Fuck, this wasn't what I wanted.

I didn't mind the dancing and the little bit of flirting, but now, this was getting to be too much.

I looked around, and I felt the sudden nerves strike me.

He pulled me closer, and soon, his alcohol-infused breath landed on my lips.

"What's the matter? Don't you like this?"

I nodded, pushing the feeling of guilt away.

"I mean, it's okay, I guess," I replied, faking a smile.

I had to find a way out of here.

His hands reached for mine and pressed them to his shoulders. He jerked his body towards me.

Okay, he's got to chill.

The anxiety grew. That, and the feeling of eyes on me.

Someone was watching me, and I knew they were angry.

Thirty-Four
Chris

I pulled up to Velvet Gold with many different feelings. Something about this place made me want to come here.

Kind of ironic because I actually *hated* this club.

I was friends with the owners, sure, but some of the people who came through here were scummy with a capital 'S'. Some didn't respect boundaries, and many of them wouldn't stop until someone called them out.

But the drinks were good.

I parked my Bugatti in one of the spaces and headed inside. The bouncer opened the gate as soon as he saw me. A grin crossed his face.

"Good to see you, Chris."

"Thanks, Artie. Hope the crowds are treating you well."

"As good as ever. Should I set up Clyde with the usual?"

"Yes, of course."

My favorite aged whiskey and coke would be ready as soon as I made my way into the VIP lounge.

I walked through the club area and saw people dancing.

Yep, just as I expected.

Lots of desperate, immature guys who were too busy trying to get a simple lay.

A man brushed against me. He mumbled a simple "Sorry" as he went by.

"Hey, watch where you're going and—"

I stopped, frozen in place.

Am I dreaming? There was *no* way that Mia was here.

And dancing with some random guy.

What the fuck was going on?

I blinked and looked around again.

The guy was gone, into a crowd of people.

I headed towards the VIP lounge and settled inside.

The bartender had the whiskey and Coke ready for me. As I drank it, my mind went back to the two people I saw dancing.

That *had* to be Mia. I recognized the hair from a mile away.

Maybe I should call her just to make sure.

I dialed Mia's number, but there was nothing. I sent two texts, but they were just received and never read.

Something was wrong.

I took my drink and then went to the main club area connected to the dance floor.

As I did, I bumped into a familiar head of blonde hair.

Wait, that was—

"You."

The woman stopped dead in her tracks.

"Hey, you're that guy from that night with Mia."

"Where the hell is she?"

"I don't know. I've been trying to call her and—"

"Okay. She was with that guy then," I muttered as I attempted to quell the growing anger that rose through my body.

Nataly brushed a hand through a couple of blonde locks.

"Oh shit, it's that guy! I have been trying to find her. He's actually supposed to be blacklisted from the club."

What? What the hell was she doing with that guy?

I had to find her.

I brushed through the rest of the crowds and practically pushed them out of the way.

Out of the corner of my eye, I saw her hair bouncing up and down in a tight ponytail.

"This way."

I moved through the crowd over to a small corner.

"Come on, you want this, don't you?"

There he was. I clenched my fists as anger swept through me.

What *the fuck* was this man doing with Mia?

He pressed his lips to her, but Mia kept pushing him away. He pressed her hands to the wall, and a hand traveled dangerously down between her legs.

Mia's eyes were wide with fright at what that bastard was doing. They grew even wider and practically jumped out of the sockets the second she saw me.

Oh, hell no.

There was *no* way I was letting this little shit touch *my* woman.

He pulled back and slipped a hand up her skirt.

"Come on, just relax. I'm sure that—"

"GET THE FUCK OFF HER!"

The man whipped around. I recognized the guy.

He was one of the bad apples that kept sneaking into the club. A guy named Damien.

The man was trouble. There were reports from multiple women of him trying to accost them for sex. Some of them were even molested by him.

And now this son of a bitch was trying to touch Mia.

"Hey man, she's my girl and—"

"THE FUCK SHE IS!" I screamed.

I reached for the guy and grabbed him.

Without a second thought, I punched the motherfucker straight in the face.

He flew back, and blood flowed from his face.

"Chris, what are you—"

Mia was mine! This roach didn't deserve her. Hell, he wasn't even a roach because at least roaches were God damn useful.

I punched him again in the face.

He fell to the ground and lay there unconscious. I stepped back and breathed heavily.

Without another thought, I grabbed Mia's hand with the one I didn't punch the guy with.

I hit him hard. It throbbed and stung a little bit.

But none of that mattered.

What mattered was her.

"Chris, let me go and—"

I threw Mia over my shoulder. I ignored the stares from everyone in the club.

They didn't understand that this was my woman, and I would stop at *nothing* to have her.

I couldn't bear the thought of her being with someone else. She was *mine.*

I mean, we might not be officially together, but I'd be damned if I let *another* man touch her like that.

I refused to give her up and to let her go.

I walked through the club. Mia's hands punched my shoulders, but it felt like nothing.

"Chris! Put me down."

"No, not until I know you're safe," I hissed in her ear.

Not until we talked about this, once and for all.

We walked past the club owner, Viktor, who nodded.

"Everything okay, Christian?"

"I'm just *peachy,* Viktor. Hand hurts a little, but—"

Viktor motioned for one of the bartenders to get me some ice.

A moment later, he pressed a small plastic bag into my hand.

"Here. Hopefully, that staves off the swelling for a bit."

"Thank you. And I'm sorry for dropping the whiskey and coke on the floor."

I realized after the fact that I did that. Viktor shook his head.

"Do not worry, Christian. Your presence at the Velvet Gold alone is wonderful to experience."

"I'm glad you think so," I replied gruffly.

Mia continued to punch and yell at me to put her down, but I didn't care.

"I'll be going now," I said.

"Alright. Have a good evening, sir."

"Give my regards to Artie. And tell him I'll give him a bonus for being such a good security guard."

"Of course."

The music stopped, and everyone watched as I left the club.

Mia's screams and hits became absolutely nothing in my ears.

I didn't care. She was dancing with a random guy. She pushed my buttons, and it pissed me the hell off.

Now, why I acted this way was still beyond me.

Was it because the thought of losing her upset me?

Was it because when I saw her react the way she did, kissing him back and his hands all over her, it made me angry?

I didn't know completely. What mattered right now was nothing else, though.

Only her.

We finally left the club, and I headed to the car. As I put her in the car, she looked at me.

"Chris, what the fuck!"

"We have to talk, Mia. And I've had enough of this shit. You want to know what you are to me. Fine. You're mine."

Her eyes widened at the words, and for a moment, she didn't say anything.

Good. She needed to shut up for a goddamn moment and let me tell her how I felt.

I didn't even bother to leave the parking lot of the club.

I had to tell her right now the feelings in my heart.

Thirty-Five
Mia

What the fuck just happened?

A haze of drunken stupor filled my head.

I half-expected Chris to leave and drive somewhere and *then* berate me.

But instead, he sat in the parking lot.

Nobody came near the car. I think he intimidated everyone.

He sure as shit did me because I was *not* expecting that.

Seeing the anger in his eyes and the ferocity that came from his lips shook me to the core.

My head spun as I tried to figure out what exactly just happened.

Chris moved to the seat next to me and stared at me.

The anger sat ignited in his eyes. My lip trembled, and both fear and desire coalesced together.

"Chris, I'm sorry about—"

"No, Mia! I can't believe I walked inside and saw that man all over you!"

"Well, because he was trying to push me to have sex with him, and I wasn't comfortable. *I* pushed him away in case you forgot that little part."

"Oh, then how come you *enjoyed* it?"

"I wasn't fucking enjoying it! I don't know why suddenly you give such a shit, Chris!"

I flinched at his words. They were so sexy, and yet, the anger made me feel an inkling of fear.

Why did Chris care so much?

Just earlier today, he *said* he couldn't do that. That he didn't want to be with me.

And now he does?

"You put yourself in danger and I'm supposed to ignore that."

I still didn't understand why he even bothered. I folded my arms across my chest.

"You're a fucking enigma, Chris."

"And you're going to get yourself hurt—"

I turned to him and balled my hands into fists.

"No, I wasn't! Sure, I didn't want him on me, but I could have taken care of myself."

"Then how come you didn't stop him?"

"Because...I was scared," I admitted, biting my lip.

I genuinely was. It relieved me to see Chris step in like that and stop the man, but still.

He acted out of line and was so much more overbearing than I ever thought he'd be.

I teared up as he glared at me, unable to say what I wanted to say.

"Mia, you could've been hurt. That's why I got so upset."

"Yeah, and why do you care? I *tried* to be there for you yesterday. And guess what you did? Pushed me the hell away."

He moved back slightly and sighed.

"Because Mia, the guilt of betrayal was killing me."

"So now it's not?"

He sighed and rubbed his temples. A subtle nod followed.

"Well now I've decided to face it and deal with it."

"What's with the change of heart?"

He paused and looked away, averting my gaze.

"I don't know. It's hard to explain."

"So explain then. We've got all night."

I was so tired of this back and forth and Chris's fickle desires. At this point, I just wanted an answer.

If he didn't want to be with me, I'd move on.

Maybe not go to the club and have sex with a random guy, but move on in other ways.

"When I saw you with him, it pissed me off. And I realized how much I want you, Mia."

I blinked, shocked by his words. His hand reached for my waist and pulled me on top of him.

"Chris, what are you—"

"I can't keep fighting this anymore. I just don't know what the fuck to do."

I didn't know what to say either.

But behind that obvious anger and his gritted teeth, I saw something else.

Hurt, masked by the furiousness that sat on his face.

"What does your heart want then?"

He sighed and looked away.

"I hurt you earlier, Mia. But I realize that I can't be without you. I know our relationship will hurt Casey, and working through that is a challenge I am willing to take on because I need you in my life."

"But you *do* want this too, then."

He nodded and took a deep breath.

"Yeah, I do. If you're willing to take back a fucked-up man like me, that is."

I smiled. He fought a good fight. I laced my fingers against his.

"Yeah. I am. And I'm glad to finally hear it."

"Why?"

"Because you've been trying to figure out these feelings for god knows how long. If you keep fighting, then you'll never have an answer. I'm glad that you finally understood how you really feel."

He nodded.

"Yeah. I do. I realized I can't *be* without you, Mia. When you left, I thought about going after you."

"You didn't, though."

"Yeah, because I didn't know what the fuck to do with myself. And honestly, I'm still trying to figure this out. But the pull you have on me is unavoidable. I feel like, if I keep ignoring it, I'll eventually go crazy."

That was exactly how I felt.

Sure, Chris was an ass, but I couldn't deny the feelings I had for him.

"I mean, I feel the same way too. I just didn't want to cross the boundaries that you've enacted."

He scoffed and shook his head.

"Too fucking late for that. I thought I could get over you and maybe just move on with life, but…"

"You can't, can you?"

He shook his head.

"Obviously not. And well, as much as I didn't want things to get complicated, we're here now."

I chuckled.

"I think we're *past* the point of not making things complicated."

"Agreed."

We locked eyes. He ran a hand through my hair.

"You know, you look fucking hot right now."

I flushed as I felt the wetness between my legs.

His alpha dominance and those pheromones he exuded as he said those words reeled me in.

"You're mine."

The thought alone made me shiver.

As I looked at Chris, I saw the broken man, but I also saw something else.

A man who cared, who felt as strongly for me as I did for him.

The man wanted this but was worried about the implications.

"So what should we do about it then?"

"I have no fucking clue, Mia. But what I do know is that I need you. And I'm tired of pretending."

I smiled.

"I need you too. I guess we'll just cross that next bridge when we get there."

"That's my plan."

He pulled me against his hardened chest.

Our lips crashed together, and a storm of emotions rushed through me.

He wrapped his arms possessively against me and held me tightly.

I melted into the touch as the ache grew and drove me crazy.

His hands reached down and touched my butt. He massaged it and playfully spanked it.

I gasped, but the desire filled my every thought.

"I'm going to show you what it means to be mine." He whispered in my ear.

He leaned down and bit down on my neck. I grabbed his white t-shirt tightly.

As he pulled back his lust-filled, desirable eyes stared at me.

"Now, you're marked by me."

"Yes," I panted. "I'm yours."

If I hadn't forgotten him already, I sure did now.

His hand reached for my dress and pushed it up to reveal the tiny black thong I wore.

"You even wore a thong like that, expecting another guy to take you tonight. Well, I'm going to make you forget all about that."

His lips captured my nipple and sucked on it hard, almost biting down on it.

I closed my eyes as he teased the nub. His other hand played with my other nipple. He pinched the nub with hard touches.

"Fuck, Chris, I need more."

"Really now? but I thought you wanted someone else?" He asked as he pulled back.

"No, please! Goddammit, I need it."

He breathed hot air against the nub, and I gasped.

"Good. That's exactly what I want to hear. Nobody else. I claim you."

That masculine, primal sound had me elated.

His lips teased my nipples again as he went back over. His tongue flicked over it hard and forcefully.

His other hand pinched them harder until they became painfully hard.

I could barely take it. I needed him to stuff me and make me his.

It wasn't just a want anymore, but a fucking need.

"Fuck me!" I practically begged Chris.

He pulled back and skated his hand down to my thong. He caressed my heat, and I whimpered.

"Really now? You want me *that* badly?"

The man had me begging like a little whore!

"Yes."

"Then tell me Mia," He breathed in my ear. "Tell me you're fucking mine and you don't want another man."

He pressed two fingers straight into my clit and teased me. I gasped, lost in the pleasures.

"I'm yours," I breathed, moaning as two fingers slipped down my panties and pushed into my entrance. He thrusted them in and out, and I closed my eyes.

Everything Chris did felt right.

As much as I tried to deny it up to this point, it was like a switch. He knew just how to turn me the fuck on and make me beg for him.

And I fucking loved it.

His fingers plunged deeply inside, and I moaned. I cried out his name as my orgasm began bubbling between my legs.

"That's right. You want this."

"I want this. Yes, Chris, I—"

"No. I won't let you cum."

I looked up, lost in the pleasure but frustrated.

"Chris, please. I'm sorry and—"

"I want you to fucking beg for it. Tell me right now."

Fuck. He was such a fucking animal.

"Please fuck me. Let me cum."

He smirked. "Fine. I'll let you cum, but I'm going to make sure you don't let it happen right away. No, I'm going to savor every goddamn minute."

The sounds alone, the alpha dominance that whisked me away, drove me absolutely crazy.

I moaned, arching my body for just more of a touch.

A bit more. That was all I needed. But he savored it, edging me to the point where I was at his mercy, and he commandeered everything.

Including my pleasure.

He looked at me, and then he slipped his pants partway off.

He brushed his member against my entrance, and I closed my eyes.

"Chris, fuck me," I pleaded.

"There we go. Know your place," He growled, nipping in my ear.

I gasped and nodded.

"It's with you."

"That's what I want to hear. You and me, together as one."

He slammed his member deep into me, and I cried out.

A mixture of minor aches and pleasure overwhelmed me as our bodies were together, united as one.

It felt right, having him inside me.

He groaned and continued to thrust all the way inside. He filled me up, and I needed every second I could get.

After a few more thrusts, he reached for my hips, and I bounced up and down.

His hand pinched my nipples and twisted them.

Pure pleasure overloaded my every sense.

My body was on fire, and I clung to him like a lifeline.

Finally, after what felt like forever, the torturous pleasure drove me to the brink as my orgasm threatened to spill.

"Chris, I'm about to cum."

"That's right. I want to see you lose it. Come for me, baby."

The words sucked me into the man's embrace. I needed him. I refused to deny myself this anymore.

I was so close. I knew that there was no way I could hold back anymore.

A moment later, I tensed up and cried out his name.

He held me there as he thrust into me, finishing inside.

We stayed like this for a bit, lost in the afterglow of our orgasms. I looked over and smiled.

"If this is how it feels to be yours, I'm not going to be able to walk soon."

Chris laughed and held me against his chest.

There was no denying it anymore. This was where I *had* to be. If I left, I would regret it forever.

We stayed entwined in each other's arms. Neither of us wanted to move. We feared that everything might disappear.

But I knew that this was where I needed to be against the man who managed to get into my heart.

That, after so much fighting, I could finally settle.

Maybe we were meant to be together.

And we would deal with the aftermath later.

Thirty-Six
Chris

"Alright. I'll see you when you get here. Hopefully, the traffic's not too bad. Bye."

I hung up the phone. It felt like a weight lifted off my shoulders.

After that night with Mia, things were different.

I talked to her at the office more freely.

The pull towards her drove me crazy, and I liked it now.

We agreed not to say anything about dating, for both our sakes. I didn't want Casey to get suspicious of us either.

Speaking of...

I looked at my calendar. We were supposed to meet up and play some badminton today. He hadn't messaged me back.

What the hell, Casey?

I sent him a text and told him that I'd be available around three.

I settled into the office and sighed. Mia should be here in a bit.

My hands rested on my desk as I began with the day's emails.

Pierre sent me the contract for another yearly partnership.

It was great seeing this. All the hard work finally paid off.

I signed the contract and then sent it back over.

I opened the rest of my emails, hoping there was nothing else. Most of it was work invitations and meeting reminders until I got to the last one.

Re: Custody appeal.

Oh, hell no. I had a bad feeling about this.

I opened the email and read the contents.

Good Day, Mr. Hamilton,

I hope this email finds you well. I am calling to inform you that Alara Tate plans on an appeal for Jacob Hamilton's custody.

With recent evidence resurfacing, we believe that the court's previous ruling in favor of your full custody of Jacob may not be in everyone's best interest anymore.

Below is a list of the recent evidence that we discovered.

Best Regards,

Cody Knack

This is getting out of fucking hand.

Alara's *desperate* to get him back. I bit my lip as I looked at the pieces of evidence.

My prescription.

In what world does a bottle of Paxil count as evidence? This is insane and—

"What the—"

Opioids? But they're fucking anti-anxiety meds!

This is insanity.

My hands shook. This had to be a ruse on her part to make my panic attacks out to be a drug addiction or something.

And it royally pissed me off.

I immediately emailed him back and told him that my legal team will contact him with my response and left it at that.

There was no way these bastards were going to win.

I sat back and sighed as I tried to figure out how to approach this.

Never in a million years would I have thought this would happen. I rested my head in my hands.

A knock at the door pulled me out of my thoughts.

"It's me."

Mia.

"Come in."

She opened the door and smiled. She settled some papers on the table and then stepped back.

"Here's the current weekly stats."

"Thanks."

Mia's brows furrowed as she looked at me.

"What's wrong?"

Fuck. I had to tell her, even if I didn't want to burden Mia with more crap.

Plus, if Alara *is* serious about trying to get Jacob back, her being a part of this could complicate things.

She could use the whole '*He's seeing a woman that's much younger than him. That's unfit.*' schtick in court.

The *last* thing I needed.

"I'm attempting to be fine. Just got some personal things I did *not* expect to see in my email today."

"Okay. Do you need my help?"

"I don't think you can help with this one. It's Alara."

"Oh."

"Yeah, she's rearing her ugly head again, trying to get custody of Jacob. You can't do anything about it. I'll just have my legal team take care of this."

"Got it. Well, if you need me, let me know."

"Thank you Mia. I do appreciate it."

I meant it. Mia's soft words of encouragement helped in even the direst of moments.

For a bit, I thought I'd' have a panic attack. Her presence was like a breath of fresh air and pulled me from those thoughts.

"Well if you need anything, let me know, okay?"

She walked over, and I stood up. We shared a quick kiss and hugged for a moment.

"I will."

"Alright."

Mia left, and as the door closed, I sighed with relief. It felt good to tell her things.

Keeping it bottled up wasn't healthy.

I relaxed slightly and then checked my phone for a response from Casey.

But there was still no response. Dammit, what was his problem?

I bit my lip, frustrated by everything. That email was the last thing I needed.

But it'll work out. One way or another.

Thirty-Seven
Mia

I headed back to my desk as my stomach gurgled. Time for lunch.

I texted Mom and asked if she wanted to get food today.

She said yes, and we agreed to meet up at the usual spot.

Hopefully this time, no awkward encounters with Chris.

Then again, after that night, our relationship was better. While we didn't outright say we were a couple, we just about were.

In the office, he'd steal small kisses and smile at me. But we agreed not to be too open about it.

I didn't want Mom freaking out that much.

Nat and Katie knew, but they supported me. Though, Nat said to be careful because he was scary that night.

Yeah, scary sexy.

Mom went to her support group early today since they wanted to meet for breakfast.

After, she went to yoga and wanted to grab a bite to eat. So we agreed to meet in a couple hours.

My phone beeped, and I looked down. It was my period tracker.

I was three days late. Weird. Usually, it came right on the dot every single month.

I have been stressed, so maybe that was it.

But then, I remembered Chris and I did have sex unprotected. Twice.

Oh shit.

I rifled through my bag and found the morning-after pill I was supposed to take still in the blister packet.

Crap! I forgot to take it. I was so stressed out by the shit with Chris that I forgot.

Now this could be a problem.

I took a couple breaths and tried keeping it together.

It'll be alright. You just had a lapse of judgment and forgot. Chill out, Mia.

It was no use. I had to know for sure.

I texted Mom and told her I could meet for 45 minutes of my lunch, and that I'd have to run to the store of the last fifteen.

At lunch, I got up and headed to the café.

When I got there, Mom waved. She sat near the same corner we were in previously.

And luckily, no sign of Chris anywhere.

That had to be a once-in-a-blue-moon thing. I settled into the seat across from Mom and grinned.

"Hey! Sorry I was late."

"Oh, no problem. The sweet waitress just got my drink order. They have this cranberry-lime spritzer, and I had to try it."

"Hey, that sounds good. I may get one myself."

The server came over, and I ordered the same drink. After ordering a sandwich, the server disappeared.

Mom looked at me curiously. "You seem happier?"

"Who me? Nah, I'm just the same as always. Overworked, stressed, and just trying to get somewhere in life."

"Well, you also look glowing," Mom pointed out as she reached out and touched my hand. "So who's the lucky guy?"

I suppressed the flush that threatened to cross my face.

"No one, Mom. I'm just doing better. Things are looking up. How are you, by the way?"

Mom relaxed slightly and rested her head on her hand.

"Oh, good. The peer support group is nice. They've helped me with a lot of things recently."

"Like what?"

"Just trying to figure out where to go next. You know, I'm thinking about going back to the hospital. I'm tired of being retired!"

"Mom, you should enjoy these years," I insisted. She meant well, but she didn't have to work.

Her 401(k) paid out so much. Mom shook her head.

"No, I don't want to. I want to do something productive. It's what Dad would've wanted."

The atmosphere changed and got tenser. I knew Mom would bring up Dad, but...

"He wouldn't want you to overwork."

"Yeah, well, he wouldn't want me to sit and wallow in my doom and gloom either, Mia."

True. Dad worked hard, and even when his diagnosis looked grim, he made sure to leave stuff behind for Mom and me.

"You could use this time to work around the house and—"

"Mia. I'm serious," Mom insisted. "I need to do this. For my sake and sanity. I could stay at home, but there are too many memories. My therapist encouraged me to go back."

"Mom, you're getting older and—"

"Who the hell cares, Mia? I'll get old when I decide to get old. I'm doing this for myself. Your education inspired me, and I want to do the same."

I nodded. There was no denying that my Mom was strong. And this push to work hard might be what she needed.

Mom retired shortly after Dad's death. While she did fill out her years, she did it because of grief for dad.

Now, she could finally move on.

"Thank you, dear. It'll be good for me. The other girls in our group are also trying this. Hobbies don't take away the pain. But maybe doing what I've always loved, helping others, will fix this."

"I think it will."

The server brought us our food, and our words soon changed to sounds of eating.

The food was good, but the nagging feeling that I *might* be pregnant sat over my head.

I couldn't be. I only fucked up twice.

Mom finished her food and sat back.

"Are you sure there's nothing different? You can tell me."

I pursed my lips. I wanted to tell her about Christian and the sort of dating thing we're doing.

But she knew him enough to make some kind of comment on it.

That was the last thing I needed right now.

"Oh no, I'm good. Just been talking to this guy."

"Oh really?"

"Yeah, it's going okay, I think. We get along well."

"I'm guessing you've finally moved on from Casey?"

I nodded. It felt good to finally admit it.

"Yeah, Mom. I have. And it's nice."

Mom beamed. "That's what I want to hear. You know that I liked Casey a lot. But he wasn't good for you."

"He wasn't. This guy, though, is really good for me."

"I'm glad. Well, if you want to invite him to dinner, I'd love to meet him."

"Yeah, I'll let him know."

We finished our food, and after Mom and I shared a quick embrace, she ran off.

I stood there, happy to get the feelings I had off my chest. The lingering worry shifted through me.

I raced to the drugstore and grabbed a pregnancy test. I had to know before I got back to the office.

After I paid for it, I went to the bathroom and opened the applicator.

Please be negative! I need you to be negative.

I peed on the stick and held it up. I bit my lip, hoping for one line.

The first line showed brightly through. Alright, it's negative so far and—

Oh no.

The second line slowly formed and soon became just as red as the first. I clutched the pregnancy test tighter so I didn't drop it.

Holy shit. *I'm pregnant, and Chris is the father.*

A million thoughts raced through me. I didn't know what to do.

Throughout the two years I dated Casey, I never had a pregnancy scare. But now, after a couple of flings with Chris, I had a positive test.

This wasn't good.

I couldn't tell Chris. I feared what might happen.

He finally accepted his feelings for me, and we were technically 'dating'. But now that I was pregnant, I feared driving him away.

He hadn't even told Casey yet about us. That was, of course, a problem. If Casey found out, that would really heat things up.

I decided I had to keep it to myself until I knew what to do.

This way, there was no possibility that Casey would discover this.

And Chris shouldn't have this extra stress to deal with on top of everything else.

I threw the test away and walked back over to the office.

When I got inside, I went to my office to check my emails.

A text flashed across the screen from Chris.

Hey. I'm going to see Casey on Friday afternoon. I'll be out of the office that day.

I texted him a quick 'OK' back with a smiley face and closed my phone.

After a couple of deep breaths, I composed myself.

Time to keep the front up, for everyone's sake.

Thirty-Eight
Chris

"Thank you. Be here in a couple hours."

"Got it."

I stepped out of the car and straightened my pants.

Normally, I hate taking my driver, but I had a few meetings to get to.

The anxiety still sat there, but it'd been better as of late. Easier to deal with, thanks to Mia.

Being with her solidified a lot of the feelings I had deep within.

And now, after confessing all this, I understood the next hurdle.

Telling Casey.

I still had no idea how to confront him on this. In fact, I wasn't sure if I was ready for that yet.

The lingering worry ate at me like a festering wound. I'd cross that bridge when I get there, though.

I walked into the Denson liquor bar.

Immediately, the bartender nodded and gestured to one of the private rooms that was an offshoot of the bar.

I stepped through the threshold and down the long hallway.

I opened the door. Casey was sitting there, smoking a cigar.

He sat with a dark-colored drink in his hands, probably a rum and coke. His legs were on the table.

The scent of cigar smoke penetrated my senses.

I furrowed my brows. "Interesting choice for cigars."

"Yeah, right?" Casey replied. His eyes refused to meet mine.

I looked over at Casey. His face turned to his left, and he gripped the drink a little tighter in his hands as I approached.

Something was wrong.

I settled into the seat across from them.

One of the servers walked over, and I ordered a double of the Emerald Isle collection with a side of coke.

After the server walked away, I looked at Casey and smiled.

"Been a minute, hasn't it."

"I got busy," he muttered.

Something was up. Casey was never this aloof towards me. I sighed as I tried to figure out what to say.

"Did something happen? You seem off and—"

"Yeah, it's you."

"Me? Why? What did I do, Casey?" I asked. My voice wavered.

"I figured it out."

"Figured what out?"

Casey sighed and placed his drink down with a clank.

"You... and Mia."

I paused. *Shit, this was not how I had planned to tell him.*

"I don't know what you're talking about and—"

"Stop! Don't lie to me, Chris."

I paused. How did he know about this?

"I'm not and—"

"I stopped by the club the other night. And I saw everything."

"But—"

"The photo op and networking event was right next door. I thought I was going crazy when I saw you two walk out together. But then..."

Casey looked down, averting my gaze.

My fingers tapped on my thigh as I tried to figure out how to diffuse the situation.

"It's not what it looks like, Casey—"

"Oh yeah? You fucking her brains out? What *is* it then, Chris? You knew I loved her and that I'm still not over her!"

"Casey, please, I'm sorry. I didn't want things to end up this way either."

The last thing I wanted was to hurt Casey like this.

When we were young I had made a promise to always protect him, no matter what. And now I had done just the opposite. He deserved so much better.

"I thought something was up when I went to your place and saw a girl leave. She looked *just* like her. At first, I dismissed it. Maybe I was seeing things. But then, after that night, I—"

Casey gripped the glass tighter.

Shit. He must have seen us that one time Mia stayed over.

My heart raced. I didn't want this to happen.

My throat tightened a little bit as the beginnings of a panic attack loomed over me.

No, this is the wrong time for that!

I couldn't let my panic attacks get the best of me right now.

I had to be strong and diffuse this situation in hopes that I could mend things with my baby brother.

"Casey, it's a complicated situation. I wasn't *trying* to see her. It was a one-night stand gone wrong. I didn't realize it was her until it was too late."

"Really now. Then how come you didn't push her away?"

"Trust me, I tried to... so hard! We agreed never to see each other again, but she got hired on as my CTO."

"And you didn't fucking fire her?"

"Grant wouldn't have it. I pushed her away again and again; she just crawled back into my life, and I hated it so much at first."

Casey folded his arms across his chest.

"Can you even imagine the level of hurt you're causing me, Chris? You're my brother, and I always looked *up* to you. We hadn't even been broken up like, what, three months yet, and you have nothing else to do but just *race* into her arms."

"I didn't do any such thing," I insisted. "You know I wouldn't have done this if—"

"If you what? Didn't get caught? Were you lusting for her during our relationship too?"

I paused. My world crumbled down upon hearing that.

"Not at all, Casey. You know that is not right. During your time together, I was still trying to move on from Alara's bullshit, trying to get Jacob back."

"And let's say hypothetically you weren't all embroiled in that. Would you have made a move on her?"

I shook my head. "No, Casey. And this all happened in a way I didn't totally understand at first. I kept pushing her away, but every time I tried, she kept appearing in my life once again."

"Uh-huh, sure," Casey retorted.

I gritted my teeth. Why couldn't my brother just *understand* I wasn't trying to hurt him.

"Casey, I never wanted this. In fact, we both wanted to keep our distance."

"So what changed then?" he asked. The venom was almost tangible when I heard it.

I sighed. He had to know.

"Well, she helped me through so much shit. She's different and—"

"Yeah, man! I know she's different! That is why I loved... no -still- love her! And that's no excuse, Chris. In fact, I feel like you just went behind my damn back and purposefully tried to hurt me. I'm only here because I had to know the truth. And, judging from the guilt -or lack of it- and your words, you don't feel any bad at all."

"Please, Casey. I did plan on telling you. And I *do* feel bad."

"Well, it's too late to fix this shit man."

Casey got up and glared at me.

"I need some space now, and I just...I gotta think about what to do next."

"Casey, I want you to know I never intended to hurt you."

I meant that. Casey was my brother, my best friend, and someone who I cared so deeply about that it hurt sometimes. I was there for him when nobody else was.

I felt like such a piece of shit seeing him like this.

"But you did. You fucking did."

Casey walked towards the doorway and turned around.

"Don't reach out to me, Chris. For now... I don't have a brother."

No! That hurt so bad.

"I'm sorry, Casey. I really am."

He didn't respond but instead walked out the door.

After I heard the slam, I sat there and looked forward.

This was *not* how I wanted this shit to go down.

It pissed me off that I did what I did.

I felt worse telling Casey than holding it back.

I didn't want him to find out like this.

It did tear off the Band-Aid, but not in the way I wanted it to.

I felt like I hurt Casey even more now by telling this.

I sat there and finished my double shot. The alcohol burned, but it was nothing compared to the regret that was burning me inside.

After I finished the shot, I left the glasses on the table and walked outside. The bartender nodded slightly.

"You leaving?"

"Yeah. I was just meeting someone there."

"I see. I hope it went well."

The answer to that should've been obvious.

I gazed around the bar to see if Casey was still there.

He was gone.

I tried to contact Casey, but my calls went straight to voicemail, and his texts did the same thing.

It was useless.

I closed my phone and walked briskly outside.

As I looked up at the dark, dreary sky, my heart ached.

I never wanted things to end this way. But I had to do this for my own conscience.

It bothered me, but the feelings I had for Mia triumphed over that.

Right now, I needed her more than anything.

Thirty-Nine
Mia

"There you are! I thought you forgot about me."

I stepped inside Mom's place and took off my shoes.

Two plates of chopped steak with a side of greens and rice sat on the table.

"Come on, Mom, you know I don't forget."

"I know, dear," Mom replied with that same dimpled smile that brought me comfort.

I settled into the seat across from Mom, and we dug into the food.

Mom looked over at me and smiled. "You're glowing again."

I gripped my fork a little bit tighter and looked up.

"What do you mean?"

"Your face! Your skin is looking clearer, and your eyes are brighter."

Oh. Yeah. I touched my cheek with my free hand and shrugged.

"Things are just going well."

"Got a new boyfriend or something?" Mom asked.

How does she *always* see through all this? I tried my best to hide the slight embarrassment when I heard her cheer.

"I knew it!"

I looked up and took a bite of my food.

"Oh, it's just someone."

"Is it Chris?"

"Mom, stop assuming things!"

"I'm not. It's all over your face. I knew it from the moment you smiled a little bit when you heard his name."

Dammit. Mom certainly cut through all the bullshit, whether I liked it or not, I suppose.

I couldn't hide it from her anymore.

Hopefully, she hadn't figured out the pregnancy yet. I wasn't sure if I was ready to tell her that part yet.

Part of me wanted to. Mom was my best friend, and she always made sure to do what was best for me.

But I was terrified of word getting out because I hadn't told anyone else about it yet.

I finished my food. A comforting silence formed between us. After I set my fork down, I looked up.

"Yeah, you figured it out. It actually is Chris."

"Good! He's a good man."

"He is. I just sometimes wonder if…"

Mom reached out and placed her hand atop mine.

"Mia dear, you've got to move on at some point. Your relationship with Casey made you happy for a while, but you can't deny yourself what you really want forever."

She was right. Even if I could, I'd eventually cave.

"Maybe you're right."

"Besides, he's looking out for you."

"More than you'd think," I admitted.

Chris might be a little rough around the edges and aloof, but he did take care of me.

"So, how long have you two been dating?"

"About a month or so."

I mean after so much back and forth, I'm not sure anymore. Sometimes I even wonder how we got here.

Mom grinned, happy to hear about my dating successes.

"This is what I like to hear, Mia. I *want* you to be happy."

"I know; it's just..."

I bit my lip as I tried to find the right words.

Sure, she wanted me to be happy. but there was the constant fear of spilling this relationship.

I wondered if Casey knew already.

We agreed to keep all this quiet, but you never know. Stranger things have happened.

"Well, do what you've got to do," Mom added. "I love hearing your successes."

"I know, mom."

"I mean it! I swear, I feel like I live vicariously through you these days."

She looked down and gripped the fork a bit tighter. A slight frown formed on her face.

"I've been trying to do the same."

"You mean with Dad?"

She nodded. "Yes. I'm trying to get out there and date. It's been years, and I need to learn to find happiness again."

"Nobody's telling you to date, though," I remarked.

Dad's death still resonated over her, even when she said she was fine.

"I know, Mia. And well, part of me wants to keep telling myself that. But there's that other part of me that wants to see what's out there. I'm not *that* old, Mia."

We both laughed. She was right. She was only fifty-five. There had to be some kind of dating pool for people that age.

"Alright. I'm not going to stop you."

"Thanks, dear. And this doesn't mean that your father's forgotten. He told me before he passed that...if I ever found someone else, he'd support me, even if he wasn't around."

Mom looked down as the somber atmosphere hung over us once more. I smiled and entwined my fingers in her hand.

"You're right. Maybe it's for the best for both of us. To move on and find happiness."

"Exactly," Mom replied. "Which is why I'm going on a date next week. I don't know what will happen, but I'm keeping an open mind."

"Good. I hope it goes well."

Mom cleared the plates and then brought out some banana bread she had baked.

Recently, she got more versed in cooking, so I was happy about that.

After she cut up two slices and placed some cinnamon spread on the table, I took a bite.

"Woah! This is so good!"

It had the perfect banana texture. There were also soft hints of nutmeg and a little bit of cinnamon added to the bread. It was the perfect dessert.

I prided myself on seeing Mom bake more.

She did when I was a kid but stopped doing it as often after Dad died.

Sure, she made dinner, but baking was a love long forgotten after Dad passed.

Now, it seemed to come back again.

As we had dessert, Mom's eyes looked over me.

"So, you're happy with the way things are going then?"

"Yeah," I admitted. "I am."

"I'm so glad. He sounds like the right guy for you."

"I think he is. I just feel like we're meant to be together. At first, I didn't want to accept it because of Casey, but...."

"Honey, if your heart tells you to follow through, you can't deny it."

"You're right," I replied, smiling.

As we finished dessert, I thought about what to do now.

There were still things I needed to tell Chris, but I didn't want to burden him.

The man had so much going on already, and this Alara mess would only make things worse.

When the time was right, he'd find out.

Mom and I spent the next couple of hours on the couch watching her favorite sitcom and spending time together.

After the latest episode finished, I stood up and stretched.

"I should get going. It's late."

"I know. But I'm glad to see you, dear. And I'm happy for you."

"Thanks Mom. I am, too."

I meant it. There was a thrill that came with admitting the truth.

As I left, my shoulders relaxed.

That's one more person who knows.

It felt good to tell her. That way, I didn't have to feel guilty acting like I hid something.

Still, there was more that I had to say at some point.

My hand clutched my stomach as I felt the slight churning.

Morning sickness hadn't reared its fully ugly head yet.

That was fortunate since I didn't have to worry about feeling any worse yet.

Right now, I counted my blessings, and when the time was right, I'd tell him.

Then, I'd figure out the rest.

Forty
Chris

"Arthur Franklin, head of Family-Based Safety Services."

"Pleasure to meet you," I replied as I grasped his hand. I held it tightly and gave it a firm shake.

Arthur extracted his hand and looked around.

A guy next to him with brown hair and big, wire-rimmed glasses took some notes.

"This is Tyler. He's my assistant and an intern at our facility. We would like to look around if that's okay."

"Be my guest," I muttered.

I thought my legal team could get them off my back, but it was no use.

They wanted to do at least one investigation before they could take their findings and bring them to court.

Arthur and Tyler walked inside. Arthur looked around and nodded.

"Big place. Are there child safety protections in place?"

"The kid is five, but yes. I've gated off all the places he shouldn't go."

Jacob stayed mostly in the east wing.

All of the workout equipment was in the west wing, which was locked off by a code. He'd get that code when he was old enough to use those facilities.

We walked on through, and Arthur looked around the kitchen.

"Knives are in drawers and locked up?"

"Those are my kitchen staff. I have a spare key, but for the most part, they take care of the cooking," I explained.

"I see. And they make sure to lock it up, right?"

"Yes, and if there is a problem, I'll make sure to handle that privately."

"Good," Arthur remarked. Tyler took a few notes.

They continued their tour throughout my place.

A couple of moments later, I saw a black car pull up.

There's my lawyer, George Sandler. He was the best in the area and would make sure that everything was handled adequately.

Arthur and Tyler poked through different rooms.

Eventually, they made their way to Jacob's room.

"Can we walk in?" Arthur asked.

"Let me ask him," I replied. I stepped forward and knocked on the door.

"Jacob, it's me! There's a couple of people who want to come in here and look at a few things."

Footsteps pattered to the door, and Jacob opened it.

"Hi, Dad. Hi..."

"Arthur. And this is Tyler."

"Oh. Dad, what do they need with me?"

I refused to tell Jacob the truth that his mother was trying to bring our case back to court again.

I faked a smile.

"They're doing some inspections on the place. They might ask you a few questions."

"Oh. Okay. I was reading this book."

Jacob walked back to the bed and sat down.

I looked at the copy of a simplified version of Charlotte's Web book that laid half-open.

"That's a pretty hard book to read," Arthur said with a subtle nod.

"Not really. I love reading!" Jacob replied with a smile.

"That's good. And everything with your Dad is good?"

Jacob frowned. "Yeah. Dad is amazing! He takes care of me and spends time with me a lot, even if he does work a lot at his office."

Tyler scribbled down a few notes. I felt like they were looking for something, anything to get me on.

Well, they wouldn't find it. Not on my damned watch.

Alara was lying, and if this was all that it took to put her in her place, then so be it.

"And when Dad isn't around, who takes care of you?"

"Grandma! She's so nice. She doesn't understand the pictures I send to her though."

"He's got a camera that he uses to take pictures and send to her on his phone."

"Isn't he a little too *young* for one?"

I grabbed it and showed it to Arthur.

"It's for kids. Only me and my mother are in it."

I scrolled down and showed them the two numbers.

The keypad was locked, so Jacob couldn't contact anyone else.

"I see. Very well."

Arthur and Tyler looked around a bit more and then they left.

Arthur maintained the same neutral expression he had during the beginning.

Meanwhile, Tyler scribbled furiously. What he was taking notes of, I didn't know. I had no intention of asking, though.

They continued through the house until they got to the end of the hallway where the locked door was.

"And Jacob doesn't know how to get in, right?"

"Correct."

"Very well. I guess that's it then!"

We walked outside. Arthur's eyes turned to my Bentley which I had left on the driveway earlier that day.

"Standard procedure. We have to look inside."

"Go ahead. The best you'll find is a car seat."

They walked to the car. Arthur opened the back door and saw the car seat, along with a book.

"Very clean."

"I keep it that way. Are we done here?"

"We should be. I can safely say that—"

"Arthur! Sir! There's something in the glove box."

Arthur walked to the front. I stiffened slightly and looked at what Tyler had in his hands.

A bag? What the hell is that?

Arthur looked them over and then held them up.

"Chris, would you mind explaining what these are."

"I have PTSD and take Paxil. I take anti-anxiety medication and—"

"These are not anti-anxiety meds. In fact, these don't look like any drug on the market. Tyler, get the kit."

Tyler walked back to the truck.

A moment later, he grabbed a beaker, a bottle of water, and some testing strips.

He filled the beaker with water and then dipped the pill inside.

After a couple minutes, Tyler placed a testing strip inside. When it was ready, Arthur pulled it out.

"I knew it."

Arthur put the testing strip in the evidence bag and turned to me.

"Chris, do you understand that you have Fentanyl in your car?"

"I'm sorry, there must be a mistake. I have a prescription for Paxil," I replied.

George, my lawyer, walked towards us.

"My client does have diagnosed PTSD and anxiety. I can assure you he takes drugs for that."

"That isn't what these are, though. Chris, I'm sorry, but we're going to have to take this as evidence."

My body stiffened. Anger formed all around me. It pissed me the hell off.

"I see."

"I'll get this to the evidence lab. But we'll have to take your case to court. I'm sorry."

"I'll be handling the case from here. Chris is a good man, and I can promise you that whatever this is has to be an apparent mistake."

"I know. I'll contact you if there's anything more we can do."

Tyler and Arthur got in their truck and drove away.

As it went off in the distance, I stood there.

A mixture of anger and fear bubbled up inside of me.

I turned to George and shook my head. "George, this has to be a mistake. I didn't—"

"I know you didn't, Chris. And I can assure you that I'll build a strong case to defend you. But it will be hard to prove."

"I know. And I don't need that," I admitted.

"I'm on it. I'll tell you how things go once I get a response from their team."

George walked to his car and drove off a moment later.

I stood there, angry and frustrated by it all.

Why did this keep happening?

First, the shit with Casey, and now this.

I wanted to scream.

I stormed off inside and closed the door.

I took a couple of deep breaths as the anger rose. I felt like I was going crazy.

Then, just as I felt the anxiety about to top off, my phone buzzed.

Hey, I wanted to come see you. Is it a good time?

I looked down.

Mia.

The one person who kept me sane. A saving grace like no other.

It still worried me if Casey did come over, and they'd see each other.

But right now, I couldn't give that thought too much energy.

My son's custody was on the line.

I typed back a quick 'yes' because, at that moment, I knew exactly what I needed.

Her.

Forty-One
Mia

I knocked on the door to Chris's place. A moment later, the door opened.

It was a guy with jet-black hair and tanned skin.

"You're looking for Master Chris, right?"

"Yes. Where is he?"

The man motioned inside. He gestured to the left-hand side.

"He's in the west wing. He said he didn't want to be bothered unless there was an emergency, but..."

"It's okay," I reassured. "He said it was okay."

The man nodded and disappeared down another corridor.

I still wasn't totally used to Chris having a full maid and butler staff.

It reminded me of the power and control that he had.

I marched to the end of the hall and then up the stairs I looked down the large hall. There was only one door open.

I assumed *that* was where I needed to go.

I approached the threshold and saw Chris inside with his head in his hands. His fingers clenched tightly.

Something was very wrong.

"Chris."

He looked up, and for a moment, his hands relaxed.

"Oh, it's you, Mia. I'm glad you came over."

"I am, too. Sorry, I meant to come over sooner, but…"

The sickness finally kicked in. I guess I couldn't avoid it forever.

Then again, it'd been a month and a half since I got pregnant, so I guess it made sense.

"You're fine. Honestly, I don't know what else to do."

"What do you mean?"

He walked over to the small couch next to the desk.

I looked around at the place. Piles of books sat along the shelves. The room was dimly lit save for a small lamp at his desk.

"This is an interesting room."

"It's my study," he remarked. "I rarely come up here, but I needed some space to figure out what to do next."

I thought about asking him what happened but then stopped myself. Knowing Chris, he would tell me eventually.

I sat down, and he moved next to me.

For the first time in a bit, I saw something in Chris's eyes.

Vulnerability.

I reached out and squeezed his hand. He relaxed into the touch.

"Thank you for coming, Mia. I need this right now."

"Of course," I gently encouraged. "You've been through a lot, haven't you?"

A dry laugh escaped him. "That obvious?"

"You don't hide it from me these days," I pointed out.

Ever since we had that heart-to-heart, Christian finally opened up about his feelings.

"It's about Jacob. You know how Alara's trying to take me to court, right?"

"Yes, you told me. I'm guessing she's lying."

"Worse," he admitted.

What the hell is worse than lying?

"CPS came here today, and well...they're claiming I use fentanyl, and I'm unfit to be a Dad. Well, they haven't claimed it yet, but I am sure that's the direction they're going in."

I sat there, shocked at what to say.

"But you don't! I've been around you. You haven't even been using the Paxil that you usually take."

I was proud he didn't rely on them. This all sounded absolutely insane.

"I don't use it," he replied. "But somehow it ended up in my car. I asked the staff, and none of them knew a damned thing."

"I see. Shit, this is bad."

"It is. And I just, I don't know what to do anymore. The thought of losing Jacob has me—"

He stopped. He gripped the couch and looked forward.

My fingers brushed against his palm when I felt the racing heart.

Chris clutched his throat and took a couple of deep breaths.

I held him tightly against my arms and gently pulled him to my chest.

"I know it's stressful, Chris. I'm right here with you. We can go through this together."

His heart continued to quicken. My fingers latched tighter against his shoulders.

Our bodies stayed against each other as I gently whispered soothing words of encouragement in his ear.

Finally, he settled. Christian looked up, his eyes wide with fright.

"I'm worried, Mia. I don't like to talk about it, but I am. I never wanted this."

"You'll beat this allegation. You're not alone," I encouraged.

"Thank you, Mia. Sometimes, it feels like you're the only one who is on my side."

"Well, maybe that's all you need. Someone in your corner, ready to help you when you need it the most."

Christian smiled. "Maybe so."

He pulled me into his arms tightly.

His lips pressed to mine, and I kissed him back. He dominated the kiss, and we stayed like this, slowly making out for who knows how long.

Eventually, Christian pulled back and caressed my hair.

"You always have the right thing to say, just when I need it the most."

"Maybe that's why we're meant for each other," I teased.

"That and so much more. Mia, you've heard all about the shit I've dealt with, and you haven't run away. It's nice to have a confidant I can just tell so many things to without being judged. It's refreshing."

I smiled. There was something I needed to tell him, but I wasn't sure how to even approach it.

"Well, I'm here. You don't have to face the world alone, and I promise that no matter what, we have each other."

"We do, Mia. We sure fucking do."

He kissed me again, and all thoughts disappeared as our lips and tongues danced with one another.

His hands reached down and caressed my butt in the jeans I wore.

"Damn, you've filled out," he said.

I froze for a second. *Shit! He might realize that—*

He growled and playfully spanked my butt.

"And I love it. Whatever you're doing, keep it up."

"I will. Since you like it so much."

"You drive me fucking crazy."

"As do you," I whispered.

He kissed down my neck and nibbled on the flesh.

I closed my eyes and moaned, gently rutting against the obvious erection in his pants.

I moved my hips in circles, and he groaned. His hands reached for my hips and gently squeezed my waist.

"Mia…I don't know how long I can last."

I looked at the door. Sure, we were in a whole different wing, but…

"Jacob's not allowed over here. He's been reading all afternoon." Chris finally whispered, as if pulling me from my thoughts.

"Huh. Good to know," I replied.

Chris's hands made quick work of my shirt and tossed it behind me.

His hands caressed my curves and moved towards my stomach.

When he pressed his fingers there, I hesitated. *Would he know?*

As soon as I had that lingering thought, he moved his hands further upward toward my breasts and pinched them under the bra.

I closed my eyes as the pleasure wafted over me. Little gasps and moans followed.

He kissed and nipped at my neck with little touches.

I clung to his shoulders and dug my fingers in. My hips continued to press to him.

"Your sounds are so fucking beautiful."

"You make me go crazy, Chris."

"I'm the only one who can."

He nipped at my neck, and my hips pressed downwards.

My back arched, and Chris took that moment to push my bra up just enough to get a taste of my nipple.

He flicked his tongue with small, languid strokes.

Every time he did this, I melted against him. It felt so right.

His other hand pinched my other nipple and played with it against his hands.

I moaned, slowly coming undone.

After a few moments, Chris moved back and slid his hands down to the fly and zipper of my pants.

He slowly rubbed me through there, and I bit my lip in an attempt to stifle my moans.

"No. I want to hear you," he commanded.

As if on cue, I moaned and pressed myself against his fingers.

I reached for his pants and pulled on the waistband.

"Chris—"

"What baby?"

I couldn't get any words out of my mouth at that moment.

I slid off of him and pulled off my jeans.

As I reached for my panties, he spoke. "Leave them on."

"But—"

"I like it when you're still partially dressed, and I get to take you in a disheveled state," he said with a low growl.

I gasped, completely enamored in the man's words and lost in every single syllable uttered.

I climbed back on top of him and teased the tip of his member with my entrance. I didn't plunge it in, but then, eager hands gripped my hips.

"I'm claiming you."

"Then do it. Take me," I whispered in a breathy, almost challenging manner.

He grunted and slammed my hips down against him.

I threw my head back, immediately enraptured by the fullness of his large member.

His hands moved my hips up and down, but then I held the top of his shoulders and smiled.

"Let me have a little fun."

I rocked my hips a little bit, gently enjoying the way his member managed to fill up every nook and cranny within me.

I gasped as his member twitched inside. It stuffed me so damn well.

Ever since I got pregnant, it felt like my senses were dialed to eleven.

He twitched inside me, and I clenched, tightening around his rod as he penetrated my core.

His hand massaged my clit with slow, languid strokes. At first, they moved in a back-and-forth motion, but as my body rode him up and down, faster and faster, he changed his strokes to circles.

All I felt was pure and utter bliss from the moment he touched me in this way.

"That's right. Moan for me. Show me how much you like this," he whispered in my ear.

The guttural sound of delight that followed told him everything.

A couple of minutes later, he reached down and grabbed my hips, slamming deep and hard into me.

His member jackhammered all the way inside, and I felt the stiff rod completely opening me to him.

The ache grew. The pleasure built, and I was so fucking close already that I could barely hold back.

"I'm so close, Chris! I can't hold back!"

"Then fucking don't. Show me how much you love my cock."

As he thrusted inside, my walls tightened around him.

His thumb pressed tightly against my clit as I cried out his name.

As I finished, he growled and then spilled inside me.

We stayed like this for a long time. I didn't want to move but instead wanted to embrace him like this forever.

Finally, reality settled in, along with the obvious dripping between my legs.

I pulled off and pushed my panties to the front. Chris smiled and hugged me tightly after I got them on.

"Thank you, Mia. Not just for that but…the words of encouragement."

I hugged him back just as tightly and smiled.

"Anytime."

"Right now, in this moment, you're the best goddamn thing to have."

After we shared one final kiss, we went back down to the kitchen. Jacob was at the dinner table.

"Mia?"

"Hey. I came to see you and your Dad."

"Oh, okay! I started to read that book you recommended to me," he replied with a grin.

"Charlotte's Web?"

"Yeah!"

"How do you like it?"

"It's so good," Jacob gushed. I can't wait to tell you all about it."

"Well, I'm happy to hear it," I replied.

We sat at the dinner table together and had dinner.

Jacob knew a little bit about Chris and me, but he didn't know we were dating; well, assuming five-year-olds would know what dating was.

We planned to tell him at the right time. For now, though, there were other worries.

The lingering possibility of custody battles is one.

I stole a glance at Christian.

Despite the smile he put on for his son, I knew he was fighting some inner demons and worries.

Which was why I knew I had to be there for him.

Chris needed all the support he could get in this trying time.

And I planned to give him every bit of it I could.

That included not overwhelming him any further by dumping my own worries on him, worries that had to do with his little one in my tummy.

Forty-Two
Chris

"Alright. I see. Thank you, George. I'll send you my current evidence that shows I'm a good father, and the prescription so you can document a copy. Thanks."

I hung up the phone and sighed.

This was *not* how I wanted to spend the next month of my life.

It'd been two weeks since child services came to my place.

And unfortunately, I got a verdict on the case.

I scrolled down and eventually found the name I was looking for.

Bradley Cravins, PI.

Bradley was one of the top private investigators in the country. He knew where to find evidence that would otherwise be left unseen.

I dialed his number, and two rings later, he spoke.

"Christian. A pleasure to hear from you again."

"Likewise. Unfortunately, I don't come bearing the best news."

"How so?"

"My case is going back to court," I began. "You know how two weeks ago I mentioned the shit with fentanyl."

"Yes. And we agreed not to take action until after we got confirmation."

"Correct. Well, I just got word from George. The case is going back to court at the end of the month. We need to place all our findings in place by then."

"I see. And do you think that—"

"I do not use those drugs. I sent George my test results the other day. Even he thought it was absurd, since there was nothing amiss there. So, I can tell you right now that someone planted it."

"I see. And the test confirms."

"I took the drug test just yesterday. And I took one right after the discovery. Both times, it was negative. So you tell me."

"I see. Well then, I guess it's my turn."

"Yes. I need you to start figuring out who put them there and why. I don't care what means you must take. Just get to the bottom of this. And fast."

"Will do. So nothing's stopping this."

"If there's anything stopping, let me and my lawyer know. We'll both take the initiative to handle it."

Bradley chuckled.

"Good to know, sir. Thank you. I'll be in touch. It might take a week or two, but…"

"As long as I have this by the end of the month, I don't care if it takes 100 hours. Just do this for me," I insisted.

"Got it."

I hung up and looked at my schedule.

Shit, I've got that meeting with Brendan in thirty minutes. My phone beeped, and I looked down.

Hey, so I know it's my day off, but I'll be near where your next meeting is. Maybe we can meet up for drinks. Or I'll come see you tonight.

I smiled. Mia was so sweet, and she always checked on me. It brightened my day.

She was at a spa today. She took the day off because she said she needed it and had some PTO.

Which was correct. But what intrigued me was she mentioned her body hurt.

What could've happened? I thought about asking her, but I figured she'd tell me tonight when she got to my place.

I texted her back 'sure' and then looked at my other calls and messages. Most of them were from other colleagues.

Not a single message from Casey.

After what happened, he didn't respond to anything.

He didn't block me, but he never took my calls or responded to my texts.

It frustrated me and made me feel even guiltier.

That, on top of the bullshit with Alara, had me on edge.

I needed a fucking break.

That was why taking some time off and possibly going out to sea sounded more attractive than ever before.

Maybe at the end of the month, after this shit with Alara was done, I could take a few days and go out there with Jacob and Mia.

It would be a good way to celebrate the end of this hellish chapter and the beginning of something new.

I grabbed my things and headed out in my Bentley to the building on 34th.

After the valet parked the car, I stepped inside.

As I walked into the gilded lobby I decided to just focus on this deal right now.

A woman with reddish-brown hair and brown eyes behind glasses typed away at the computer.

She looked up and gave me a friendly half-smile.

"You here to see Brendan?"

"Yes. I'm Christian Hamilton. We had an appointment."

"Oh yes! He told me. Go to the elevator and press the button on the eighth floor. He'll be waiting for you."

I gave a goodbye and headed inside.

As the doors closed, all that was on my mind was one thing.

Work and making sure that the next contract is settled and signed.

Forty-Three
Mia

"Ugh, that's the *stuff*." Katie moaned as the massage therapist rubbed her back.

"You're telling me. It feels like my knots have knots!" Nataly added.

I nodded and shuffled slightly.

The massage therapist pressed her hands tightly against the middle part of my back, and I gasped.

"Oh, you've got a very tight knot there," she chided.

"Please, get it," I almost begged. It felt almost good after she massaged it a little bit.

I never realized how much I needed this until after I sat down.

Then again, I'd been carrying more weight, and my stomach was filling out just a little bit.

Not enough to be considered pregnant, but it got closer and closer to that point.

I still didn't know what I'd do when it came to telling Christian.

I'd soon be showing, even during sex. I couldn't chalk it off to a stressful weight gain.

It was a miracle that he hadn't noticed anything yet.

The weight gain had been speeding up, and so far, I didn't know what to do with myself.

Other than of course, it just bears it.

The massage therapists worked throughout my back, and after the litany of "You need to take care of your body better" from a few of them, I finally sat up.

"You feel it, don't you?" Katie asked.

"You think? I didn't know those knots even existed."

"Ugh, you're telling me. Mine kept telling me to stop dancing. What nerve! I would never," Nat replied.

"I think the day you stopped clubbing would be the day hell freezes over," I teased.

"Yeah, definitely. Clubbing has been my life for far too long," she gushed.

I rolled my eyes. I didn't agree with all of Nat's ideas, but I supported her as best as I could.

We got our slippers and robes on and headed to the hot springs. This spa was killer.

When Chris found out I was going with friends, he paid for everything.

It shocked me, but he said I deserved it.

What a treasure! I still felt like the luckiest girl in the world, even if there were some things I still needed to figure out.

We settled into the hot springs area. Well, they were more like a private jacuzzi and didn't get all that hot.

I couldn't do the hottest pools cause of the baby, according to what the doctor said.

As I settled in, Nat and Katie both looked at me with playful smiles.

"So, how are things? You look like a different person," Nat said.

"Good. It's just..."

I bit my lip. I had to tell them. They were my friends, and they might be able to help.

"Well, what is it?" Katie asked.

I gestured to my stomach.

"You two have probably seen that I gained a bit of weight, right?"

"I just thought you'd been eating better. You know how it is, a girl gets with a guy, and suddenly she gains weight and is happy and shit," Katie mused.

"It's not that," I admitted.

I took a deep breath as the anxiety washed over me. If I told them, would they be upset?

"It's Chris and me. I'm pregnant."

"What!" Katie said, splashing some water.

"You're fucking serious, right?" Nat added.

I nodded. "Yeah. I'm almost two months along, but..."

"So, does he know?"

I shook my head. "I don't know what to say."

"That's going to be a problem," Nat muttered. "He should know."

"Guys, we *just* got together. The man just finally professed his real feelings to me. I don't want to rush things. Plus, you know, there's the Casey thing."

Casey and I were always pretty careful. I was on the pill back then, and also Casey took the extra precautions to use condoms.

He was adamant about not having kids, which also contributed slightly to the eventual breakup.

As for Chris, I didn't know what he thought about having kids.

Sure, he had Jacob, but was he ready for another?

"I know, but still. You should tell him. I'm sure he'll be elated."

"Well, I am not so sure about that. He's also going through a lot with his ex-wife."

"And you coming in, bringing it up, might be just what he needs to feel better!" Katie insisted.

I shrugged. "I don't think that's how it works."

"Mia, girl, you've got to tell him. You will be starting a whole new chapter of your life with this guy! It's the least you can do."

"I know. Don't remind me," I replied.

It's not that I didn't want that. It's just that I feared maybe we were moving far too fast. The fear that he might not feel the same way loomed over me.

"Anyways, I'm not going to force you, but for your own sake, you should," Katie admonished.

"I'll think about it."

Nat and Katie finished their soaks and stood up. Katie stretched and sighed.

"Man, that really fixes the muscles!"

"It does. Anyways, we're going to have to head on out," Katie said.

"Why?" I asked.

"I have to get to work. And Nat here..."

"Has a date tonight! I didn't want to spoil your mood."

"It's all good. Good luck out there," I replied with a smile. I was happy that both of them were figuring out their lives, even just a little bit.

After we said our goodbyes, they disappeared. I got out and headed to the changing room. As I did, I looked up.

Smoke?

What the hell was going on?

The smoke rose throughout the dressing room, almost choking me in the process.

I coughed and covered my nose.

Quickly, I got the rest of my clothes on and walked through the hallway.

The smoke plumed and got even larger, almost stifling me.

I tried the elevator, but it didn't work.

Shit!

Embers formed to my left.

It was the sauna. It was on fire.

I had to find a way out. I walked to the stairs and tried to open them. We were only on the third floor, but the door was locked.

Seriously?

I tried pounding on the door, kicking it with all my might.

Nobody heard me.

I ran towards the window and waved my arms, hoping someone would see me.

Nothing.

Shit this wasn't good.

I grabbed a couple of the stones from the hot baths and threw them against the window. The glass was strong, and nothing made a dent.

I went back to the door and tugged on it, trying again.

The smoke grew larger and became almost black around the area.

I tried to stay upright, but it was no use.

My legs buckled. I refused to breathe in too much. *The baby.*

I tried to hold my breath, but the smoke burned my nose.

I walked around, using a couple more of the stones to break something open.

Everything I did ended up in failure.

Complete, utter failure that seemed to go absolutely nowhere.

My knees gave out, and eventually, I fell to the ground.

Choked coughs and sobs emitted from my lips. But there was nothing I could do.

My throat grew drier.

I tried to get towards another doorway, but every movement felt as if rocks sat atop me.

Finally, when I got about five feet from the door, I coughed, collapsing.

Fuck, I needed help.

I reached for my phone and dialed Chris. He was in a meeting, but maybe....

"Hey Mia, how are things?"

"Chris, I'm—"

I coughed, unable to get it out.

"Mia, what's going on?"

"Help...me..."

Those were the only words I could get out before I fell unconscious and the flames surrounded me.

Forty-Four
Chris

"I'm *very* impressed with the lineup and current changes you've made to the company, Christian."

"Happy to hear it."

Brendan folds his hands on his lap and nods.

"I've already sent the contract to your legal department. I'm excited for this long-term partnership."

I stood up and shook Brendan's hand confidently.

"I'm happy to hear that."

After the final touches, I left Brendan's office.

I looked at my watch. It's still early, and meeting Mia for a late lunch or early dinner wasn't completely off the table.

My phone buzzed, and I looked down.

Mia.

Guess she wanted to see if I was out yet. I pressed the button and held it to my ear.

"Hey Mia, how are things?" I began.

"Chris, I'm—"

A series of sharp coughs emanated from her lips. I heard the sound of something crackling in the background.

"Mia, what's going on?"

"Help…me…"

The line clicked off. I looked forward and saw the spa that Mia went to.

When she mentioned she'd be going there, I thought it was convenient. We could meet up for lunch after the fact.

But now, when I looked at the building, one block down from where I was standing, all I could see was a huge plume of smoke, along with embers.

Holy shit!

I sprinted outside and rushed to the valet.

"I need my keys!"

"I'm getting them. Your car's right at the entrance and—"

"I'll get it myself."

I grabbed my keys out of his hand and rushed down to my car, parked right at the entrance.

My heart raced with every passing second.

I jumped into my car and raced down the street. I had no time to waste.

When I arrived at the scene, I stormed to the door, but the receptionist put her hand up.

"I'm sorry, sir, but there's a fire, and we can't let you in."

"My girlfriend's in there!"

I didn't even wait for their response.

I rushed inside, immediately smelling the smoke.

I grabbed the handkerchief in my pocket and held it up as I looked around.

Okay, the fire seemed contained on the third floor.

I spotted a staircase door next to the elevator and pushed on it.

As I rushed up the stairs, the smoke became heavier.

When I got to the third floor, I fiddled with the handle. It was locked. Why the hell is the emergency staircase locked?

I kicked the door right in the center and it bent.

I hit the door again and got it open only to be greeted with a heavy plume of smoke over the air.

Shit, it's really bad.

All I saw were flames.

I remembered my training, finding the areas with the least amount of fire damage and the shallowest embers.

As I walked through the pathway, I stamped out a couple of flames in order to get a path back.

When I got towards the center, I saw Mia on the floor, unconscious.

No! Am I too late?

I scooped her into my arms and held her tightly against my shoulders.

And just as I walked back towards the door, the roof where she lay collapsed.

If I were only a couple seconds later...

I shook that thought away. I wasn't going to test my luck.

I held her and raced down the stairs as fast as my feet could.

The reception area was still clear by the time I got to the doors.

Firefighters paraded inside and up the stairs. A couple in the basket went to the window to put out the embers.

A man with silvery-gray hair stared at me with wide, shocked eyes.

"You're the one who went back in."

"I had to, sir. For her," I replied, holding her.

Mia's chest rose and fell, but her breathing was shallow. "Where's the paramedics? I need them to take her now!"

The man pointed to the ambulance.

I raced over and got Mia on a stretcher. I climbed in after her.

As it barreled through the city, I held Mia's hand. *Please be okay. Please don't die on me now.*

A million thoughts raced through my head as I tried to keep it together.

She would make it, and I would make sure of it.

When the truck stopped at the hospital, they wheeled her in.

They brought her to a room, and a ventilator was placed on her throat.

I stood there and watched. A million thoughts swam through my head, most of them of total worry.

If Mia died here, I'd...

"Have a seat," a voice said.

I looked behind me and saw a woman with light blonde hair and golden brown eyes.

She gave me a small smile and gestured to the seats next to the door.

"I can't. Not until I know she's okay."

"She's in the best hands. Doctor Gibbons is the best ER doctor," the nurse encouraged.

Her confidence helped with the agonizing feelings.

I sat there, looking down as I tried to figure out the correct thing to say.

What *if* she didn't? I hated these morbid thoughts, but...

I paused, taking a moment to compose myself.

No, it was useless to think this way. I had to stay confident and—

The door opened, and the doctor stood there.

"You're the man who came with Mia Thornton, right?"

"Yes. Christian. I'm her boyfriend."

"Thank you for getting her when you did."

I tapped my finger on the door where Mia was.

"Is she going to be okay?"

"Yes. She and the baby are both doing fine. I'd like her to stay overnight to make sure her vitals stay normal."

Baby? What the fuck?

"What did you say?"

The doctor walked back inside and brought out a piece of paper. An image of an ultrasound.

"We had to do an ultrasound to make sure there was no internal damage to her. She's alright, and the baby will make it."

I clutched the picture. My hands shook.

Was Mia pregnant? And she didn't even tell me?

I looked at the doctor curiously.

"How far along is she?"

"About two months now. The baby's still healthy and has a heartbeat. We'll check respiration."

"I see," I mused. "Thank you."

"No problem. I'm here if you need anything else. For now, let her rest."

She walked away. I stood there, feeling as if everything I knew wasn't real.

I was about to be a dad again. The thought reeled me.

I was going to have another kid, all while my life slowly crumbled apart.

I wasn't ready for this, especially since my relationship with Casey was soured.

It would only make things worse.

Not to mention the custody battle.

But why didn't Mia tell me? Why'd she hide such huge news from me?

Maybe she didn't know. She was still early.

And maybe a baby was a good thing for us after all.

But right now, I needed to see her.

I needed to know if she knew because if she did...it would hurt so much more.

Forty-Five
Mia

I survived.

Chris got to me in time. *Again*.

I turned to my left and saw him sitting there.

He *was* my hero. Without him, I might have…

I shook my head. I didn't want to think about that.

The fact that he'd saved me not just once but twice was refreshing enough.

I shifted a little bit and saw Chris sitting there.

But, instead of a smile of relief on his face, he stared.

"Hey, Christian. Looks like I made it—"

"You did," he muttered.

"What's wrong? You're acting so strange."

"Yeah, well, I guess you just call on me when you need me. And you leave me out of it when it comes to big decisions."

What the hell was he talking about? I wanted to ask, but as soon as I could, the doctor entered.

"You're awake, Mia," she said.

"I am," I breathed.

"Well, I'm happy to say that you're healthy. And so is the baby."

The baby. I froze up and caught Chris's cold eyes on me.

Fuck. He knows.

I never wanted to hide it from him forever. But now, it made me look ten times worse.

Like I trapped him.

The doctor took a small look over me before she disappeared.

As the door closed, I caught Chris's icy blue eyes, looking me up and down.

"Chris, I'm—"

"Mia, you fucking knew you were pregnant, right?"

I couldn't hide this from him forever. I gave him a subtle nod.

"Yes, Chris. I'm sorry."

"Wow. You didn't even bother to tell me?"

He didn't bother to raise his voice. Not that he needed to.

I felt the animosity from a mile away.

"I never wanted this to happen, Chris. I just know you're going through a lot."

"Yeah, and I thought that you were better than this. I can't believe you!"

"I wanted to tell you! I swear and—"

"So why didn't you! I thought that you and I were..."

He looked away. I reached out for his hand.

"Chris, please talk to me."

"No. You didn't trust me. You didn't believe I'd take responsibility for this. First, Casey finds out about us, and now this. I feel like my whole life is turning upside down."

He clenched his hands into fists.

I sat there, ruminating over what he said.

What happened to Casey? I thought they were fine.

"What do you mean? About Casey?"

He turned to me and scoffed.

"He knows, Mia, about us. And he cut me off. My baby brother, the one I promised to always protect, cut me the fuck out of his life!"

Oh.

"I didn't know that."

"Yeah, you don't cause you were too busy hiding everything from me. What else are you hiding, huh?"

"Trust me! I wanted to tell you, but I didn't know when the right time would be. I didn't want to overwhelm you."

"Right," he mustered. "But now, it feels like you *tried* to hide the truth from me."

"I was not, Chris. Please, we can talk about this."

He shook his head.

"No, I've betrayed Casey, and your pregnancy only made it worse."

It always comes back to Casey.

"Casey doesn't have anything to do with it! He never wanted kids, Chris."

"Oh, and you didn't use protection with me because you thought a child was the *best* solution to our already precarious relationship.?"

"No, Chris. You know that's nonsense. I never planned for this. I never wanted things to transpire this way either," I admitted.

"Yeah, well, they did. And while I am glad you are safe. I need some fucking space."

I sat up on the bed.

"I know this is a bit stressful, Chris, but I want this baby. And I want it with you. Don't you want the same?"

He pursed his lips.

"I don't know. It's all too much too quickly."

The words killed me as my fists clenched in anger. He didn't *want* to be a part of our child's life.

"Fuck you Chris. I thought you'd be more accepting, but you're obviously not. I know things will be better and—"

"Well, I don't know if they will be, Mia. Right now, everything feels like a fucking lie. And I regret finding out this way."

He stepped back. He folded his hands across his chest.

"My custody hearing's not till the end of the month. I need some space to figure everything out."

"So you're just going to leave."

"I need some time to process all of this."

I shook my head. Hearing him talk this way sounded so cowardly. Nothing like the man that I knew and fell in love with.

"I thought you were different, Christian. That you'd understand why I couldn't tell you."

"I thought you were different too, Mia! But now you've put me in this shitty situation."

Christian stormed off and slammed the door. I sat in bed, tears filled in my eyes.

Why did I hide it? Why was I such a fucking coward?

It hurt hearing Christian push me away like this.

I took a couple of breaths, but the anxiety settled.

I ruined everything.

I sat in the hospital bed, unsure of what to do next.

After all that happened, he pushed me away. He tossed me aside like I meant nothing to him.

And now, I had to raise this child myself.

The doctor knocked on the door and stepped inside.

She had a small smile on her face, but it did nothing to ease the tension.

"Hey! How are you?"

"Could be better."

She reached over and gently touched my shoulder.

"I heard the last bit of what he said. It'll be okay. I'm sure this is scary for him. But he'll eventually come around. What you need to focus on right now is yourself."

I nodded, feeling hollow with every word.

The doctor didn't know the truth and just said this to make me feel better.

It crushed me inside.

All that time and effort, the push and pull between us for so long, was for nothing.

I hurt Christian. Far more than I think Casey ever hurt me.

I reached for my phone and tried to contact Christian, but it went straight to voicemail.

I placed the phone on the bedside table as the emotions overwhelmed me, and I did the only thing I could do.

Cry.

Forty-Six
Chris

I pulled up to the house as the anger overwhelmed me.

I gripped the steering wheel and let the emotions out.

Which involved screaming my head off for a good two minutes.

I had no idea how to process any of this.

Mia hurt me. She hid something huge from me, something I had the right to make a decision about just as much as she had.

Now after realizing what happened, I committed the ultimate betrayal.

I hurt Casey by dating Mia. And now, with her being pregnant, it would only make everything worse.

I feared what telling him might bring forth.

I didn't want to think about it, but the thought invaded my mind.

I took a couple of breaths and looked forward at my house.

I couldn't stay here. I had to leave.

I needed space from everything and everyone. Well, everyone other than my son, of course.

I walked into the house. Jacob would be home in a half-hour.

I had to take him and get the fuck out of here for a bit.

"Everyone leave!" I yelled.

The staff looked at me.

"But sir, we've—"

"I don't need your services for the time being. I will contact you when I need it."

The staff nodded and quickly scattered.

As the last car pulled out of the staff quarters on the western side of the property, I saw one of the drivers come to the front with Jacob in it.

Jacob walked out, grinning from ear to ear.

"Dad!"

I embraced Jacob and held him tightly. He looked at me curiously.

"Dad, is everything okay?"

I put on a strong face. *Nothing was okay.* I had to figure things out.

"Everything's alright, son. I was thinking you and I go on that trip I mentioned."

"You mean?"

"Yes. The one on Daddy's yacht," I encouraged.

Jacob gasped.

"We haven't been there in forever!?"

"I know, and I'm excited to take you. Come on, Jacob, it will be a father and son trip."

"Yay!"

Jacob hugged me tightly. I hugged him back as tight as I could like he was my lifeline.

He didn't need these burdens.

I knew of some great places to sail around and show him.

I reached for his shoulders and gently held them.

"It'll be a good trip for the both of us."

Jacob nodded.

"Okay, Daddy!"

"Alright then, go pack the toys you want to bring."

Jacob raced upstairs and packed his toys. I joined him upstairs and packed his clothes.

Finally, I got my own stuff, only taking just what I needed.

I left all my work at home. I refused to bring anything with me.

After Jacob had his bag, we walked to the door.

"Alright, son, get in the car and buckle up," I instructed.

"Okay!"

Jacob raced to the car and sat inside. I held his things as all the feelings washed over me.

I hated this.

I hated that after letting Mia in, she kept such a huge secret.

I hated that Casey was out of my life. And I hated that I betrayed him.

I got in the car and drove over to the pier near the national harbor, which would allow us to sail all around the East Coast.

Finally, some time away and a chance to forget. At least for now.

Jacob got out of the car and clutched his things. His eyes darted about, bubbling with excitement.

"I'm so excited to go! We're gonna see those fishies again!"

I'm glad I can at least give Jacob happiness, even if I can't be happy.

I faked a smile. "Of course, son! You and I are going on an adventure!"

"Yeah, I love adventures!

"Haha, of course," I replied, forcing a smile.

Running off with Jacob and getting a chance to figure out these thoughts was all that I needed right now.

We walked down the pier to my boat, which sat at Dock One.

The Queen of the Ocean. It was a yacht that I purchased years ago, and I usually kept it in a private harbor.

But, after I mentioned to the staff I'd be taking it out soonish, they got it ready.

When we got to Dock One, I walked all the way down towards the private quarters.

There, it sat bobbing in the water.

"Over here, Jacob."

Jacob raced onto the yacht, and I followed him.

I walked over to the control deck and turned on the ship motor and engine.

"Uhm Dad?"

"What is it?" I asked, masking my annoyance.

"Are you okay? You're not happy and we're at your favorite place!"

I didn't know how to answer that.

"I'm alright son. Once we're on the water, I'll feel better."

Jacob beamed.

"Okay!"

I checked the kitchen quarters. There was enough food for a couple weeks.

That should give me enough time.

I had to be back at the end of the month for the hearing.

At that point, maybe I'd have some idea of what the fuck to do with my life.

I settled into the captain's chair, and after I double-checked with Jacob that he was okay, I started the yacht.

The engine roared to life and then simmered down to a small purr. Just the way I liked it.

I pulled away from the dock and undid the mooring ties.

As I steered towards the exit, I looked back at the mainland.

Being here was nice; it helped me with figuring out my shit. And processing everything that happened and what to do next.

I wanted to be with Mia, but then I kept remembering how I committed the worst betrayal.

Agony and regret simmered over me. But, as we floated along the shoreline, slowly pulling away into the vast, beautiful ocean, I relaxed a little bit.

At this moment, I just needed some time alone with the one person who was the only constant in my life.

And the one who mattered the most.

My son.

Forty-Seven
Mia

Nothing.

That was all that I've gotten for the last week and a half. Nothing from Chris.

His phone was off. Even texts weren't going through.

I looked around the office and at a couple of his favorite places. Not a single glimpse of Chris was found.

Was he okay?

I sighed and put my phone down.

My stomach churned, and a moment later, I grabbed the wastebasket to puke.

After I finished, I bagged it up and tossed it in the bathroom. I could've just gone there, but the last couple of times, I didn't make it.

And I *refused* to keep possibly embarrassing myself while I tried to do my job.

I tapped my fingers on my desk as the anxiety washed over me. *Where the hell did he go?*

A knock at the door roused me out of my thoughts.

I marched over and opened it. There was Grant standing there.

"Mia, there you are."

"Have you found anything?" I asked, attempting to mask the desperation.

He shook his head.

"Nothing. I've had a couple people from legal do some digging. They said they saw a boat in National Harbor with him on it a week and a half ago, but he was gone before they could do anything."

"And I'm guessing nothing since then?"

He shook his head. "No. And I'm worried. What if something happened to him?"

That was my worry too. Chris normally told everyone if he was going to be out of town.

The man never took vacations. He mentioned he planned to, and a couple of his advisors had mentioned that he'd been so stressed that he needed a vacation. But the stubborn bastard never took them.

This was bad.

"Shit."

"Listen, I've got our security team looking for them. We may also want to contact the police."

The police? How are they going to help?

"He's a grown man. He can take care of himself."

Grant shook his head. "There's criminals out there that want to kidnap wealthy people all the time. Take them hostage for ransom. It happened before to another billionaire here in town."

Shit, maybe he was right.

"Okay. I will after this…"

Jacob was with him, too. That worried me just as much.

VALENCIA ROSE

What was he trying to do with his son?

Grant rested his hand on my shoulder.

"It didn't skip me how you two have become closer in the last few weeks."

Oh shit. So now he knows too.

He continued, "It will be okay. He's well-known and can't disappear forever. We'll find him."

I nodded, masking my frustration with a smile.

"I know. Thank you, Grant."

He closed the door, and I went back to my desk.

I tried to do some work, but it was impossible.

After I called the police and reported this, and also talked to his security team, exhaustion overwhelmed me.

I couldn't stay here.

I clocked out early and went to Chris's place. Maybe he finally showed up there.

When I approached, the gate was open, and an older woman with silvery-blonde hair and blue eyes looked around. Her body, while frail and bony, had numerous surgeries.

It was Esme, Christian's mom. She looked like she was fresh out from plastic surgery.

She knocked on the door and looked inside the window.

"Come on, Chris, where are you."

I stepped forward, feeling the awkward tension with every single step.

Esme turned around, eyes wide with surprise.

"You!"

"Hey Esme, it's been a while."

"What are you doing here?"

"I came to see Chris. I was wondering if he showed up."

Esme shook her head and gently touched the pillar.

"No. He gave me a key to open the place, but there's no sign of him or Jacob. They must have left in a hurry, from what I saw in Jacob's room. His toys were tossed around haphazardly, all over the floor."

She sighed and shook her head.

"What are you doing here?"

I paused, unsure of what to say. I couldn't just tell her I was seeing her son, right?

"Chris and I, we…"

She nodded slowly.

"I see. You were the girl that made him happy."

I stood there, agape and shocked at her words.

"What do you mean?"

"He mentioned he was seeing a girl. I wasn't expecting my other son's ex."

Her eyes leveled a similar icy glare to Chris's towards me.

Great, I was on her shitlist too.

"Esme, it's not like that. I had moved on."

"I know, dear," she gently stated. "It's just, I'm surprised it was you. Casey's still heartbroken over what happened."

"I know. But we weren't made for each other, that's all. I made this decision. Chris and I, we…."

I looked away. The feelings were there, and they threatened to overflow.

I loved Chris. And I was so worried about him.

I had not been able to sleep, and I had tried to get the nagging feeling out of there.

Esme rested her hand on my shoulder.

"Listen, I might not be happy about this. But in that small time you two dated, he seemed happier. Less stressed."

"He was. He hadn't used those prescription pills for anxiety as much."

"I noticed," she replied. "You're a good woman, Mia. And I hope that we can find him. I'm worried he got himself into something stupid."

"I am, too."

Esme called her private security team to help with searching for Chris. They agreed to give Esme real-time updates on where he might be and what they'll find.

She closed her phone and turned to me.

"I know we'll find him. And if someone did kidnap him and hold him for ransom, I will pay it."

I smiled. "Thank you Esme."

"You're welcome, dear."

She reached out and touched the palm of my hand.

"I'm not too keen on you two being together, but if you're able to make my son happy, then I'm happy."

"I will make him happy. We just got to get him back."

I left Chris' estate as a conflict of feelings erupted over me.

My phone rang, and I looked down.

Casey?

I paused. Do I take this? Part of me didn't want to because I had moved on. But I had to know why he was calling.

I pressed the green button and held the phone to my ear.

"Casey."

"Hi, Mia. Listen, I'll cut to the chase. I know about Chris and you. And that Chris is gone."

Fuck. His voice was hollowed, devoid of any emotion.

"I'm sorry, Casey, I'm—"

"Mia, I'm upset that you moved on that fast, but what's breaking my heart is that my brother did that. He was my best friend… and I always looked up to him. I'm just devastated. I don't know how to deal with this."

I didn't know what to say. I sat there as I heard his voice on the other line.

"But he is still my brother, and I love him, Mia. And even though he hurt me so deeply, I want him back. I cannot just simply forget the only constant figure in my life who has always been there for me— well, until now. So I'll help in the search to find him. And then I'll sit down with him and have a word, man to man, to figure out how to navigate this shit you two put me in."

"I appreciate you making an effort to understand this whole thing."

"Well, I'm worried about him, and I don't want something bad to happen to him."

"It won't," I reassured him.

"I doubt it. But we shall see."

He hung up the phone.

A flurry of emotions sat in my head.

What the hell do I do next? I didn't have the answers to that.

But for now, I had to find him.

And hopefully, when Christian came back, we could talk about it and find a solution.

Forty-Eight
Chris

The boat bobbled in the water. Blue was as far as my eyes could see.

We weren't too far, just near the Keys in Florida.

But it relaxed me since the water was clear, and the sun shone brightly.

Jacob sat on the deck and read. In his hands was some Maximum Rides book I'd never heard of.

I was just glad the kid was reading.

Jacob looked up at me and smiled.

"Dad, when will we go back?"

That was a good question. I had no idea. It had been almost two weeks.

There were still so many questions and not enough answers.

Betraying Casey was the worst part.

There was also the possibility that, when I got back to shore, the authorities might take Jacob away.

I left, all during a suit that felt unreal. I sighed.

"I'm not sure, son."

Jacob walked over and sat in the chair next to me.

"You look a bit scared, Dad, but you have me."

"What do you mean?"

"You're the strongest dad ever! And I love having a strong Dad."

My heart melted upon hearing that.

How did Jacob know how to say the right thing at the right time?

I smiled.

"Thanks, son. I'm doing my best."

"I know, Dad. And you deserve it!"

I chuckled. "Well, I'll try."

Jacob walked back to the book he was reading.

I walked to the edge of the boat and looked down.

An abyss of nothing. Limitless potential.

It made me wonder just what else could happen.

I walked to the open part of the boat and touched the water with my hands. It was cold but felt soothing to me.

My restless heart refused to be contained.

What now? How could I tell Casey any of this?

The sound of pattered footsteps pulled me out of my thoughts.

Jacob sat there, and he looked out.

"I thought you were reading?"

"I was, but I wanted to see you," Jacob began.

"Why's that?"

"Because you look sad, Daddy. And I wanted to make you happy!"

I smiled. "I'm happy when I have you around, Jacob."

We sat in silence as the water continued to flow.

Jacob took a deep breath and looked up at me with a smile.

"I like Mia, Dad."

"Oh, you do?" I asked, holding back the emotions at the mention of her name.

"She's really nice to me," Jacob said. "She'd be a great mommy."

That only poured more salt on the wound.

"I know, son."

"Are you happy with her?"

I knew the answer to that. Even though I tried to avoid it, the answer was obvious.

"Yeah," I admitted. "I am happy!"

"I like it when Daddy's happy."

I chuckled. "I'll try to be happier then."

"Okay!"

Jacob and I spent the rest of the evening together, making small talk.

The emotions reared their ugly heads. Many of which, I tried to simmer for so long.

The fear of betrayal lay over me, but there was also that innate desire.

The more I thought about it, the more the desire to be a good father for the child on the way awakened in me.

And, this time, I wanted to raise a kid with someone who would put their family first. Someone like Mia.

There was also something else. The more I sat here and thought about everything, the more I felt this other emotion trying to set itself free from the depths I had buried it.

An emotion that I had pushed aside and avoided for too long.

Love.

I *loved* Mia. I could not avoid it anymore. When she was in my life, I felt whole and happy.

I wasn't sitting here with a void that couldn't be closed.

Instead, I felt a new lease on life. A refreshing second chance.

Until I ruined it again by running away from her and everything else.

No, I wouldn't forego my chance at happiness for a second time. I needed this.

I knew Mia loved me, too. With every passing day, she stayed by my side and with me, even when I almost suffocated her.

And she didn't want to get back with Casey ever again. She had clearly stated that to me herself.

I shook my head and laughed.

I was such a goddamned fool. I knew what I had to do now.

I walked over to the navigation room.

Jacob's footsteps pattered behind me. He stood in the doorway curiously.

"Daddy, where are you going?"

"Back home," I replied. "I think we've been out here for a little too long."

I had to get back soon anyways. My hearing was in a week, and I still didn't know what to do.

Facing reality was the next step. Hiding away in fear and shame would get me nowhere.

It was time to face the truth, about the feelings I had.

I steered the ship back to the harbor.

As we landed, I grabbed my phone and opened it for the first time after a long time.

My phone bombarded me with calls and texts from people worried about me.

Including Casey.

I hovered over his name to give him a call. A moment later, my phone blared with a call from Bradley.

In an instant, I picked it up.

"Bradley?"

"Jesus Christ, Christian, where have you been?"

"It's complicated. What's the matter?"

"Well, I looked through some of the security footage you sent me. I also had a patrol out there examining the area. We found some startling footage."

"What?" I asked.

Bradley didn't say anything for a moment. After he coughed, he spoke.

"Alara was the one who planted the fentanyl. We caught her on tape with someone else. It was very brief, but it was during that time when you were out with Jacob at the science center."

That motherfucker! I clenched the phone tighter as I tried to quell myself.

The last thing I needed was an outburst.

"I see. Get that information and evidence ready. We're bringing that to court."

"Okay. And is everything alright? I heard you went missing and—"

"Everything's fine now," I reassured. "I just needed some space."

"Understood. Well, welcome back, sir."

"It's good to be back."

I hung up the phone and looked at Casey's name.

I pressed the button and waited for two rings before I heard his voice.

"Chris! Where the hell have you been?"

"It's a long story. But we need to talk. I want to clear the air and—"

"I agree. I wanted to talk to you too."

Forty-Nine
Mia

"He'll come back, dear. I know he will."

I put my phone down and sighed.

I looked at the food. Mom made a ribeye steak with potatoes and asparagus spears, but I didn't even feel like eating.

Ever since Chris disappeared, I haven't wanted to.

I managed to force a nutrition shake down my gullet to feed the baby.

But when it came to actual food, I just couldn't.

Maybe it was the growing regret of what went on. Or maybe it was my own fear.

"I don't know," I muttered.

Mom rested her hand on my shoulder and massaged it.

"I know it's worrisome, but if something happened, maybe he went to fix it before he came back."

I doubted that's what happened.

"I don't know. I just feel so…"

"Insecure? Unsure of what to do?"

I nodded. "Yeah. And I feel lost."

Mom nodded. "That happens, hun. He probably needed to figure out his own lot."

I touched my stomach on instinct. Hiding the pregnancy caused this.

I was at fault.

I worked with Casey and Esme to try to contact him, but there was nothing. Casey was at least cordial during all this.

Still, the pain from before stung, and I could sense the tension.

I never brought it up, for both our sakes.

As for Esme, she at first wasn't too keen on me helping.

But over time, when I mentioned I was using his work security team to help, she relaxed a little bit.

The air was tense, but we tried our best.

"Mom, it's not that," I started.

"What do you mean?"

Tears welled up in my eyes.

"I tried to make everything work! I thought that maybe, now that I figured out my feelings for Chris, things would be easier. But...I screwed up."

I bit my lip as the words threatened to fall from my lips.

"You screwed up how?"

I looked at Mom. She was so sweet and understanding, but I feared what she might say.

"I messed up. I'm responsible for this?"

"But how?"

It was time to come clean.

I raised my baggy shirt a little bit to reveal the small protrusion of my stomach.

"Mom, I'm pregnant with Chris's baby. And I didn't tell him."

There we go. At least I finally got it off my chest.

I half-expected Mom to be surprised. Instead, she laughed.

"I knew it."

"Wait, how?" I asked, shocked that she picked it up.

"Remember when I said you were glowing a few weeks ago, dear? I'm a mom; I pick up on these things."

I smiled. "I see."

"So you didn't tell him?"

I shook my head. "No, I feared that it would ruin everything. Since we'd only just started dating and he was so protective of Casey."

"I see. Well, guess the cat is out of the bag then."

"You mean the baby."

We both laughed. Mom settled and rested her hand against mine.

"Well, whatever you do next, I'm here for you. I'm happy my little girl's going to be a mom. And I promise, as the grandma, I'll make sure she's fully taken care of."

"Thanks, mom. I don't plan to leave you with the child or anything."

"Nonsense! It didn't work out with that guy. Maybe I'm just destined to be the supportive grandmother who wants only the best for her babies."

"Maybe so. Either way, I feel so much better having told you, like a weight's been lifted off my chest."

I was still worried about Chris, though. Nobody could find him. I swear if someone took him.

Mom laced her fingers against mine.

"Whatever the case, I know it'll work out. You're happy, Mia, and I can sense that this man is the one for you."

"How can you be so sure?"

"I can tell. You smile differently when you talk about Chris. It's like the universe brought this as a sign."

I nodded.

"Maybe so."

I finally managed to eat some food.

The regrets still hung over me, but there was a calmness that I felt.

Even though I didn't have all the answers yet, at least I knew one thing for sure.

No matter what, I'd have the support of my mom throughout these times.

Now, if only Chris could come back.

Fifty
Chris

"Alright, Jacob, go have fun in the playroom."

"Okay, Dad!" Jacob said.

He raced into the country club kids' room, where the other kids played.

Immediately, they talked to him, and he joined in their game of tag.

I smiled. At least Jacob could be a kid for a bit.

The playroom was where the children of some of the clientele went when their parents needed to talk business.

I walked over to one of the small lounges nearby.

Inside was Casey, who looked at his phone. He looked up with a hesitant stare.

"There you are," he stated.

"Sorry. Had to drop Jacob off."

"All good."

I sat down across from him.

The anxiety spiked through my body, but I knew one thing was for sure.

I had to do this. To face the truth and get it off my chest.

The fear hung over me like a gaping wound. The fear of losing my baby brother for good.

But the only way to face fear and to clear it all away was to tell him everything.

"Casey, I want to start with, I'm really sorry for worrying everyone."

"Yes, you worried everyone sick, including me. You disappeared, Chris. Where the hell did you go?"

"Out to sea," I replied curtly. "I didn't know where else to go. I did something, and I realized that I screwed up big time."

Casey nodded. "You did."

"I'm not asking you to forgive me."

"It's not that," Casey admitted. "It's just you betrayed me, man. I was so pissed and heartbroken when I learned the truth. And worst of all, you didn't tell me. I had to find out that way... You were my best friend, Chris, a kind of a father figure for me, and next thing I know, you're screwing my ex, whom you know I still loved."

I nodded. "I understand your frustrations. It was a shitty thing of me."

Casey sighed. "Yeah, it was."

"I want you to believe me when I say I feel terrible for what I did, Casey."

"It was a terrible thing to do, Chris. But I've thought about it too. These last few weeks have been really hard on me."

"Why's that?"

"Well, after having you by my side to guide me through thick and thin, I suddenly didn't have you anymore. You were always the only constant in my life and these past few weeks without you made me feel like I was lost."

That was true. I was always there for him when he needed it. At least I tried. We'd have conversations at all hours of the day.

"Well, I felt lost too. The thought of losing my little brother drove me crazy."

"Not anymore. You're not going to lose him. Your little brother had a proper sole searching week and saw what the real things are that truly matter in life."

He continued calmly, "Although I loved Mia, she made it very clear to me that she wouldn't get back with me. And if you two make each other happy, then I should get over my emotions and support you. I mean I know that you haven't been happy since god knows when."

He looked up, and a small smile formed on his face.

"And I want you to be happy." he continued.

"Why?" I finally asked.

"Because Chris, you deserve happiness. You've been through so much shit. Fucking raised me and then went halfway around the world to fight for your country. You're a fucking legend."

"I'm not."

"You are man. But it's more than that. I guess maybe Mia was right. I am an immature and impulsive fuck."

Casey took a sip of his whiskey and coke and looked outside at the golf course.

"I guess I kind of realized this right before one of my races. I haven't settled down. Everyone else has. Mia wants stability. Hell, she wants kids. And I don't know what the hell I want."

I nodded. "Yeah, about that..."

Casey's eyes widened. "Wait, don't tell me—"

"She is. She's about two months along."

Casey's jaw dropped. I mentally berated myself for saying this.

"Damn. Looks like she really did find the one."

"I'm sorry, Casey."

"Don't be. I realized that you are better for Mia. I need to learn to be a better man and stand on my own two feet. I know by now that Mia likes to be with a guy who has his shit together instead of having to raise a silly man-child like myself."

"Come on, dude, give yourself some credit now. You've made it in the world of pro-racing."

"Yeah, but I guess my outlook on women kind of sucks. I wanted Mia to do what I wanted, and I rarely gave a damn about her feelings, looking back. It made me realize that I need to do some growing up."

I nodded, understanding the situation.

"You're still a great man, Casey. And the fact that you know what you need to work on tells me you're already on your way to becoming a more mature man."

"Well that means a lot. Thanks, brother. I'm going to try to be and hopefully, I'll nab a girl that loves me as much as Mia loves you. She's moved on, and I need to do the same."

I smiled.

"Hey, just don't be too upset. You've done well for yourself."

Casey laughed sardonically.

"I know you say this, but I feel like I can do better."

"Well, you can. And no matter what, I'm here for you, man."

Casey got up. I walked over and hugged him tightly.

He was my brother. My best friend. Someone I dropped every goddamn thing for.

And I am so glad to have him back in my life.

And now, I felt like I could finally do what made me happy.

I stopped living for others, and with Mia, I could finally live for myself and do something that not only makes others happy but me as well.

"I love you, man."

"I love you too, Casey. And I promise that, no matter what, I'll be in your corner, cheering you on."

"As will I."

Fifty-One
Mia

"Okay, Grant, I'll send over those files when I get there."

I hung up the phone and drove my new car, a sleek Ford Fusion, over to the workplace parking garage.

As I parked, I thought about everything I needed to do today.

All of the meetings and contracts I had to send to Grant loomed over my head. There was so much, and our team was thinned out.

No word from Chris yet, other than the security team mentioning his boat was back. Whether he was still on it, I didn't know.

I tried not to let it get to me.

Katie and Nat were supportive, and even though we couldn't go out to drink, they made time for me.

As for Mom, she already started to prepare to be a grandma. It warmed my heart to see her like this.

I got to the lobby and looked around. Nobody was here yet.

Strange. I wasn't that early, was I?

I walked to the elevator and opened the door.

As it went up, I felt an odd, almost familiar presence hang over me.

The doors opened, and I walked to my office.

I grabbed my key to unlock it when I realized the door had already been unlocked.

What the hell? I always lock it when I leave.

I opened the door, greeted by a familiar face I thought I'd never see again.

"Chris..."

I dropped my stuff on the ground and rushed on over.

He pulled me into his arms and held me tightly.

A million thoughts raced through my head, but they were all silenced by his warm, inviting embrace.

I hugged him tightly and relished in the feeling of his hardened body.

It comforted me and helped soothe all of the aching thoughts that I had.

We looked up, and our eyes met. For a moment, I didn't know what to say.

Words weren't' needed to convey our thoughts.

Chris kissed me passionately, and I immediately held him even tighter.

Our tongues danced, and he bit on my lip.

I gasped, and as he pulled away, an impish half-smile crossed his face.

"Bet you thought I wasn't coming back."

"Well—"

"I'm sorry, Mia. For so many things. For running off like that. For getting upset about the baby and saying all those terrible things. For…everything. I was stressed out and I took it out on you when I should have stayed and been there for you, for both of you."

I stood there, unable to form words.

"But how did—"

"I needed to do some soul searching, or shit, and figure out what the hell to do next," he explained.

"So what do you want now?"

He tugged my waist and pushed me against his body.

"You. You, Mia, and our baby. I love you, and I'm tired of holding back anymore."

The words shocked me to the core but also warmed my every being.

I looked up and smiled.

"I love you too. But this time, you'll stay. Right? Even when it gets hard, you have to stay and fight with me."

"I know and I will," he promised. "I talked to Casey. He knows about us. And, well, the baby. He apparently had a soul-searching phase of his own and came to the conclusion that you and me are a better fit for each other. So he's accepting of it now and is happy for us."

That was both such a relief and a shocker.

"I'm, uh, glad to hear that."

"What's the matter?" he asked, utterly confused.

"Nothing. I'm just surprised he took it so well."

"Well, he's done some growing up too. He realized I am happy when I'm with you and, as brothers, we both want nothing more than for the other to be happy."

"That's good to hear."

"Indeed. And that means I can finally do what I want. Which is to be with you."

Chris stepped away and closed the door. He grabbed my hand and brought me to the desk.

"Chris, what are you—"

He pushed me down. I laid there, splayed out.

My pen box fell to the ground with a clunk.

He kissed me passionately and moved his hands upwards my suit jacket. As he undid the buttons, I closed my eyes.

All I wanted right now was him.

Chris pulled back and traced his fingers against my black bra.

"Why don't we have a little bit of fun before the rest of the office gets here. It's been a while," he whispered into my ear, a naughty smirk on his lips. He licked the shell of my ear, and I shuddered.

This was what I needed.

To be taken and penetrated by this utterly amazing man who loved me.

That wanted me just as much as I wanted him.

I wrapped my arms around his shoulders and pulled him down.

"I thought you'd never ask."

Our lips came together again, and soon, he pushed my jacket apart.

He didn't get rid of it like the last time, but instead pushed his hands underneath my back bra to my nipples.

Little touches from his fingertips danced against my sensitive flesh. I closed my eyes and moaned.

"They've gotten bigger."

"Yeah, comes with pregnancy."

"Good. I get to watch you become the beautiful mother to my child."

I moaned, aroused and filled with love.

His hands pinched and grazed my nipples.

I mewled, balling my hands into fists with every sensitive touch from his fingers.

His lips moved down, and after he pushed one of my bra cups away, he pressed his lips to the tip.

As he suckled on the flesh, I arched my body, begging for more.

The heat resonated deep within. Our bodies came together. I moaned and gasped, aching for more.

"Come on, Chris, stop teasing," I pleaded.

He pulled back and slid his hands to my nylons.

"Why should I."

"Because I can barely last. And I know that you can't either."

He chuckled. "You're right."

Chris pushed my legs apart and moved between my legs. Little laps from his tongue danced along my folds.

Fuck that felt good. The man knew just where to touch me, both on my outside and also right against my entrance.

He alternated, and his thumb played with my clit. He pressed the nub against his fingers as his tongue continued to savor, tasting the sweet juices that dripped from me.

He reached for my hips and pulled me tighter around him.

My thighs hugged each side of his head and kept them there until he savored every last drop.

I gasped, holding his head there.

Fuck, I was so close. I needed it and—

Chris pulled away, and I groaned.

"Why?"

"Because I want to hear you cum with me inside you," he whispered.

Dammit, those words, with the lust dripped over them, drove me crazy.

"Get to the window and turn around," he instructed.

I sat up, surprised.

"But someone might see us."

"Let them. I want them to know just how much I love you."

My heart skipped a beat as I heard this.

I spread my legs apart, and soon, he slammed inside.

He held my hips tighter, and I gasped. Clawing the glass panes.

Fuck he felt so big and familiar. The inviting sensation of his rot all the way inside of me created an ache that I couldn't shake.

He groaned, and as he slammed his hips against me, penetrating my core with his member, I rolled my head back.

All rational thought disappeared. All that escaped me were moans.

He pressed me against the glass pane. I fogged up the windows, and as he held me there, garbled sounds of pure, unadulterated desire formed against my lips.

I needed more.

I met his thrusts with my hips, and he grunted.

His hand slipped downwards towards my clit.

"Tell me you want it. Tell me you want to cum."

"I want it, Chris! Goddammit, I'm—"

He pulled my head back, and I pressed my hands to the pane.

A scream of pure delight escaped my lips as I felt the sudden, rapturous pleasure of my orgasm race through me.

It shocked me to the core, drove me crazy, and made me realize just how much I loved this man.

He took care of me, and I knew Chris would be there for me and our baby, no matter what.

Christian thrusted a couple more times, finishing inside me.

We stayed like this, entwined together in pure bliss.

That was until my legs gave out.

I fell to the ground, flushed with embarrassment. Christian laughed.

"Too much?"

"No, it's not that. You're absolutely perfect," I gushed.

Christian pulled me into his arms, and I stayed there. His warm, inviting hugs helped ease all of the pain.

After a little bit, Christian pulled back and looked at the clock.

"Duty calls."

"It does."

He didn't make a move, though, to move us.

He rubbed his hand over my growing stomach and I interlaced our fingers together. "This feels right now that we're together now."

"We are," I said.

His hand reached up and traced my cheek. "And I wouldn't have it any other way. I love you, Mia, and I promise that no matter what kinds of bullshit life throws at me, I'll face it with you by my side."

I held his hand and squeezed it.

"Yes. We're a team, and we'll conquer it all together."

He sighed as if he remembered something.

"And that includes dealing with Alara's bullshit in court next week. Once I know I have Jacob safe with us forever, we can focus on our sweet, growing little family."

"We will win the case and Jacob will be with us forever, Chris. I know that. And then we can build our own little heaven here; you, me and our two little kids."

And that, I meant from the bottom of my heart.

Fifty-Two
Chris

"He's lying! I swear by it."

The judge looked at the security footage once more and then looked at Alara.

Her fire-engine red hair's got gray streaks in it. Her skin, which used to be supple and full, now sat with wrinkles all over the place.

"The evidence is right here. It's all obvious," her lawyer said.

"I understand, but we also know Mr. Hamilton has something as well for the jury. Mr. Sandler?" He looked over to my lawyer, George.

Alara's battle was the longest month of my life. She kept not showing, giving excuse after excuse.

It drove me crazy.

Their main argument was that I was a drug addict and not fit to raise a child.

But George had me have drug tests for the last few weeks to support my case.

Not only that, but Mia also gave testimony on me being clean.

But the most important piece of evidence was the security footage my personal investigator had found.

George walked over and stood in front of the defense stand.

"Your honor, we have clear evidence demonstrating that Ms. Tate is lying with regard to her accusations."

The crowd chattered and the judge slammed the gavel.

"Order!"

George then handed him a flash drive containing the file.

"This is a file, clearly demonstrating security footage of Ms. Tate placing the evidence."

He looked it over, and then nodded.

There was another couple of hours of back and forth between the two sides, arguing their case.

With Alara unable to respond with any fact-based answers to any of George's questions, her cross-examination was a clear win for us.

Eventually, the judge said, "Alright. We have heard all the evidence and arguments from both parties now. I will have the jury convene and come back with a decision."

And with that, the jury went to the back room, and a break transpired. Alara glared at Mia, but she smiled and turned to me.

"She's caught."

"I know. She won't get out of this."

To my surprise, only fifteen minutes later, the judge came back and ordered the court to be seated.

"I've spoken with the jury, and we've come to a conclusion in this legal battle."

The judge was an older man with a large gray beard and thin gray hair.

The bags under his eyes were a clear indication that even he was tired of this case. He'd been there since the initial testimony.

"The jury and I find Christian Hamilton to be a fit father to Jacob Hamilton and grant him full custody of Jacob until he turns eighteen years old. The court also finds Alara Tate guilty of fabricating evidence, false testimony, and perjury of the court. She will be sentenced to fifteen months in prison and will then be on probation for the duration of one year."

With that, the gavel slammed down, and I smiled.

Alara glared, angry as hell.

"This isn't over, Christian," she yelled.

"You lied, Alara. And yes, it is over." I calmly responded.

Two of the police officers near the entrance of the court escorted Alara off the court.

As they left, I turned and looked at Mia.

She grinned, holding her hands together. And then she raced over and gave me a tight hug.

I took a moment to bask in her scent.

She grew more perfect by the day.

It relieved me to have her by my side.

Mia and I walked out of the courthouse.

She looked over towards our car. "Ready to go home?"

"Yes, I want to see Jacob and just spend time together as a family. I can't thank you enough for being by my side."

Mia smiled.

"That sounds like a perfect ending to this long day. I love you Chris, and now, we can finally begin our new chapter together."

"I can't wait for that."

We went back to the house, excited for the future. One that we would share together, filled with everlasting happiness.

At home, I gave Jacob bits and pieces about Alara and the trial.

He still called her a witch. I did not tell him how fitting I found that description for her.

He grinned. "Yay! I get to stay with daddy! That's awesome."

That it was; Jacob was safe, and he finally got to live a normal life.

He hugged me.

"I'm glad, Dad! I didn't want to live with her."

I chuckled. "I didn't want that either."

And now, I could finally move on.

Fifty-Three
Chris

SEVEN MONTHS LATER

Seven months had passed since the court date.

Emmy was born, and Jacob was thrilled to have a little sister.

Jacob stared at Emmy as she slept.

"Daddy, she sleeps a lot."

"She's a baby. And you have to go to bed too."

"Aww."

"Hey, remember what we said about going to bed early. If you went to bed on time for a month, we can go to the racetrack."

Jacob's eyes widened.

"Racecars!"

I chuckled. "I'm sure Uncle Casey would love to show you."

Jacob raced to the bedroom.

As he got ready, I walked over to Mia, who watched Emmy's sleeping form.

"She's beautiful," Mia gushed.

"She is. Just like her wonderful mother."

"You're not the worst father yourself," she said with a naughty smirk on her lips.

I touched her hand and looked out the window.

These past seven months have been stressful but worth it.

I stayed with Mia throughout all the changes, and when Emmy was born, she became even more beautiful.

I couldn't think of any other place I wanted to be.

"You haven't had one in a while, have you?"

I shook my head. I haven't had any anxiety medication in three months.

It was because of Mia. She helped me naturally overcome the stress.

It seemed like when I was around her, my problems melted away.

After the kids were in bed, Mia and I went up to the stargazing balcony.

As we got up there, I looked up at the stars.

"It feels good to be back up here again."

"It sure does," she admitted.

The stars twinkled brightly. So did that desire, which grew stronger with every pressing second.

I had to tell her. There was no way I would ever let Mia go. She was my ride-or-die and my forever.

"Mia," I began. "There's something I want to tell you."

She looked curious about it.

"OK...what is it?"

I took her hand and squeezed it.

"We've been through so much together. A lot of back and forth, as we figured out what we wanted."

She nodded.

"And through all of the obstacles, I learned what real love was. And I discovered real love through you."

She leaned in and smiled contentedly.

"I learned it through you as well."

"Which is why there's something I need to ask you right now."

I stood up and got down on one knee.

Her eyes widened, and those hazel pupils became more beautiful than before.

In the moonlight, they shimmered in an almost ethereal beauty.

"Mia, will you spend the rest of my life with me? Will you marry me and enjoy this adventure together."

Mia looked at the ring, which sparkled in the box.

It was a princess-cut 3-carat solitaire diamond ring and one that would sit perfectly on her hand.

"I thought you would never ask. Of course, I'll marry you!"

She stood up, and I placed the ring on her finger. I kissed her hand and looked up.

"I can't wait to call you my wife. Now we can finally start the next chapter of our life. This time, without any stops."

She smiled. "I'm so ready for what's to come."

I pulled Mia into my arms and kissed her passionately.

Under the night sky, I had the perfect woman next to me.

I couldn't remember the last time I'd been this happy. This relaxed.

I didn't have to fight anymore.

It was the life I always wanted but couldn't see how I could get there.

And now, I finally got what I wanted, with the most beautiful woman in the world.

Epilogue: Mia

THREE YEARS LATER

"Be careful! Don't go too far out!"

"We won't, Mom," Jacob said. "Come on, Em, let's look at the seashells!"

"Shells!"

Emmy and Jacob walked along the shoreline. I smiled and placed my magazine down.

"They'll be fine. If they go out too far, I'll get them," Chris insisted.

I looked at Chris, who looked just as delicious as he did the first time I saw him.

His swim trunks hung low against his body and highlighted his hips. His muscles stayed fit and cut and were a wonder to behold.

He was scrumptious.

A teasing smile crossed his face.

"Like what you see?"

"Always."

"Well, I can say the same. I now have a super-hot wife that comes with me to the Caribbean just cause I want to have a little vacation."

"Look at you. Finally taking vacations," I teased.

"Hey, being a husband awoke me to it. And plus, we're going to experience the joys of parenthood again soon."

I touched my stomach, where a small protrusion formed.

We had our wedding, and things were great, but we both wanted to give Em and Jacob another sibling.

Which, of course, led to baby number three. We were about three months along, so I was starting to show, but not a ton yet.

I was so blessed. I got to raise three kids with the love of my life.

"Yes, we get to have that fun again."

"Yes, but this time we're more prepared. Although you already kicked ass with Em."

"I tried my best," I replied. "She's a great kid."

"An amazing one," he complimented.

We watched Em and Jacob walk around and grab some shells.

I turned and looked at Chris. "So, how's Casey doing?"

"Good. The guy finally settled down with that Crystal girl."

Casey found a girl named Crystal who was perfect for him. She helped curb his impulsivity, and they were about to get married.

"Good. I'm glad for him. He deserves it," I said.

I still cared about Casey, even though we weren't meant for each other. So, seeing him do good was a win in my book.

"Yes. And you're rocking it so well at your own company now too."

I was indeed.

A few months after Em was born, I decided to build my own tech startup. It was successful, and Chris and I worked together with mutual clients.

"Speaking of which, I'll be taking another maternity leave soon."

"Hey, if they screw up during your absence, I'll cover for you."

"I'm flattered," I teased.

We both laughed and enjoyed the presence of one another. I looked up and gazed at the man above me.

"I love you, Chris."

"I love you too, Mia, and I'm glad that I can say this every single day."

"I am, too."

We were meant for each other, even if, at first, we didn't realize it.

But now, after so much we've gone through together, the truth was apparent, and it made me happy to admit it.

As for Alara, after she got out of jail, she disappeared with some guy.

So much for her claim to care about Jacob!

But I was not complaining. She never bothered us again, and that was a relief.

For the rest of the day, we lazed on the beach and watched our kids.

It was the perfect family vacation and the perfect start to the next chapter of my life.

A chapter that I'd get to share with the best man on the planet.

One filled with not just love, but also appreciation and respect for one another.

THE END

Did you like this book? Then you'll LOVE my other book "Secret Baby For My Bestie's Ex-SEAL Dad", a steamy enemies to lovers billionaire romance, in the same series "Billionaire Silver Foxes' Club", available to read for FREE on Kindle Unlimited here.

Here is a short description of what "Secret Baby For My Bestie's Ex-SEAL Dad" is all about:

When I got this job, I didn't know I would end up crying in pleasure, splayed on my arrogant boss's desk, who also happened to be my bestie's off-limits dad.

The first day walking into the office, I discovered my new billionaire ex-navy SEAL boss was the same grumpy man who hated my guts for years.

Right from the start, he had it out for me.

His never-ending last-minute job demands should have made me hate him back but, instead, I found myself daydreaming about his rock-hard body and all the things he could do to me.

Yet, I tried hard to stay away from him; after all, he was twice my age and my best friend's dad.

Until, during a late evening shift, he savagely overtook me in his office, like I was his every dirty fantasy.

But *that* wasn't all... things got even more out of control when two life-changing little pink lines appeared.

***

"Secret Baby For My Bestie's Ex-SEAL Dad" is a sizzling enemies to lovers, billionaire boss, age gap romance in the Billionaire Silver Foxes' Club Series. Each book is a complete stand-alone with no cliffhangers and a satisfying happy ever after.

Click the link below to grab your copy of "Secret Baby

For My Bestie's Ex-SEAL Dad" and check out a sneak peek into this sizzling book on the next page:

https://www.amazon.com/dp/B0CJBGJ2PC

Sneak Peek Into "Secret Baby For My Bestie's Ex-SEAL Dad"

Below is a sneak peek into "Secret Baby For My Bestie's Ex-SEAL Dad", which is available here:

Prologue: Lucas

I don't know how it happened.

How I ended up with my lips against my daughter's best friend. Someone who was young enough to be my daughter.

I know I should have stopped, especially since I was her boss. My daughter would have been furious.

And yet, no matter what I tried to tell myself, I was unable to pull away from her.

We were smiling at each other, and I looked down at her lips for a second.

My lips closed the distance, touching softly against hers.

The kiss was chaste and gentle, and I groaned, enjoying the sweet touch of those lips. They were perky and soft, perfect for a kiss.

I ran my hands through her long hair. As I deepened our kiss, pulling her closer, she squeaked in response.

I expected Natalia to pull back, but she didn't.

She moved back after a good minute, surprise on her face.

"What was that?"

I had no clue. But Natalia looked utterly delectable right now.

As much as I wished to hold back these feelings, I refused to. I reached out, caressing her cheek.

"We can keep this our little secret. Just for tonight."

She nodded.

"Right. Our secret."

VALENCIA ROSE

***

To find out what happens next, click on the below link and read for FREE on KU:
https://www.amazon.com/dp/B0CJBGJ2PC

About the Author

Valencia Rose is an Indie Author who loves to create a world of love and happy ever afters for her readers to escape from the crazy times we currently live in. She loves to breathe life into sizzling hot stories revolving around Sexy Billionaires, Alpha Bosses and Dominant Playboys who will stop at nothing to achieve their happy endings with their feisty heroines, when they want and how they want.

When she is not writing, Valencia loves to play the piano and also travel with her husband and two little girls to explore fun new activities with them.

If you like sensual steamy page-turning contemporary romance books, make sure to sign up here for Valencia's Romance Book Club to receive FREE Advanced Reader Copies (ARCs), first dibs and discounts on her latest releases.

And as a new member of Valencia's Steamy Romance Book Club, you will receive a special gift from her; your very own copy of one of her steamy romance novellas, called "Bad Boy Professor".

Click on the link below to join and download your copy for FREE!

https://dl.bookfunnel.com/8h4cfh6qfv.

"Bad Boy Professor" is a Grumpy Billionaire Off-limits Romance. Here is a short look at what happens inside that book:

That moment you realize your hot professor is the sexy bad boy you slept with last week...

So here is what happened: I was hard on money and met this sexy tattooed playboy who claimed my body without even saying a word.

Fast forward to a week later, my smart, sexy-as-hell, but arrogant Professor walked through the class door!

I didn't know whether I should squeeze my thighs or throw up in my purse because it was him... And he recognized me too.

Next thing I knew, that first one-night stand turned into a passionate relationship. But we had to stop it because I could be expelled. He could lose his job. We could lose everything.

The problem was we couldn't keep our hands off each other. We were in way too deep.

***

Sign up now by clicking on the link below to get your FREE copy of "Bad Boy Professor":

https://dl.bookfunnel.com/8h4cfh6qfv

Printed in Great Britain
by Amazon